Stay

Stay

D. A. Flowers

Cover design by D.A. Flowers
Cover images ©Adobe Stock Images

This book is dedicated to the kids in my life. I look at them, each with their own individual personalities, and it inspires me to be better. I love you all.

Eliza Wilton

I scurried to class like a little mouse, keeping my head down, hoping that would be enough to keep me from being noticed. I couldn't wait to escape into the little hole that would provide me with cover from the predators in the hallway; the door to Mr. Jamison's classroom was only a few yards away. *Almost there,* I thought to myself as I clutched my books close to my chest like they were a protective shield. My curls bounced up and down with my stride like little brown springs. I'd almost made it when the group of girls in front of me stopped abruptly and I collided with one of them, almost knocking the girl down.

I knew who it was immediately. The shiny, perfectly curled, long blonde hair paired with the expensive, fitted designer dress and overpowering but pleasant perfume was a dead giveaway. *I bumped into Caroline Bancroft,* I thought as I stood there feeling scared and wondering if it was going to be my last day alive. *Why couldn't it have been anyone but her?*

Caroline was the meanest girl in school, at least to me anyway. She had all the teachers convinced that she was a perfect little southern belle, but I knew better. I had a long history with her, and none of it included her having manners.

In the split second that I had before Caroline spun around to rip me a new one, I had a flashback to the eighth grade. Caroline convinced her two friends to dump a bucket of water on me at the beginning of first period. Never mind the fact that I had nothing to change into. The worst part of the prank was that they soaked my hair. My 3C hair shrank up into a helmet-like mess after being wet for a while. I'd used the school phone to call and beg the Wiltons, my adoptive parents, to come get me from school but they refused. I had no choice but to walk around like a furry, wet dog and the kids were brutal as they teased me.

By the middle of the day, my clothes were halfway dried, but my hair had gotten worse. The school nurse tried to help me comb it out, but she wasn't familiar with styling ethnic hair. Neither was I unfortunately. My adoptive parents were white. They never treated me poorly because of my race but they also never bothered to learn about black girls' hair. That means they'd never taught me how to take care of it. As the nurse combed my hair out, it went from a helmet to a terribly frizzy, uneven, messy afro. The girls, even the black girls who should have been more compassionate, teased me incessantly for the rest of the day.

My flashback was broken when Caroline and her two groupies, Tinsley and Jessica, stepped up to me. I wilted like an old flower as I quickly looked down, hoping Caroline would just let it go while knowing full well she wouldn't. I knew she was about to make a scene.

"Eliza Wilton," she said slowly with a smirk as she pulled one of my curls. "Aren't you going to apologize, Mutie!" She said that part loudly, so she'd get everyone's attention. It worked. People around us stopped, stared, pointed, and whispered.

I stood there, clutching my books with a scared look on my face. I'd never been much of a talker which is what earned me that nickname. I preferred to listen and observe, a survival technique that usually kept me out of harm's way, but at that moment, it felt like I was directly in the path of harm.

"You owe my friend an apology, *Mutie*," said Tinsley in her shrill voice that reminded me of chalk scraping across a board. She crossed her arms and tapped her shiny, black heels. She stared at me, and it felt like she had lasers for eyes.

"I'm...sorry," I managed to stutter out. It came out so low, it was barely audible. I tried to squeeze my books closer to my chest, but they were already as close as they were going to get.

"That's not a real apology," said Caroline. "It doesn't count if I can't hear it, Mutie."

As if things weren't embarrassing enough, Ethan Rohe, the quarterback of the football team, the Alpha's son, and the bully who originally gave me the nickname of Mutie, came strolling down the hallway with his two groupies. He was an even worse bully than Caroline and I seemed to always be the center of his attention when he was feeling particularly mean. I wanted nothing more than to disappear at that moment. I tried to dart around Caroline before Ethan got to us, but Jessica and Tinsley blocked my path.

"Where are you going? You have to pay for what you've done since you don't want to apologize properly," said Jessica. Suddenly Caroline pushed me so hard that I stumbled backward, dropped my books, lost my footing, and landed on the floor. My books slid all over the place. The entire hallway of students erupted into laughter. I hit my elbow and grimaced at the pain. No one bothered to help me up.

Ethan and his boys walked by me and stared at me with smirks on their faces. "She's mute *and* she's clumsy," Ethan said as he walked by. He kicked one of my books. It slid over and the corner of it hit me on the leg. I winced at the blow and the other two boys laughed as they kept walking by. Caroline, Jessica, and Tinsley joined them, and they all went into Mr. Jamison's classroom.

I hate them all, I thought as I got up and dusted off my pants. I tuned out the laughs and the finger-pointing. I picked up my books, having to dodge a few people as they nonchalantly walked past me. I finally made it into the classroom where a few students were still laughing at me. Some of them whispered and pointed. I went to my desk at the very back corner of the room and sat down.

I hate them all and, in a few months, when I graduate, I'm leaving and going far away, I thought. *Somewhere I can be alone and away from these horrible people.* According to my adoptive parents, my parents had been rogues. I understood why. At least, I imagined I understood why. I didn't know the real reason they were rogues, but if they endured even half of what I had endured during my almost eighteen years of life, I could understand why they'd left their pack. Being alone was better than being treated like crap every day.

I settled down and thankfully everyone quickly forgot about me and moved on to more interesting conversations. The bell rang and Mr. Jamison hopped into action. I was too busy reflecting on my life to pay attention to him.

My home life was only slightly better than school because my adoptive parents, Skylar and Star, mostly ignored me rather than treated me poorly. They only took me in out of pity when I was three years old, and they were sure to remind me of that constantly. "You're lucky we have good hearts," Star would often say. "No one wants a rogue around, especially when they don't know why you're a rogue. You're lucky the Alpha didn't order your death."

I was found by the pack's Beta, Luke Tomlin, hiding behind my dead father's body on the side of the road, trying to keep warm under his fur. My mother was found a few yards away, also dead. Both had been brutally murdered, and no one ever bothered to find out why. According to Luke, they were unable to find any identifying information about me, so they let my adoptive parents name me. I never knew why they chose the name Eliza. They never told me, and I never asked.

When Luke found me, according to him, I didn't make a peep. I didn't cry. I just looked at him. I once heard him refer to me as "the most pitiful thing he'd ever seen." Perhaps he thought I wouldn't remember that comment because I was young, but I was five at the time and I never forgot it.

Luke wasn't the only adult who seemed to think it was okay to say mean stuff to me. On one occasion, Skylar said, "it might be a good thing your parents died. Maybe one day you can shed that rogue title and become a member of the pack. Well, an accepted member of the pack." After a couple of seconds, he added, "probably not, but with them being dead, you'll at least have a shot." Little did Skylar know,

I had no intention of joining the pack. I knew at a young age that I wanted to leave.

I didn't hear Mr. Jamison ask for everyone to pull their homework out. I was staring at my desk, lost in my thoughts when I finally heard, "Eliza!" I jumped and looked up at Mr. Jamison glaring down at me. "Homework, *please*," he said, stretching out his hand. The class laughed and Ethan yelled out, "she's mute, clumsy, and deaf!" This made the students laugh more.

"That's enough, Ethan," said Mr. Jamison with very little authority in his voice. Ethan was the Alpha's son, so he didn't get the discipline that he deserved for his behavior. Most teachers would scold him lightly, but he was basically free to torment me and other students as he pleased.

Mr. Jamison collected my homework and walked back to the front of the class. He put the stack of papers on his desk and refocused his energy. "Group projects!" Mr. Jamison exclaimed. Many of the students groaned. No one really liked group projects. Especially me.

"You're going to start a business," he said. "Well, at least you're going to start one on paper. That means you need to come up with an idea for a product or service and figure out how you're going to sell it. This is going to require a lot of research, so you'll need to set up study groups and split the project up between all group members."

The students began looking around, wondering who they'd partner up with. Many of them were already signaling their friends. I tried to shrink back in my chair, hoping no one would look at me or pick me. *Maybe he'll let me do a solo project if no one wants to partner with me,* I hoped.

"Ah, ah, ah!" said Mr. Jamison. "I will be assigning group members."

The classroom came alive with objections and chatter. Mr. Jamison held his hand up. "Settle down, settle down. I want to make sure you're working together on the project, not hanging out with your friends. You can do that on your own time."

He grabbed a paper from his desk and began reading out the assigned groups. I felt goosebumps rising on my arms and neck. *Please don't put me with Caroline and her lackies*, I thought. *Anyone but them.*

I got my wish. I wasn't partnered with Caroline or any of her friends, but I was partnered with the next worse person I could think of. Mr. Jamison read the group members' names out. "Ethan Rohe, Emily Weaver, Justin Perro, and Eliza Wilton." My heart sank and I felt like I was going to die right there in that cheap, plastic chair.

"Okay, for the remainder of the class period, you'll get with your group members and decide what you want to do for your business. Make plans, assign tasks, and if you have time, start some research. There is a project guide in the online school portal with more instructions."

No one moved.

"Now, guys. Get with your group members now," said Mr. Jamison, finally putting some authority in his voice.

There was a rustle of talking as everyone got up to rearrange themselves into groups. Many of the female students glared at Emily and me as we moved to sit with Ethan. He was next in line to be Alpha, making him the most desired guy in school. All the girls wanted to be on his radar, especially since he'd be shifting for the first time soon and looking for his mate. All of them except for me, that is. I would have gladly traded spots with any of those girls.

As the four of us pulled our desks together, I felt my anxiety begin to rise because I ended up sitting right next to Ethan. I fully expected the group session to turn into an hour of torture for me. Even worse, I'd have to participate in the discussion. That thought was even scarier than the thought of being teased.

The guide in the school portal said that in order to get credit, all group members would have to present a part of the project to the class. It's not that I couldn't talk or that I was shy, it's just that I didn't *like* talking, especially to all those people who obviously hated me. Public speaking was something that I dreaded and usually avoided at all costs. I wanted to be invisible, and talking in front of a group was the complete opposite of that.

"I guess this means we automatically make a bad grade. Maybe even fail," said Justin. We all looked at him for clarification. "Mutie here won't talk. That's twenty-five percent of the grade right there."

"Don't call me that," said I said quietly.

"C'mon guys, don't start. Let's focus on the project here," said Emily. "Let's figure out what we're going to sell."

I noticed that Ethan kept glancing at me in a weird way and wrinkling his nose, almost as if I smelled bad. *I'm pretty sure I put on deodorant today*, I thought. *Please, not something else for him to tease me about.*

"What about clothes? That might be profitable since people are always ripping them up when they shift. Creates repeat customers," said Justin with a shrug.

"That's actually a pretty good idea," said Emily.

"Yeah, but it's lame," said Ethan as he plopped back in his chair. "You can find clothes anywhere. We need something exciting. Something that's going to stand out."

"Puppies," said Emily. "Everyone loves puppies."

"Absolutely not," said Justin. Ethan looked at her and shook his head to say no.

"We could sell sports cars," said Ethan.

"Uh, yeah...maybe," said Emily. "It's just that, you know, realistically, not everyone has the money to buy...sports cars."

Ethan sighed. He looked at me. "Well, what do you think, Mutie? Any ideas?"

I grimaced at the nickname, but I cleared my throat and responded. "Services," I said so quietly that they all leaned towards me to try to hear what I said.

"Speak up, Mutie" commanded Ethan.

I cleared my throat and tried again. "A service. What's the one thing that everyone wants more than anything?" They looked at me with question marks. "A mate," I said. I felt my cheeks get hot with embarrassment although I wasn't sure why. I looked down at my desk as I talked. "We could start a mating service. Like speed dating parties or something. I haven't thought of all the details yet, but—"

"—that's actually a really good idea," said Ethan. "I think you're on to something." The other two students nodded in agreement. *Wow, he agreed with me,* I thought. I was sure he'd laugh at me and tell me I was stupid.

"So Mutie's got something up there after all," Justin said.

"Stop calling me that," I said.

"I'm just joking, sorry," said Justin. I was sure his apology wasn't sincere.

Emily said, "so how would we turn that into a service. I mean, people usually find their mate on their own, you know when you smell them." She glanced at Ethan and gave him a little smile. Justin rolled his eyes.

"That's true, but not everyone finds their mate," said Ethan. "Even worse, some people reject their mates." Ethan, Emily, and Justin shuddered at that thought. Being rejected by your mate, especially a true mate, was one of the most painful experiences a werewolf could go through. Some people never recover from it.

"Yeah, like Mr. Templeton, the guy that lives at the edge of town," said Emily. I heard his mate rejected him like 75 years ago and he's never found another. He just lives his days out alone with no real purpose in life like a useless rogue wolf." Emily gasped and blushed. "Sorry, Eliza, I wasn't referring to..." she trailed off and looked down. "Sorry." I didn't say anything in response. I was used to people bringing up my past.

"Second chance mating service," said Ethan. "For rejected wolves. That's actually kinda pitiful."

"Maybe leave out the rejected part," I said quietly. I glanced at Ethan. "You don't want to insult people." *I can't stand Ethan, but he is hot,* I thought as I looked at his hypnotic green eyes. *Wait, what am I saying? It's Ethan Rohe...eww.* I blushed and looked back at my desk quickly.

"Yeah, I guess you're right," Ethan said. "They won't give us their money if we hurt their feelings." He chuckled. "I mean, we could always force them give it to us, but that might be bad for business."

"Okay, so we have a good idea, guys," said Emily. "It's a start. We just have to do a lot of research to narrow it down. Let's exchange numbers so we can text later." She looked at Ethan and blushed. "You know, about the project." Justin rolled his eyes again.

Ethan, Justin, and Emily exchanged numbers. Then they looked at me. "What's your number, Mutie?" said Justin. Yeah, not a genuine apology.

I took in a deep breath. "I don't have a phone," I said.

Their mouths dropped open. "Cap," said Justin.

"You don't have a phone?" said Emily. "What the hell? How are you making it through life?"

"Makes sense that Mutie wouldn't have a phone," said Ethan as he rolled his eyes.

"Stop calling me that," I said but all three of them ignored me that time.

"Well, Mutie, how are we supposed to communicate with you about the project?" asked Justin.

I sighed. It was no use. "You can email me," I said. The Wiltons had a desktop computer that they let me use for schoolwork. I wrote my email down and pushed it to the group. They looked at each other with an expression that said, "you have to be kidding me," but they each took a photo of the email address.

"We know who the weakest link is going to be," said Justin.

"Guys, stop it," said Emily. "It's fine. We can email her. Whatever."

"Okay, so we're all going to think of ways to refine this idea, right?" asked Ethan. "Everybody comes up with at least one refined idea and we'll pick the best one."

Mr. Jamison interrupted the class. "The bell is about to ring, so put your desks back and pack up."

Everyone complied and a chorus of sliding desks ensued. I noticed as I stood up that Ethan wrinkled his nose again. I moved the desk back and quickly walked back to the safety of my corner. I didn't want to give Ethan a chance to insult me about body odor in front of the entire class.

Less than a minute went by before the bell rang. I sat for a few seconds, giving everyone around me the chance to leave before I stood up. I was nervous that others would catch a whiff of whatever Ethan smelled. As everyone filed out of the classroom, I grabbed my books and headed for the door. I noticed Ethan glance at me with a weird expression and another wrinkle of his nose before he disappeared into the hallway.

What is his problem? I wondered. I pushed it out of my head, dismissing it as another one of his bullying tactics and headed to my next class, praying that my odor wouldn't offend anyone else that day.

The rest of the day went by smoothly. There was only one more moment of teasing and it passed quickly. As usual at the end of school, I walked home alone. That was something I'd started doing the day the Wiltons refused to come get me from school. I lived about three miles away, but I enjoyed smelling the fresh breeze and looking at the serene surroundings as I walked. There was something comforting about the solitude of it, especially after enduring the hell I endured at school every day.

As I began walking in the cool, crisp March air, I noticed a new, very light scent in the breeze that I'd never smelled before. It was so light that I couldn't make out the notes, but it wasn't a bad scent. In fact, it was intriguing. It seemed to be everywhere. I stopped and looked around, trying to figure out what I was smelling.

New flowers? Perhaps one of the girls was wearing a new perfume or one of the guys was wearing a new cologne? Air freshener?

As I looked around, I accidentally locked eyes with Ethan who had apparently been looking at me. I felt a rush of embarrassment, so I turned away from him and quickly started walking home. *Don't let him follow me, please.* I took a chance and looked back. He had turned around and was walking to his car.

After a while, what was usually a peaceful and refreshing walk home ended up being a marathon for the thoughts in my head. Why was that scent so enticing? Why did it seem that Ethan smelled it also? Why was I suddenly getting lost in thoughts of his mesmerizing eyes? I turned these questions over in my head as I made progress on my almost two-hour walk home.

2

Never Get Close Again

On the way home, I passed a lot of nice houses with well-manicured lawns. I saw people watering their gardens or washing their cars as if they didn't have a care in the world. There was a family outside playing T-ball with their little one. An elderly couple sat on their porch in rocking chairs and engaged each other in what seemed to be an amusing conversation. The mailman made his rounds, dropping mail in beautifully bricked-in mailboxes while smiling and waving at neighbors as he went by.

Walking through that beautiful suburban neighborhood everyday made me uncomfortable. It was a life I knew I'd never live—immaculate homes, loving families, safety and security. It was a tease worse than the teasing I endured at school each day and further reinforced my desire to run away. These people were the well-off people in the pack—Gammas and other high ranking pack members. The neighborhoods of Omegas were nothing like this. There was no one outside watering their lawn or playing games. They were too busy trying to work and survive.

The territory of the Moon Valley Pack was massive and stretched for almost thirty miles between the Black Moon River and the beginning of the mountains. The majority of the pack lived within a ten-mile radius of the Alpha's house which was located right in the center of the territory. Omegas lived on the outskirts of this radius, and you would absolutely know when you crossed over into their neighborhoods.

I didn't mind my scanty neighborhood. In fact, I wished I lived even further away from the elites. After all, who wants to be constantly reminded of what they'll never have? *I'll be able to live as far away as I want when I graduate*, I often thought to myself. That thought made me strong enough to endure all that crap at school. *Just get through it and put it behind you*, I'd tell myself. I'd even considered quitting school altogether if I shifted for the first time before graduation. As far as I was concerned, a rogue wolf didn't need a high school degree.

I walked into the old gate that was in desperate need of repair in front of the Wiltons' small yard. It squeaked loudly every time it was opened, alerting all surrounding houses to visitors if they cared to listen. On that day, it alerted Cameron and Cassie, the Wiltons' two kids.

"Eliza's back!" screamed Cass from inside the house.

"So what?" screamed Cam back to her. I walked into the house where 12-year-old Cass was sitting on the couch watching *Renegade Nell*. "Hi, Eliza," she said with a smile. Cass and Cam were like my siblings although they were spoiled brats...well, as much as an Omega family can spoil their kids. We'd grown up together and despite their parents' indifference to me, they'd grown attached to me even though they sometimes acted as if I was the stepsister. In a way, I was.

"Hey, Cass," I said as I continued on to my room.

"Mom's got some bad news for you," she said casually.

I stopped. "What is it," I asked.

"I dunno," Cass said with a shrug. She never took her eyes off the television.

I went to my room which was really a repurposed closet and dropped my things on my tiny bed. Then I went into the kitchen where Star was making dinner.

"Hey, Star," I said quietly, trying to sound somewhat cheerful despite the pit I was feeling in my stomach.

"Oh, you're back," Star said with obvious disdain.

"Is something wrong?" I asked weakly. "Cass said you had bad news."

Star stopped what she was doing. "Oh, Eliza. I...was going to wait for Skylar to get here before I told you. Cass talks too much."

"What is it?" I asked. "Just tell me. What did I do?" I had a feeling I already knew what was coming. The Wiltons never hid the fact that I was just a payday for them, and I would be turning eighteen soon. That meant the money was going to stop.

"This is hard. It really is," said Star. "You know, we care about you so much..." *That's a lie,* I thought.

"...but it's been hard. The money we get for you is barely enough and we have two pups to think about now. So, and I'm sorry for this...you're going to have to move out on your birthday."

"But that's in two weeks!" I exclaimed. That was the loudest I'd ever spoken in my life. "I haven't even shifted for the first time yet!"

"I know, I know, it's so inconvenient—"

"—I don't have any money—"

"—but we can't have a grown person living here for free. We just can't afford it."

"Why did you wait till now to tell me? Why didn't you give me time to prepare? I could have gotten a job!"

I was close to tears. I knew why they didn't tell me. They were afraid I'd leave before they got the last check. They knew they were going to kick me out and didn't bother to give me one dollar of *my own* money.

Cam and Cass were standing in the doorway looking at me with tears in their eyes. Apparently, they were just as surprised as I was.

"Eliza, I'm sorry, but you have two weeks to find somewhere to go." Star opened a drawer and pulled out an envelope. "This isn't much, but it's a start." She handed me the envelope. There were five twenty-dollar bills in it.

"What about school?" I asked. I couldn't hold back my tears any-more. They dropped down my cheeks like a waterfall. "I still have three months until I graduate. Can I at least stay until I finish? I'll stay out of your way."

Star sighed. "Let me talk to Skylar. See what he says. I can't make you any promises."

I knew it was Skylar who wanted me gone more. Star was just telling me what I wanted to hear because she wanted the conversation to end. I gave her what she wanted. I took the envelope and went to my room. I closed the door and cried harder than I'd ever cried before.

I had been looking forward to leaving the Wiltons and the Moon Valley Pack for a long time, but now that I was being thrown out rather than leaving on my own, I was hurt. I knew the Wiltons didn't care for me very much, but I never imagined they had that much of a cruel streak. They were the only family I'd ever known since I didn't remember anything about my parents or where I came from.

How could they do this to me? I thought as a bawled my eyes out. *I have no one. No one loves me.* I cried a few minutes more, then forced myself to think differently.

Stop crying, I said out loud to myself. *You're strong. You don't need anyone. They'll be the last family you ever know. When you leave, you'll never get close to anyone ever again, so you won't be hurt again.*

The pep talk helped only a little. I at least stopped crying, but I dry heaved for a little while until I could get control of my breathing. There was a light knock at the door, like a small hand had caused the interruption. I was in no mood to deal with Cam, Cassie, or even worse, both of them, but I knew they were probably just as confused and hurt as I was. Cam was probably more confused than his sister since he was two years younger than her. I opened the door and both kids stood there peering at me with uneasy curiosity. When they saw my red, swollen eyes, they both started crying. I pulled them to me, and I couldn't help but shed more tears.

"Why is Mom and Dad doing this?" asked Cassie. "Is it because we ate all the candy and blamed it on you? We'll come clean if it means you can stay," she said.

I chuckled. "No, it's not that. This has nothing to do with you guys. It's just time for me to...go be an adult so your parents can focus on taking care of you."

"Will you come back to see us?" asked Cam timidly.

I wiped his eyes and paused before I answered. I didn't want to lie to him. "I'll never forget you," I said. "You're my little brother. And you're my little sister." I did my best to muster up a smile and I ruffled Cam's hair. He hated when I did that, but this time, he didn't swat my hand away like he would usually do. "C'mon guys, stop crying. Everything is fine. I'm really tired. I need to get a nap. I'll play the game with you when I get up." They nodded and left me to my little room.

Pretending to be the protective big sister zapped the rest of my energy. I spent the rest of the day in my room thinking until I finally fell asleep, and I didn't wake up until the next morning.

...

I left for school early because I didn't want to cross paths with the Wiltons. I bought breakfast on the way to school—a sausage, egg, and cheese McMuffin from McDonald's—since I had money for the first time in my life. The taste was amazing! *I wish I'd bought two,* I thought as I took the last bite.

I wasn't in the mood for a repeat of yesterday's bullying, so I got to Mr. Jamison's class well before the bell rang. I sat at my desk in the dark with my head down. Before I knew it, I had fallen asleep and was being woken up by someone who was shaking me. My first thought was that it was Caroline or Ethan coming over to bully me, but I relaxed when I saw it was Mr. Jamison.

"You're bright and early," he said as he walked to the front of the room and put his briefcase on his desk. I didn't say anything. I just looked at him.

"Is everything okay?" he asked. I nodded and looked down at my desk.

Mr. Jamison looked at me for a moment. "You're probably nervous about your first shift. It's coming up soon, right?" I nodded.

"There's nothing to be nervous about. I mean, it's going to hurt, that's true. But you'll be fine with your parents to guide you through it," he said.

That statement stung me deeply. I cleared my throat. "I don't...have parents," I said quietly.

"Well, yes. The Wiltons adopted you," he said. "In any case, you'll have someone there, so you can relax."

I didn't want to start the day off by crying in front of everyone, so I just nodded in agreement rather than trying to explain the situation to Mr. Jamison. The bell rang, saving me from the rest of the awkward conversation.

Students started coming in and I made sure to keep my eyes down so I wouldn't be noticed. Unfortunately, it didn't work. Ethan, Justin, and Emily walked over to me. Ethan thumbed at Samuel, the guy that sat in front of me and he promptly got up and walked away. Emily stood on my left and Justin stood on my right. I looked back and forth between the three of them with confusion. *Are they about to beat me up or something?* I wondered.

"What happened to you yesterday?" Ethan said in an annoyed tone. I didn't understand. I frowned.

"You told us to email you, but you didn't respond," said Emily. *Crap, the project,* I thought.

"I...I'm sorry. I had a lot going on," I said quietly.

"You don't even have to talk to send an email, Mutie!" Justin said. "I'm not failing this project because of you. I need a good grade on this to pass," he said.

"Hey, Justin. Calm down. You don't have to yell at her," Ethan said.

Whoa! Did Ethan just stick up for me, I thought.

Justin sighed. "Whatever, man, but if she doesn't pull her weight, I'm not taking the hit for it. I've worked hard to graduate with honors and I'm not letting Mutie here mess that up." He and Emily went to their desks. My anxiety level tripled. I was sitting face to face, alone with Ethan the jerk for the first time ever. I didn't know what was about to happen. *Is he going to tease me? Push me out of my desk? Pull my hair?* At least a dozen ways Ethan could bully me went through my head at the speed of light.

"I can tell something is going on with you," he said, "so I'll give you a pass this time. Just keep in mind that your actions affect us all," he said.

"I will," I said quietly. "It won't happen again." I felt like I had just been scolded by a parent. *Not that I know what a real parent is,* I thought. Ethan got up to go to his desk and I noticed that strange scent from yesterday. It was light, almost undetectable, and definitely unrecognizable, but there was no mistaking it this time. The scent was coming from Ethan. *It must be a new cologne,* I thought. *I like it.*

The class went by smoothly, but Mr. Jamison had us working in groups again. I was quiet for most of the session, only putting in my opinion when I absolutely had to. I noticed Ethan staring at me a few times with a look of confusion on his face. He didn't tease me once during the entire class. Justin must have noticed also because he followed Ethan's lead and didn't call me Mutie at all during the group session.

The rest of school was a typical day. There was name-calling, hair pulling, and during the transfer to the last block of the day, someone tripped me in the hallway and made me drop my books. Everyone laughed at me and that was one thing too much with the way I was already feeling. I decided to ditch the last block of school.

As I walked home, I thought about my first shift. The full moon was that night and if I was going to shift, it would likely be then since most people shifted on the full moon closest to their eighteenth birthday. I'd be able to take care of myself better with my wolf inside, so I prayed to the Moon Goddess to let my first shift happen. I was about to take a huge risk, and I needed all the favor I could get.

Once I arrived at the Wiltons', I decided I didn't want to spend another minute living in that house or living in a town of people who hated me. I put my faith in the Moon Goddess, packed my few belongings in one of Cam's old bookbags, along with some food from the pantry, and left the Wiltons' house, with plans to never to return again. My life as a rogue wolf started with the creak of the old gate slamming behind me.

3

Going Rogue

I walked for a mile along the road, then decided to turn off and make my way through the woods. I'd never been in that part of the territory before and had no idea where I was going, but it seemed off the beaten path which was just what I wanted. My desire was to be away from everyone, so going to an isolated area was the goal. I found a place deep in the woods that was well hidden and covered by thick foliage at the top of the trees surrounding it. The small clearing was circled on three sides by bushes. It was there that I made camp and decided to wait for my shift...if it would happen.

Later that evening, I guessed a little after six according to the waning sunlight, I made a small fire to keep myself warm. Days in early March in South Carolina were tolerable and that day had a high of sixty, but at night temperatures would sometimes go down into the thirties. This is something I hadn't considered when I packed. I didn't bring warm layers or an extra change of clothes. I didn't even bring a coat or jacket. *Some street smarts,* I thought to myself as I scooted as close as I could to the fire. I ate some of the food I'd taken from the Wiltons' pantry. Sardines and crackers were hardly a meal, but it was better than shifting on an empty stomach.

The small fire wasn't enough to keep me warm as the temperature continued to drop. I shivered as the cool air bit my skin. Goosebumps filled my arms and legs, and my nose felt like a small block of ice. I drew my legs to my chest and hugged myself for warmth. When that didn't work, I laid down and curled up as close to the fire as I safely could. I could feel the heat stinging one side of my body as the other side was assaulted by the cold air. I felt like an unevenly cooked roast. *Please let me shift,* I thought. *I can't survive out here without my wolf. I beg of you Moon Goddess. Have mercy on me.*

I lost track of time as my body began to freeze. I started shivering uncontrollably and my breathing became labored. This lasted for what I guessed was half an hour, then my body stopped shivering. *That's a good thing, right?* I wondered as I sat up. I didn't feel cold anymore, but I was exhausted. *My body must be worn out from all the shivering.*

I closed my eyes and thought about what I was going to do if I didn't shift. I was pretty sure I would die. I'd freeze to death right there in that little enclave of bushes and no one would even care. I doubted that anyone would even look for me. My remains would wither away and maybe years later some hunter or hiker might find my bones.

Just as I was about to drift off to sleep, I felt a strange sensation. First, it felt like an inner warmth which, considering the frigid temperature, I was thankful for. The little heat somehow comforted me despite the gloomy situation I was in. Then, the warmth spread over my entire body and I felt a prickly feeling all over. *I'm about to shift,* I thought. *It's really going to happen.*

The next feeling was a stark contrast to the warmth. It was absolutely awful. I felt my bones begin to bend. It hurt like hell. I screamed out as they continued to reshape themselves. Then...SNAP! My femur broke. The sudden onset of pain was almost too much to bear as bones began snapping all over my body. It was pure torture. I screamed for dear life as tears blurred my vision.

Just when I thought I couldn't take anymore, the pain subsided quickly, and other changes began to happen to my body. Fangs grew in my mouth, knocking out the two teeth whose place they took. Beautiful, shiny, thick brown fur grew from my skin. I grew a bushy tail. I shifted into a werewolf with piercing brown eyes. The Moon Goddess had favored me when I needed favor the most, saving me from what would probably have been a cold and lonely death that night.

I felt stronger than I'd ever felt in my life. I was happy to meet my wolf because I now understood that I would never be alone again. It was like having another being in my body—not one that talked to me or controlled me or anything, but just another presence inside me that loved me and accepted me no matter what.

When I got my bearings and rested for a couple of minutes, allowing every trace of pain to subside, I walked around the fire to test out how well I walked on all fours. To my surprise, I didn't need any practice. Walking on four legs seemed to be a natural instinct. I panted, stuck my tongue out, and licked my snout. I growled and bared my teeth. I looked at my bushy tail and had the desire to touch it. I chased it in a circle once, remembered how ridiculous my neighbor's dog looked when he did it, and opted to just shake it instead.

It was time for the most important test. I started running slowly and I quickly realized that my leg muscles were extraordinarily powerful. I took a few minutes to run through the woods, testing out my power and speed. I was *fast*. It was exciting to fly past all the trees and bushes. I thought that running past them so fast would make them appear like a blur, but my eyesight was exemplary. I could see every detail of every leaf even as I passed them at such a rapid pace.

When the moon reached its highest point around midnight, I took some time to give thanks to the Moon Goddess. I howled, happily and thankfully. Soon, my howls were joined by a few other howls in the territory. Apparently I wasn't the only one who had shifted for the first time.

I spent the night running through the woods in my wolf form, testing all my heightened abilities and senses. I could see things clearly for at least seventy-five feet ahead of me. I could hear sounds clearly and distinctly, sounds that I never even knew existed. I spent time just sitting in one spot and listening to all the different sounds the woods made. I heard animals and insects. I could hear the slither of snakes and the pattering of squirrels. I could hear sounds that were unrecognizable to me. *I'll figure out what they all are,* I thought to myself as I listened with fascination.

The most amazing sense that I enjoyed was a heightened sense of smell. I could smell at least a hundred different odors. Some scents were good, and some were bad, but I relished the bad ones because I was so enthralled by the crispness of them. I could smell distinct scents from miles away and I longed to identify them all.

I was no longer cold despite the freezing temperature. I suspected that my fur had something to do with that, but I thought that maybe it was simply an inner warmth. *Does this mean I'll be overheated in summer?* I wondered, but I shrugged it off and decided to figure that out some other time.

My fear of...well...everything had subsided and for the first time in my life, I felt powerful and invincible. I felt loved knowing that my wolf would never leave me. *What more do I need? This rogue wolf life is going to be amazing*, I thought.

After a lot of running and at least an hour of exploring the outskirts of the pack territory, I decided on the perfect place to cross the territory border. I returned to my camp for a rest. I may have had heightened abilities but using them all made me tired. That was one thing my wolf form had in common with my human form. Both forms needed sleep. I settled in for a few hours of shut eye, staying in my wolf form to keep warm, and decided that I would leave the pack territory for good when I woke up.

A few hours later, I woke up feeling energized and ready to go. I was hungry, so I decided to change back to my human form temporarily so I could eat food from my bookbag. That was easier said than done. I realized I didn't know how to shift back. It took a little while, but I eventually found the trigger.

To my surprise, I was still warm in my human form so I only need to shift back to eat. Sardines and crackers again. Not a great breakfast, but I would make do with what I had.

I ate breakfast naked. The clothes I had on before my shift had been ripped to shreds. I decided to change back to my wolf form for cover. Plus I liked being in my wolf form. *No pain this time. That's awesome*

I thought. I grabbed my bookbag with my mouth and headed for the mountains beyond the pack's territory.

I stopped twice on my way and ate sweet berries from the bushes. I wasn't sure if they were edible, so I attempted to use my keen sense of smell to sniff for any parts of the berries that might seem dangerous. Every part of the berries smelled yummy, so I took a chance and gobbled them down with satisfaction.

I stopped another time to drink from a cool stream. After drinking from the stream, I realized how good the running water felt over my paw. I frolicked in the stream for a while and splashed around while trying to catch some of the fish that darted around me. It took a few tries, but I finally caught one and ate it. *A bit unorthodox for my human side,* I thought, *but it tastes good, and I need to get used to eating like this if I'm going to be out here on my own.*

For the first time in my life, I had a consistent few hours of peace without anyone teasing me, hurting me, or bothering me. *No more Caroline. No more Ethan. No more fake love from Star and Skylar. Just me. I'm the priority now.* The peace and joy that I was experiencing further reinforced the idea that I should be a lone wolf. I loved every moment of it.

I finally reached the very edge of the pack territory. This was it. I was about to embrace life as a rogue. Once I crossed over, I would be exiled forever since the Alpha's number one rule was to never go into the forbidden mountains. For just a brief moment, I thought about how lonely I might be and how I may never find my mate, but a life of peace seemed to be a much better choice than what I had suffered since I was adopted fifteen years ago. No one in the pack ever liked me anyway. Leaving would be no one's loss. I thought about this, and it fueled me to cross the border.

While I had never been in this unclaimed territory, I'd heard stories about the dangerous wolves that lurked in and around the valleys. I felt a little nervous, but how bad could it be with sunrise right around the corner? I slowly plowed my way through the valley, working hard to keep my wits as I went.

As I walked, I began to smell something coming from behind me. It was the scent I'd smelled at school, but stronger. *Much* stronger. *The scent I'd smelled on Ethan,* I thought. I could make out the notes this time—a cedarwood and pine combination with a hint of orange. Even with a forest full of trees behind me, that scent stood out. There was something unique about it that I couldn't quite put my finger on.

The closer the scent got, the more my senses tingled. I stopped. I wanted to continue with my rogue journey, but that scent was driving me crazy. It made me want to turn back. It seemed that the scent was getting stronger and stronger, as if it were following me. *It's not the scent that's following me,* I thought. *It's a person. A wolf.* I turned around and peered into the darkness and saw a wolf bounding behind me.

As I stared at the wolf with the attractive smell, I didn't notice the dark, looming figure advancing slowly on me from the front. If I hadn't been distracted, I might have detected the dangerous wolf before it got too close. By the time I noticed him, it was too late. He lunged at me, and I didn't even have time to get out of the way. *What a short life as a rogue,* was all I had time to think as the wolf closed in on me with malice in his eyes.

4

True Mates

It was hard sneaking away from the celebration. I felt the shift coming and it wasn't something I wanted to do in front of everyone despite the fact they were all there to support me. In my opinion, a first shift was a private moment. More importantly, if it hurt, I didn't want to be a screaming punk in front of everyone. I had an image to maintain.

I went into the woods and found a quiet spot nestled between a group of trees and bushes. I took off my clothes because my father had warned me they'd be ripped to shreds if I didn't, and I waited. It happened just like my parents said it would. First, intense pain from my bones cracking and rearranging themselves, then a sudden awareness of, well, everything. The pain sucked, but everything else was mind-blowing. I felt power surge through me unlike anything I could have imagined.

After I shifted and got my composure, I went back to the celebration, clothes in tow in my mouth, and everyone was thrilled to see me in my wolf form. There were plenty of gasps, lots of applause, and a few people who ruffled my fur.

"Your future Alpha, ladies and gentleman," my father said proudly.

For the purposes of the party, I changed back to my human form which was surprisingly easy and pain-free. I dressed and headed back to join in on the fun. We partied for hours into the early morning. After the last of the guests left, I was tired and so was my family. They opted to go to bed, but I decided to ignore my fatigue and go enjoy my wolf. He'd been almost begging me to shift back the entire party.

I ran for miles, taking everything in. I could see small details that I'd never noticed before. I could hear sounds that I never knew existed. I could smell everything. That's when it hit me. The scent that I'd been smelling at school. Eliza's scent. It stopped me in my tracks. The scent was mild like she was far away, but I could now distinctly smell each note. She smelled sweet, like lilac and peppermint, but in a way that was a unique combination, unlike anything I'd ever smelled before. *But why is she so far away? Where is she?* I wondered.

The scent was making me crazy and horny. I knew what it meant. Eliza was my mate. *Mutie,* the girl whose life I made miserable in school was my mate. I instantly recoiled at that thought. *I'll never call her that name again. It was so awful of me to call her that,* I thought as shame crept in.

I didn't have a choice but to follow the scent. My wolf was going crazy inside for her. The feelings that were surfacing were just as intense as all the senses I had developed. As I walked towards her, I thought of all the awful things I had done to her over the years, and the fact that she might reject me. I wasn't strong enough to handle a rejection yet. I'd just turned for the first time and a rejection would weaken me severely. It might even kill me. Yet, I sensed something wasn't quite right, so I kept looking for her.

As I walked deeper into the woods, I began to grow uneasy. No one in the pack ever came out into the territory this far. *Perhaps she changed and like me she just wanted to run around and enjoy her new abilities.* As much as I wanted to believe that, I knew that wasn't exactly the case. The Alpha in me, which seemed to develop as quickly as my other senses, could tell that it was something else. I suddenly realized why. Her scent wasn't getting closer. It was getting further away. *Where are you going, Eliza?*

I could smell her scent in a trail. I came across what looked like a camp site. There was a fire that had been recently put out and I could see a spot on the ground where someone had slept. I walked over to it.

Eliza. She was here. Did she stay out here all night? Was her family with her? Where is she now?

I sniffed the air, trying to pick up her trail again. It seemed to wane, so I had to concentrate hard. I picked up a whiff of it near the stream, but that didn't make me feel better. The stream was even closer to the edge of the pack territory. An alarm went off inside of me. *She's leaving. She's leaving the pack! She's leaving me!*

Why shouldn't she? The entire pack had treated her like an outsider. She was the daughter of rogue wolves, so it would make sense that she chose to be a loner. That's probably why she never talked to anyone very much. Maybe she was always planning to leave.

I had to stop her. I had to beg for her forgiveness. I'd been waiting for my true mate all my life and I wasn't about to lose her now.

It was harder following her trail downstream, but I finally came to a place where her scent left the stream and went back into the trees. This made it much easier to track her and the trail was leading to...*the mountains! No, Eliza! It's dangerous there!*

The mountains were full of evil, rogue wolves who had no morals or code of conduct. There wasn't much food in the mountains, so they'd resort to cannibalism if necessary. They didn't take kindly to outsiders.

Something told me that Eliza was about to be in big trouble, so I took off running as fast as I could. Panic began to set in as I smelled something else—someone else. Someone foul.

Eliza, turn around, I shouted through my mind. *Turn around!* But I knew she couldn't hear me from this distance because we hadn't mated yet. We hadn't solidified our bond yet. The thought occurred to me that we might never do that, but I pushed it out of my head and focused on getting to her.

Her scent was intoxicating. It was getting stronger which meant I was gaining on her. Then I saw her a couple of miles ahead of me. It was amazing how much my vision sharpened from shifting. I could see that she was moving, and it was as I suspected—towards the mountains.

I didn't care how tired I was. I pushed myself to my limit to get to her because I could smell the rogue wolf hiding in the shadows, waiting for her to cross out of the safety of my territory. *Why can't she smell him? Is she distracted?* For the first time in my life, I felt fear as Eliza disappeared into the dark valley.

As I got closer, I saw Eliza look back at me. I also saw the dark wolf advancing towards her, but she didn't see him. *Run Eliza! Run!* But it was too late. I ran for dear life and leapt in the air at the same time the dark wolf leapt in the air.

...

I gasped as the large, dark wolf descended on me. My short life flashed before my eyes as I stared at the sharp, outstretched claws that were going to rip me to shreds. It seemed the dark wolf was moving in slow motion, and it took forever for him to get to me, but I still wasn't fast enough to dodge him. I could see the underside of his belly and all of his sharp teeth as he seemingly hovered right above me. I was sure my life was over, but right before he landed on me, another wolf with beautiful, light brown fur flew from behind me, over my head, and knocked him out of the air just in the nick of time.

The light brown wolf landed almost gracefully between my attacker and me. He growled at the dark wolf as he tumbled along the ground from the blow. The two wolves bared their teeth at each other as the dark wolf quickly recovered from the ground. I bared my teeth also, even though I was terrified. The wolf that had saved me was bigger and stronger than the dark wolf. The dark wolf must have thought that he would lose the fight, seeing as it was two against one, so he backed up a few steps and ran off into the darkness of the valley.

I stared at the wolf's back, realizing that the scent I had been smelling was emanating from him in waves. He smelled so good! I knew I should have been focused on the obvious danger around us, but all I could focus on was this brave wolf who had just saved my life and his intoxicating scent. He was the wolf that had been following me, but why? And why was I so attracted to him?

He turned to me. He was much larger than I was, and I wouldn't have been able to fight him off, but I knew in my heart that he wouldn't harm me. His green eyes were kind, and he stared at me with adoration. I was panting, but it wasn't from fear. There was something about this wolf that was making my heart race. After a moment, he spoke to me through a mind link, albeit a weak one.

Leave, now, he projected.

Ethan? I stared at the newly transformed Ethan. I couldn't believe that he had come to my rescue. Ethan, the jerk who'd given me that awful nickname and treated me like dirt for most of our high school years, had saved my life and now he seemed eager to protect me.

. Why are you here—

—no time. Leave, now, he projected to me more forcefully than before. I grabbed my bag from the ground and ran back towards the pack's territory. Ethan followed, right on my heels, constantly looking around for any predators.

As we ran, Ethan kept getting extremely close to me at times and I thought it was on purpose. The closer he got to me, the more my heart raced. I knew there was only one reason I would feel this way, but I didn't want to believe it. *Not Ethan. Anyone but him,* I thought as I vehemently tried to deny what I was feeling.

We didn't speak much as we ran because our bond wasn't solidified yet. We could get simple thoughts to each other, but we would need to mate to be able to fully bond and have full mind link conversations. *I'm not mating with him,* I thought but my wolf was saying otherwise.

After we were safely in the pack territory a good distance, we slowed down and walked. Ethan tried to nuzzle me a few times but each time I pulled away. *Life has already been so cruel to me, and now my mate is Ethan Rohe. Will the cruelty never end?*

Ethan stopped in a clearing when he felt that it was safe to do so. "Need to talk," Ethan said through the mind link. He tried to nuzzle me once again and once again, I pulled away.

"No clothes," I said.

"Hide in grass," he replied, "please, Eliza."

I didn't want to shift back, but he was right about us needing to talk. Ethan turned away and I walked into the tall grass. I shifted to my human form, but stayed down so Ethan could only see my face and shoulders.

Ethan had shifted to his human form also, but not in the grass. When I turned, I caught a glimpse of his naked body before gasping and looking down at the ground quickly. It was too late–the image was in my head, and I felt myself getting aroused. *No, Eliza. It's Ethan Rohe. No!*

We were both silent for a few moments, neither of us knowing what to say to the other. Finally, Ethan broke the tension.

"Eliza, I've been really shitty to you. I know it's not worth much, but I'm sorry."

I was surprised by his apology. Ethan had never apologized before, not once. Not even the time he tripped me while I was carrying my lunch tray. I fell and the food flew everywhere. I scraped my elbow. Everyone in the cafeteria laughed at me and no one helped me up. I remembered looking at Ethan as I picked myself up from the ground and he and his jerkwad friends just laughed. After that, I avoided the cafeteria at lunch time for the rest of the year.

"I know you were trying to leave. I don't blame you," he said. "But you're my mate, Eliza. Do you feel it?"

I didn't say anything, but I sighed. I didn't want to feel it. I didn't want Ethan to be my mate, but my wolf was longing for his touch.

"Please stay," he pleaded. "Let me make it up to you. I'll do whatever it takes. I've been waiting my entire life to feel this bond with my true mate."

I had decided early on that I never wanted a mate. Everyone I had ever met mistreated me, so I'd always planned on being a loner. Now that Ethan was my mate, I wanted a mate even less. How could I love someone who was so awful to me? I didn't think I could forget the pure torture he put me through for the last four years. I didn't think I'd be able to get past all those memories.

"Eliza? Say something..."

Mutie, I immediately thought.

"...baby. Will you give me a chance?"

Baby. He called me baby, not Mutie! My heart fluttered. Then I thought, *this must be what it feels like to have bipolar disorder. How can I want him and not want him at the same time?*

"Eliza? Please, say something. Anything." He looked at me with pleading eyes. *Beautiful, intense, green eyes* I thought.

"I can't stay," I blurted out. He recoiled at that statement, and I felt a little tinge of pain inside. "It's too painful. Too many memories. Not just from you. From everyone."

Ethan sighed heavily. It came out almost as a sad moan. "I know a lot of that is my fault. I'm ashamed of how I've hurt you," he said. Ethan sat down and put his head in his hands.

I could almost feel his heartache. It looked as if he were going to cry. *An Alpha crying? That doesn't happen, ever,* I thought. But, of course, he wasn't the Alpha yet. One thing was clear—he was truly sorry for all he had done to me and a part of me wanted to forgive him. But it wasn't enough. He was only sorry because I was his mate, not because he'd suddenly had some epiphany about how much of a bully he was. My entire life was one giant ball of pain, and I just wanted peace. I truly felt I could only get that if I was alone.

"Even if I wanted to stay, I can't," I said. "I have nowhere to live." I hung my head shamefully.

"What do you mean," Ethan asked. "What happened to your house?"

"The house is fine. I just don't have a home anymore. I don't think I ever did. My parents...adoptive parents, kicked me out."

"They kicked you out right before you shifted!" Ethan's eyes went dark. "Why would they do that?"

"Because I'm turning 18 and the checks are going to stop coming. It's fine, really. I wanted to leave anyway," I said. I noticed that my voice cracked as I said it. I cleared my throat.

"I can't believe they did that to you!" Then after a beat, "wait. Did you have to shift out here, alone?"

A wave of emotion came over me as I nodded. Tears dropped from my eyes. I had been so strong since I left the Wiltons' house and unwilling to let the situation affect me, but admitting what happened to someone out loud finally made me feel the betrayal in full force. Perhaps it was admitting it to my true mate that made me feel it. My emotions were all over the place.

The Wiltons' house wasn't much, but it had been my home—my safe haven for 15 years and they just put me out like I didn't matter. The dynamic between the Wiltons and me was never great, but they were the only family I knew. I realized that I missed them, especially Cam and Cassie. The fact that I would never see them again crossed my mind and that hurt more than I was willing to admit. At least until then, when I was talking to my mate and I seemed to be unable to control myself.

I didn't realize that I had started sobbing heavily. I was lost in my thoughts when I suddenly felt warm arms around my naked body. At first, I was surprised, and I was going to push him away, but my sorrow got the best of me, and I just cried into his chest.

"It's okay, baby. Everything is going to be alright. I'm here and I will never let anyone hurt you again," said Ethan as I let out fifteen years of pain onto the chest of one of the people that had hurt me the most.

5

Our First Time

After I finished with my massive cry I felt a little better. I looked up at Ethan with my swollen eyes. He had been patiently holding me. He pushed some of my curls from my forehead and kissed it. Then he leaned down and kissed me on the lips.

I felt fireworks erupt inside and I forgot all about not wanting Ethan to be my mate. I leaned into the kiss, and soon I felt Ethan's tongue part my lips. It felt so good to be in his arms as he caressed my body.

His hands slid down my waist to my hips. He sat back, stretched out his legs, and hoisted me onto his lap. I straddled him and I could feel his erection trapped between our abdomens. A warm, moist sensation developed between my legs. We continued kissing, tongues dancing in each other's mouths as our naked bodies pressed against each other in the grass.

I stopped to catch my breath, and I said shyly, "I'm a virgin." He smiled warmly at me. "So am I," he said.

What? My mouth dropped open. "You? You're a virgin? You could have any girl at school that you want! You didn't...with any of them?"

"Well...I made out with some of them. I'll admit, I received oral a couple of times."

I pressed my lips together. I'm pretty sure I was blushing.

"Hey, they were offering! But I wanted to save the real thing for my mate. I wanted to save myself for you." He caressed my cheek and kissed me gently. "Eliza, I had this whole plan. I wanted to wait and take our time. I wanted our first time to be extra special," he said, "but holding you like this, I don't know if I can wait." He kissed me again and his hands explored forbidden parts of my body. It felt good and even though I knew it was too soon for us, I was powerless to stop him. The attraction was too strong.

"One thing, Ethan." I managed to squeak out as I paused for breath. It was the first time I had said his name during the conversation, and it felt strange coming out of my mouth.

"Anything," he said.

"I'm not ready to be marked," I said. "I need time." I saw a flicker of disappointment in his eyes.

"I understand," he said.

I initiated a kiss, and Ethan didn't waste time taking over. He placed me on my back and crawled on top of me, between my legs. I wrapped my legs around his waist. I moaned as I felt a light pop when he went in. It hurt at first, but the pain quickly went away. *This is the most wonderful feeling in the world,* I thought as Ethan made love to me.

We made love for only a few minutes before a strange sensation started building in my core. I got warm inside, not like when I shifted, but a more intense and concentrated warmth. My body shivered and an abrupt feeling that started in my vagina washed over me and took my breath away. "I take it back," I said out loud. "*This* is the best feeling in the world!" I closed my eyes and enjoyed every moment of my very first orgasm.

...

I wasn't prepared for how good it would feel being inside of her. She was so wet and warm. It was heaven and I never wanted to come out. *We're going to be doing this a lot,* I thought. *If I can convince her to stay.*

I kissed her and ran my fingers through her curls as I tried to figure out the best timing of my movements. I was nervous at first, hoping that I was making her feel as good as she was making me feel. Suddenly, her body started shivering and she shouted, "I take it back! This is the best feeling in the world!"

That startled me and I almost stopped, but suddenly I felt this intense wetness surrounding my member. It felt so good, it drove me wild. Before I could stop myself, I was shooting my seed deep inside her.

"Fuck!" I shouted as I felt the energy leaving my body. My arms were trembling, and I almost collapsed on top of her. We both stayed in that position for a moment as we caught our breath. I was completely embarrassed.

"I'm sorry," I said breathlessly as I tried to recover.

"Sorry for what?" Eliza asked. Her eyebrows rose up as she looked at me curiously.

"I came too fast. It's embarrassing," I said. I tried to avoid eye contact with Eliza but I'm sure she could see the shame in my face anyway.

"It's okay," she said. "It felt good. It felt right. Please don't be embarrassed. I loved it." She put her arms around my neck and for a moment, I saw love in her eyes. That was all I needed...a shred of hope that she was mine.

I looked at her and smiled. Then I felt my horniness coming back. I leaned over, still on top of her, and kissed her. That made my manhood hard again. I pushed it inside of her and once more we started making love.

This time it lasted a lot longer. We laid on the grass for at least half an hour pleasing each other. *I'm not losing you,* I thought as we made love. *You're mine and I will fight for you.*

She orgasmed once more, this time moaning much louder than the first time. Her shivering body turned me on so much, but I was able to control myself a little better this time. The thought occurred to me that she might get pregnant. It was way too soon for us to have a pup but if it would make her stay, I was fine with it.

I looked into her eyes, and she looked into mine. "I love you Eliza." She looked startled. Her mouth opened but she didn't say anything.

"You don't have to say it right now, baby. I know you need time. Just know that I love you and only you."

I got up and helped her off the ground. There was grass all over her back side and all over my knees. I helped her get it off, then I kissed her. I felt myself getting hard again.

"I need to stop kissing you for a while," I said. "Otherwise, we'll never make it back to town." I chuckled but Eliza just stared at me. "What? What is it," I asked her. I couldn't help but look at her naked body. *Shit, I want to be inside her again. Control yourself, Ethan.*

She smiled briefly and I realized that our bond had strengthened, so she could probably hear my thoughts. That turned me on too, so I was going to embrace her and make love to her again, but she stepped back from me.

"Eliza?" I asked in confusion.

"I'm sorry, Ethan," she said. "But I'm not going back to town." Then she suddenly shifted back to her wolf form, and I knew she was preparing to run away from me.

...

I looked at Ethan and I could feel my wolf's disapproval of what I was about to do, but there was no way I was going back. I was finally free. It's what I wanted my entire life. I was in love with Ethan and there was nothing I could do about that, but just because he was my mate didn't mean I was suddenly going to want to settle down and be his mate.

I turned around and took off, hoping the head start meant that he wouldn't catch up to me. I was wrong about that. Before I even made it 30 yards, Ethan had shifted, caught up with me, and leapt in front of me. *Gosh he's fast,* I thought. *Well, he is the Alpha's son, so I guess that makes sense.*

Yes, that makes sense, Ethan said through our mind connection. I had forgotten that we could hear each other's thoughts, and the ability was stronger now that we had made love. If we mated, it would be unbreakable, and I'd probably never have another thought to myself no matter how hard I tried. I wasn't sure if I wanted that.

Eliza, please don't run away from me. I don't think he realized that the way he said it seemed less like a request and more like a command.

I'm not running away from you, I projected to him. *Well, maybe I'm running away from you a little bit, but I'm not running away from only you. I'm running away from the pack. I've always wanted to go back to my rogue roots. I've dreamed about it since I was little.*

Ethan walked over to me and nuzzled me. A part of me wanted to stop him because every touch made me want him more, but that was also the same reason I couldn't stop him.

Why? Why would you want to be a rogue? I mean, I know your parents were rogues, but you'd be alone. You would be an outcast. Unprotected. At least here I can make sure you're safe.

I'm an outcast now, Ethan. At home. At school. Everywhere. I just want some peace in my life. I...I don't want a mate. I backed away from him a little. I could tell from the way Ethan's eyes shifted that my statement hurt him. It wasn't a real rejection, but the statement still hurt him. In fact, it hurt me too.

I'm sorry. I didn't mean to hurt you, Ethan. I'm just being honest. I've always said that—

—please, stop, he projected in a beseeching tone. *Look, Eliza, daylight is coming in. We both need some clothes. We both need food and rest. Please, just come back, at least for today. Let's get some sleep and we'll talk later. I give you my word that I won't mark you.*

He wasn't wrong. I needed all those things since I didn't do a great job of packing. Plus, the fact that I almost got ripped to shreds in the valley meant that I might need to come up with another game plan anyway. I sat down and hung my head.

I don't have anywhere to go, I said.

You can come to my house.

That statement got my attention loud and clear. I snapped my head up. *Your house? The Alpha and Luna's house? But they didn't invite me—*

I'm inviting you. It's okay. You can sleep in my room, but if you don't want to you can sleep in a guest room.

Ethan, your parents hate me.

They don't hate you! Look, I'm not taking no for an answer on this. Just come back with me.

Not taking no for an answer. Is he going to force me to go back? I wondered.

No, I won't do anything to hurt you, he projected back. *I'll just follow you anywhere you go, so you may as well come back.*

Stupid mind link, I thought. Ethan sort of snorted. *Ugh, stupid mind link,* I thought again. *Okay, fine, I'll come back with you for now, but this doesn't mean I'm staying, understand?*

Yes, I understand, he projected sullenly. *Let's go.*

I grabbed my bag and we both took off running towards Ethan's house. *No, the Alpha's house* I thought as a sinking feeling developed in my core. When we got there, we changed to our naked human forms and Ethan snuck me in through a window. Luckily, it was still early morning, so no one was walking around. Ethan got me into his room undetected. He put on some clothes.

"Wait here. I'll be right back," he said. He didn't have to tell me that. I was terrified of going anywhere in that house. I waited in his room for about ten minutes before he finally came back with some clothes for me.

"Who's clothes are these?" I asked.

"My sister's," he said.

"Oh my God, I can't put these on. She'll kill me!" I tried to shove the clothes back to Ethan, but he wouldn't take them.

"It's fine, Eliza. I swear to you. You're my mate so no one will lay a hand on you."

I took a deep breath. I felt like I was signing my death certificate by putting on Stacey Rohe's clothes, but I had to put on something. I looked at the tag on the pants. Size 8. Ethan watched me dress as I put the clothes on. They fit nicely and I was a bit happy that we wore the same size clothes. It made me feel less fat.

"Ethan?"

"Yes, baby," he said as he caressed my cheek.

"I think I should sleep in a guest room." I could see the disappointment in his face. "It's just that...well I'm really tired and if I sleep in your bed, we'll probably never get to sleep." That was the truth, but there was another part that I didn't say. I didn't want us sleeping together and having sex because it would cloud my judgment. I also didn't want to disrespect the Alpha and Luna's house.

"You're right, and I'm tired too. Okay follow me, quietly."

Ethan snuck me into a room that was just two doors down from his. I wondered what was behind the door between us. When we got into the room, he grabbed me by the waist and pulled me to him. He kissed me passionately and I felt fireworks all over my body again.

"Good night, baby. Well, good morning." We both chuckled.

"Good morning," I said. Ethan let me go and left the room. I settled into the large bed, surprised at how comfortable it was. Just as I was thinking about how I'd never slept in a bed that large before, I drifted off into darkness.

...

I lay in my bed, desperately trying to figure out what I would have to do to get Eliza to stay in the Moon Valley Pack. *I mean, I could lock her up*, I thought, *but that wouldn't get her to love me. In fact, she'd probably hate me even more.*

I sighed. *Why did I have to be such an asshole to her? Why?* I wasn't going to figure out how to get her to stay when I was exhausted, so I forced myself to go to sleep. I only slept for three hours, but it was enough for me to at least be able to think a little more clearly.

I woke up to the sound of yelling down the hall. *Eliza!* I jumped up and ran out of my room. The door to the room Eliza was sleeping in was open. I went inside and saw my parents and siblings staring at her. She was huddled in the middle of the bed with the covers drawn to her like they were some kind of shield. She looked frightened as my parents were demanding to know why she was there.

"Hey, stop yelling at her," I shouted. Everyone turned to look at me.

"Ethan, is this your doing? Why is this rogue sleeping in our house!" my mother yelled.

I felt anger surge in me. "Don't call her that," I said. "She's not a...she's my mate." They all gasped collectively.

"Your mate?" asked my mother. "Eliza Wilton is your mate?"

"Yes, and from this point forward, she will be treated as such. No one, and I mean *no one* is to hurt her ever again," I said.

My family looked at Eliza. They seemed to still be in shock. I walked passed them and sat on the bed with Eliza, shielding her from their view. I knew she didn't want to be stared at like some museum exhibit. *I'm scared Ethan*, I heard her say in my mind.

"At least you had enough sense to sleep in separate rooms last night," said my father as he glared at me. "It's too soon for pups." That was all he said as he turned and walked out of the room. My mother followed, glancing back once right before she shook her head and disappeared around the corner. I knew that their cold and callous exit meant they didn't approve of her and that a serious talk was coming later.

Stacey and Lennox, my two oldest siblings, looked at each other and, to my surprise, laughed. "I'm pretty sure she hates you," said Stacey. "You've treated her so badly all this time."

Why does she have to remind me? I thought.

"This is going to be interesting," said Lennox.

"Stop it," I said. "We're going to work it out." *I hope we will*, I thought to Eliza. She didn't respond.

"Whatever, bro," said Lennox. "Mom and Dad will never approve of this, but I'm happy you found your mate."

As they turned to leave, Stacey stopped. "Is that my shirt?"

I felt Eliza's panic, so I answered for her. "I gave it to her to put on last night. She didn't have anything with her to sleep in."

"Ah, the shift, right? Your first one?" Stacey asked. Eliza nodded. "It looks good on you," she said. "Keep it." Stacey turned and left the room.

Eliza let out a deep breath as if she'd been holding it in the entire time my family was in the room. "They hate me," she said.

"They don't hate you," I said. "Stop saying that. My sister even let you keep the shirt."

"Oh great, I should be so happy she gave me her hand-me-downs," she said sarcastically.

"I didn't mean it like that," I said. I leaned over for a kiss, hoping she wouldn't reject me. She didn't.

"I appreciate your hospitality, Ethan, but I'm uncomfortable here," she said. "You don't have to force your family to like me."

"Eliza, I don't think you realize…" I trailed off, trying to put into words what I was about to say.

"Realize what?" she asked.

"*You* are my family," I said. "I mean yes, my family is still my family, but you are the most important person to me in this whole world. It doesn't matter what anyone says or thinks. Not even my parents."

"Ethan—"

"I know, I know. You still haven't decided to stay, but I really can't imagine doing this without you." She dropped her head and didn't respond, so I decided to change the subject.

"C'mon," I said to her. "We're skipping school today."

"Where are we going?" she asked.

"First, to shower, then to your house," I said.

"My house? You mean the Wilton's house?" I asked. "I can't, Ethan! They kicked me out, remember?"

"It's your money that paid for that house, so it's your house. We're going." I held out my hand to her and she reluctantly took it.

"We're not going to shower together, are we?" she asked. "Your parents…"

"The thought hadn't even crossed my mind," I said with a smile. *Yes, it did,* she thought. "Okay, maybe just briefly," I said with a laugh, "but it's probably best if we don't."

"I agree," she said.

I took her to one of the bathrooms, and I went to mine. When we were showered and dressed, with Eliza in another one of Stacey's outfits, we headed to my car. "This car is really nice," she said as we pulled off. "I've never been in a car this nice."

"It's a Mercedes AMG GT," I said. "I got it last year. Do you like it? I could get you one."

"Oh, uh...no. I mean, yes, I like it a lot, but I don't know how to drive," she said.

"I'll teach you. I mean, if you let me," I said. She smiled at me but didn't say anything. I hoped it was a good smile.

Eliza seemed a bit nervous the entire trip. *She must feel this way often,* I thought, forgetting again that she could hear my thoughts. She responded with, *yeah, pretty much all the time.* That made me feel bad because I knew some of it was my fault. I'd really done a number on this poor girl, and I knew it would be my responsibility to help her heal. *We'll change that,* I projected to her. *I want you to be happy all the time.*

Once we got to her neighborhood, I was surprised at what I saw. I had never been in the outskirts of town before. The Omegas' neighborhood was much shabbier than mine. There were a few decent houses, but most of them looked more like shacks. *Is this how the omegas have been living? This is terrible.*

It's not so bad, she projected back. I looked at Eliza, unable to hide my guilt. It wasn't my fault that they were living like this. After all, I wasn't the Alpha. However, just knowing that I added grief to their hard lives by bullying them made me feel ashamed.

"I'll be a better Alpha," I said to Eliza. "I'll be a better person."

We arrived at Eliza's house. It was a small, shabby house that was only a step above a shack. The faded blue siding needed to be replaced. The grass was just as faded as the siding and looked like it was desperately thirsty. Even the windows seemed old and trite due to a few holes in the screens that covered them. The fence and gate were in dire need of attention. The only thing that really looked nice was a patch of flowers in the yard. They were a beautiful, bright, bold array of yellow, red, and blue colors and were a stark contrast to the faded and withered property.

"I know it's not much," said Eliza, "but I've called it home almost all my life."

I nodded. "Then let's go."

I didn't know the Wiltons very well and I wasn't sure what I was walking in to. Plus, there was the fact that I wasn't the Alpha yet, so I couldn't exactly command them to let Eliza stay, but there was no way I was leaving without making sure my mate had a roof over her head.

6

Eliza Goes Home

Despite Ethan being with me, I was nervous walking up to the place I'd called home for most of my life. I still had my key, but I wasn't sure if I should just open the door or knock. I looked at Ethan, still mentally trying to grasp on to the fact that he was here with me, by my side. I took a deep breath and was about to use my key when the door swung open.

"You owe us a bookbag you little thief!" said Skylar as he opened the door. He had a scowl on his face until he noticed Ethan. "You...you're Ethan Rohe, the Alpha's son," said Skylar. He suddenly looked nervous as he scratched his head.

I looked over at Ethan and I could tell he was angry. More importantly, I could feel that he was angry. I got nervous, wondering if things were about to escalate.

"What did you just call her?" asked Ethan. His fists were balled up. *Surely he couldn't be so mad that he was about to strike Skylar,* I wondered. It was ironic because Ethan had done so much worse to me in the past, yet here he was about to defend me from a simple insult.

"Uh, nothing," said Skylar nervously. "It was a joke. We joke like that sometimes, right Eliza?" Skylar chuckled nervously and looked at me, probably hoping I'd back him up. I didn't say anything.

"What brings you here, young Alpha?" said Skylar. I'm sure he was desperate to change the subject. "It's an honor to have you here. We weren't prepared—"

"—I'm here to bring Eliza home," Ethan said, "to *her* home." Then to me, Ethan said, "let's go inside, Eliza." Ethan took me by my hand and led me inside. Skylar barely had time to step aside before Ethan almost bowled him over. We stepped into the living room were Cam and Cassie were watching tv as usual. They stopped watching the show and eyed Ethan with wide eyes full of amazement.

Cassie jumped up, ran over to me, and gave me a big hug. "Eliza! You're back," she exclaimed with delight.

"Whoa, it's the Alpha's son," said Cam as he hopped up from the sofa. He walked up to Ethan. "Hi, my name is Cameron. People call me Cam."

I was glad that Ethan could put aside his anger to address Cam. "Hey, nice to meet you." He fist-bumped Cam and gave him a smile. At least he wasn't going to take his anger out on the kids. That gave me a little bit of relief.

Star walked into the living room. "What's going on...oh, it's Ethan Rohe..." She looked at me, "...and Eliza?" She looked confused about the two of us standing together in her living room. In fact, they all did except Cam who seemed to be completely star struck.

Realization hit Skylar as he suddenly understood what Ethan implied at the door. "Oh, Eliza must have told you about our arrangement," he said. I'd never seen Skylar so nervous before. "It's...you know, she's an adult now. We didn't mean...it's hard for Omegas—"

"—you put her out with no money and nowhere to go," said Ethan. His temperament changed instantly as he addressed Skylar. The moment Ethan looked at him, his anger got put back on the front burner.

"We didn't!" said Star. "I gave her money, and I told her she had two weeks to find a place. She chose to leave with nowhere to go."

Ethan looked at me. "Is that true, Eliza?" I gulped and shrank back a little. It was uncomfortable suddenly having the spotlight on me.

"Well, yes. Star gave me one hundred dollars. I just..." I looked around at all the eyes peering at me and had to fight back tears that I felt welling in my eyes. "...I just felt so betrayed that I decided to go ahead and leave. I didn't see the point in—"

"—staring at the people who hurt you for two weeks," said Ethan. I nodded as a tear dropped from my eye.

He returned his attention to Skylar. "What the hell was she supposed to do with one hundred dollars and only a two-week notice?" he yelled. I could hear the Alpha in his voice. It wasn't fully developed yet, but I could tell that once he took over the pack, his voice would be scary and commanding, impossible to ignore. Cassie jumped and scooted as close to me as she could. I put my arm around her. Cam suddenly realized that Ethan wasn't here for a friendly visit and I could see the concern for his father on his face. He backed away a few steps from Ethan and his eyes darted back and forth between the two men.

"Kids, go to your rooms," said Star. "Go right now." The kids stood still as if they were frozen. "Go to your rooms right now!" yelled Star. Finally, their feet started moving. They took off, with Cam looking back as his face dragged the floor.

"Ethan, I'm terribly sorry that Eliza has involved you in all of this," said Skylar. "I'm sure you all have your hands full running the pack, something she probably doesn't understand due to the rogue in her. This is a family dispute. We can work this out among ourselves." Skylar looked at me as if I was the problem in the room. *He doesn't realize that Ethan is my mate*, I thought.

He's about to find out right now, projected Ethan. I'd forgotten again that he could hear my thoughts.

Ethan, wait! Before I could get the thought out, Ethan had already shot across the room and grabbed Skylar by the throat. To my surprise, he lifted him in the air easily. Skylar was no small guy. He was six feet tall and weighed at least 200 pounds. I'm a little embarrassed to admit that watching Ethan display his strength kinda turned me on. *Not the time, Eliza,* I scolded myself.

Star yelled, "Skylar!" At the same time, I yelled, "Ethan, wait! Please!" Ethan ignored both of us as Skylar dangled, his feet waving back and forth. He tried to pry Ethan's hands from his neck but he couldn't.

"You've insulted my mate a second time. I should kill you right now," Ethan hissed.

Star gasped and Skylar, struggling to breath as Ethan continued to squeeze his throat, sputtered out, "I'm...sorry...I...didn't...know." Ethan let go of Skylar and he dropped to the ground with a plop.

"You all are a disgrace to this pack," said Ethan. "How could you do that to her? And right before she had her first shift! She had to shift all alone in the woods!" I thought Ethan was angry before, but his eyes turned dark, and I suddenly realized that his previous anger was only the tip of the iceberg.

"Ethan, please," I said as I stepped in front of him. "Please, I know they're wrong but don't hurt them. They're the only family I have." I touched Ethan's cheek. That seemed to snap him out of his irate trance. His eyes lightened a bit and so did my nerves.

I looked over at Star. She had run over to Skylar and was kneeling beside him as he sat on the floor coughing and holding his neck. "I'm sorry," she said. "You're right. It was wrong of us. Please, can you forgive us? Can you give us a chance to make it right?"

"I should exile you all from the pack when I'm Alpha so you can see what it's like to be thrown out like trash. I just might," he said. I winced at that statement. *Thrown out like trash. That's precisely what they did to me.*

Star's eyes widened. "No, please! She can move back in. Please, we have children."

"Not only will she move back in, but you will pay her back every dime you've ever stolen from her," said Ethan.

"What? Stolen...her money helped with bills. We used that money to take care of her," said Skylar. "We didn't steal—"

"—you are her parents! It was your responsibility to do those things! A responsibility you agreed to when you took her in," Ethan yelled. "You will return every...single...dollar to her and that's final!"

Skylar and Star looked at each other. "How are we going to afford that," said Star as she weeped. "We don't have that kind of money."

I stared at the people that had essentially made me feel unwelcome my entire life and was surprised that I still had a soft spot for them. Seeing them that way hurt me. "Ethan, wait. Stop. They honestly don't have that kind of money just lying around. They don't have to pay me back. I can get a job. Please don't be so harsh on them."

"How can you defend them after what they did to you?" he asked me. Through our mind link, I said, *I'm giving you a chance, aren't I?*

I saw a moment of surprise on Ethan's face, followed by a look of shame. That seemed to cause a major break in his anger. He took a deep breath, then turned to the Wiltons. "Eliza's forgiveness is the only thing that has saved you today."

"Thank you, Eliza," said Skylar. "I'm ashamed of how we've behaved towards you all this time." I didn't believe him. I felt that he was only saying that to save face in front of Ethan. "We need to work on fixing things as a family," he said. "The family we should have always been." I simply nodded. I couldn't verbally respond because I didn't feel that Skylar was being genuine. Ethan would hear it in my voice, and I didn't want him to get mad again.

Skylar and Star stood up. Ethan turned to me, seeming to forget about the Wiltons instantly. He smiled lovingly at me. "Show me your room," he said. "I bet you have some weird posters on the walls or something."

"Oh, uh..." I didn't know what to say. I felt like showing him my room would cause him to get angry all over again and I wasn't sure that Skylar's neck could take much more. I looked at the Wiltons. I could see they were thinking the same thing.

"What? What is it?" asked Ethan.

"Maybe another time," I said. "I think Skylar, Star, and I have a lot to talk about right now. We need some family time."

Ethan looked at me for a moment. I knew he was trying to sense if there was something more, but what I said was the truth. We really did have a lot to talk about.

"Okay, beautiful," he said. "Are you sure you're going to be okay? You don't know how hard it is for me to even think about leaving you here." Then through mind link, he asked, *are you going to try to run away from me again?*

I promise you, I won't. I'll be here, at least for now, I said to him.

That wasn't the answer he wanted, but it was the answer he got. He sighed, then leaned in and kissed me passionately. I was completely embarrassed to kiss him in front of the Wiltons. I'd never had a boyfriend, now here I was kissing Ethan Rohe in their living room. *In our living room,* I thought.

I walked Ethan outside and through the rickety gate. "I know this is home for you, but when I mark you, there is no way I can let you stay here. This place just isn't good enough for you."

"It's been good enough for my entire life, Ethan. It's fine," I said.

He sighed. "We aren't going to agree on this right now, so I'll drop it. I'll be here at seven to pick you up for school in the morning."

School! Oh my God, everyone's going to see us together! I thought.

That's the idea, he thought back. Stupid mind link.

"Ethan, everyone's going to stare at us!" I said.

"I get stared at every day," he said. "I'm used to it."

"Well, I'm not. I try my best to not be noticed," I said.

"Eliza, trust me," he said. "Everything will be fine. Things are going to be so much different for you now. So much better. Plus, there is absolutely no way I'm letting you walk two hours to school. I mean, sure walking is good for your health, but that's a bit ridiculous."

"Ethan, I—"

"—it's not up for debate, Eliza. Tomorrow morning at seven," he said. With that, he kissed me again, got in his car, and drove away. I turned around to go inside and begin "healing" with the Wiltons.

7

You Don't Know What It's Like

I watched Ethan's car get smaller as it headed down the road. Then I turned and went back through the rickety gate. *Things are so awkward now*, I thought. *Will Skylar and Star keep their word when Ethan isn't here?*

I took a deep breath, gathered my courage, and headed back inside. When I walked in, the four sets of eyes peered at me curiously, probably wondering if Ethan was coming back in. "You can relax. He's gone," I said. I could see all four of their bodies relax as the tension melted away.

"What have you done, Eliza? Why did you make us look like bad people in front of the Alpha's son?" said Star.

"I didn't make you look like anything," I said. "How was I supposed to know I'd be Ethan's mate? You think I want this? I wanted to disappear after you put me out on the street," I said.

"Well, I guess you've fixed that, huh? I guess you get to stay here rent free for as long as you want," said Skylar. He had such disdain in his voice that it was surprising.

"I don't understand," I said. "Why is it that all of a sudden you hate me so much, Skylar? What did I do?"

Skylar scoffed and waved his hand. He walked away and went down the hall to his room. He slammed the door hard.

I looked at Star, waiting for some sort of explanation. She looked at the kids. "Go to your rooms, sweeties. Let me talk to Eliza." The kids complied and Star and I sat on the sofa.

"Star, tell me what I've done wrong? I mean, I know you and Skylar have never really liked me much, but we at least got along well. Was I really just a paycheck to you," I asked with tears in my eyes. I wiped my face as they fell down.

"You don't know what it's been like," she said. "We took you in and it made us the pariahs of the pack. The family of the rogue wolf." She chuckled and shook her head. "We're Omegas. I mean, we have some status within the pack, even if it's the lowest, but that didn't matter because we're housing a rogue wolf under our roof. We were looking forward to the day where we could...fit in. Where Cam and Cassie would be treated a little better at school. Where Skylar might get better work assignments."

"How can you say I don't know what it's like? I've been treated like crap by the entire pack my whole life. I've been treated much worse than all of you. Look at all these scars!" I stretched out my arms and legs. "Scars from being tripped or thrown into things. I've suffered every kind of abuse there is, so how can you honestly sit there and say I don't know what it's like?"

"Yes, but—" started Star.

"—but what?" I almost yelled.

"You're actually a rogue. We aren't," she said. "We don't deserve—"

"—neither do I!" That time, I did yell. "I was a baby for Goddess's sake! I don't even know why my parents were rogues! None of it was my fault, but I was made to pay for the sins of my parents." I stood up and walked across the room as my tears got the best of me. "Did you ever feel anything for me? Anything at all? All these years and you've never developed even the slightest bit of love or anything?"

"Eliza, your mere presence has brought us nothing but grief," she said. She couldn't even look at me as she said it.

"If that's true, why keep me around?" I asked.

"We really needed the money and, honestly, no one else wanted you. We did you a favor. The Alpha would have had you killed," she said.

Star wasn't telling me anything I didn't know already, but it hurt so much to hear her say it out loud. There was literally no one in the entire world who loved me. *Except Ethan,* I thought, *but not by choice. He's forced to love me through some cruel trick of nature.*

"Right," I said. I was crying so hard that my nose stopped up and started to run. "Look, Star. I don't want to be a burden to anyone. I was going to leave. I really was, but Ethan stopped me. I can leave again. I'll just get some sleep, and I'll go away."

"That won't work now," said Star. "Ethan's got his eye on us now, so we're obligated to keep you here. If you leave, he'll never forgive us and when he becomes Alpha, he'll exile us!"

"No, I'll explain everything to him. I'll get him to promise to leave you alone. It's my choice to leave," I said. "I don't want to live with people who don't want me around." I took a deep breath and used my shirt...or rather, Stacey's shirt, to wipe my face. "Star, I'm exhausted. I can't keep this conversation up. I'm just going to lay down for a while."

Star nodded and she stood up. We both made our way to our rooms. I went into my little closet and laid down. Before I knew it, I had drifted off to sleep.

...

I could feel that Eliza was...uncomfortable? Sad? Tired? It was hard to pinpoint because she was so far away. I wanted to turn around and go to her to comfort her, but she was mending things with the Wiltons. I imagined that would make her emotions run high, so I kept going to the phone store determined to make it before they closed.

I got Eliza an iPhone and put her on my phone plan. I stopped and got a dozen roses from the florist my father used often, then the jewelry store to get her a gold charm bracelet. Then I headed back towards the Wilton's to give her the surprises.

Everything seemed very still when I arrived. Too still. *Shouldn't they be talking? What's happening?* I couldn't sense Eliza like I wanted to, but from what little I could sense, she was fine. *Maybe she's asleep,* I thought as I knocked on the door. I waited for a moment, and I saw someone peek out of the curtain quickly. Then, I heard a click at the door and the door opened. It was the boy, Cam.

"Hi Ethan. You came back," he said with delight. He stepped aside and walked in. "Are you still mad at my Dad?" he asked.

"No, I'm not," I said. "I have some gifts for Eliza."

"She's sleeping, but I can give them to her for you," he said.

"That's cool of you, but I really want to give them to her myself," I said.

"Okay," he said. "Follow me."

We went down a short hallway and he stopped at a small door that looked like it led to a little storage area. I could smell Eliza's scent so strongly. *Is she sleeping in a closet?* I wondered, but I already knew the answer to my own question. I didn't have to wonder long as Cam knocked on the door and I heard Eliza stirring. She opened the door, rubbing her sleepy eyes. When she saw me, she suddenly wasn't sleepy, and her eyes went wide with surprise.

"Ethan, what are you—"

"—is this where you sleep?" I asked. "In the closet?" I felt my rage growing and this time, nothing Eliza said could have calmed me down.

Just then, Skylar stepped out into the hallway. He spotted us. "Cam! No," was all he could get out because before I knew it, I had him dangling again.

"She sleeps in the closet!" I yelled. "How could you treat her like that!" I felt Eliza pulling on me. "Let him go, please," she was saying. "Please, Ethan. Not in front of the kids!" I flung Skylar against the wall, and he dropped to the floor with a loud grunt. I turned and grabbed Eliza's hand. "Let's go. We're leaving."

I thought Eliza would protest, but to my surprise, she didn't. I felt a sense of relief emanating from her. *You didn't want to be here, and I forced you,* I projected to her. *I'm sorry. I thought I was making things better.*

It's okay. You didn't know, she projected back as she picked up the phone, flowers, and small box I had dropped in the hallway.

We went outside, got into my car and left the Wiltons. The drive to my house was mostly silent until I had to express some of my pent up rage. "When I'm Alpha, I'm going to make them pay for everything they've done to you," I hissed. Eliza didn't react. She was characteristically quiet, but it was a different kind of quiet. "Eliza, what's on your mind?" I asked.

"Leaving," she said while staring out of the window.

Shit, we're back to this, I thought. "Eliza, please. I understand how the situation with the Wiltons hurt you, but you don't have to leave the whole pack—"

"—they were going to kill me," she said.

"What? Who was going to kill you. The Wiltons?"

"No. Your parents. When I was a baby, they were going to kill me, but the Wiltons saved my life by agreeing to take me in," she said.

I looked at Eliza in disbelief. If Eliza was lying to me, I would have been able to sense it, but I sensed only truth. Still, it was hard to believe my parents would murder a baby. "Eliza, there must be some mistake," I said. "I know my parents are hard, and they have to be to lead the pack, but they're not cruel."

Eliza scoffed. Still looking out of the window, she said, "you obviously don't know your parents very well."

There had to be some mistake. I pressed the gas a little harder so I could hurry and get home to get to the bottom of this.

8

Amina Sturges

I was speechless as I stared at my parents. "You were going to kill a baby?" I asked. "How could you bring yourself to do something like that? To even think about something like that?"

"Well, technically she wasn't a baby. She was three," said my father. "You have to understand, rogue wolves can be dangerous. We didn't know what happened to her parents, why they were rogues, if they were good or bad, or if their deaths would bring trouble for the pack," said my father. "We needed to dispose of the whole situation—"

"—dispose of the *situation?* We're talking about a person!" I shouted.

"Yes, we know! That's why we offered an alternative to killing her," said my mother. "We offered the option for someone to take her in. We're not monsters. Killing her would have been a last resort."

"It shouldn't have been any resort," I said.

My father chimed in. "We told them they would have to change her name and raise her as their own. The last thing I wanted to do was kill a child, but there were no takers. Then I got the idea to offer an incentive, a stipend for raising her until she was an adult. Even then, only one family volunteered. The Wiltons," he said.

"I'll admit, they weren't the best couple. They were young and immature, but we didn't know what else to do," said Mom.

I looked at Eliza. She almost seemed as if she were wilting listening to the conversation. I could feel the pain flowing from her.

"As an Alpha, I have to make decisions to protect our pack. *Our* pack. She wasn't a part of our pack, but I still gave her a chance to live. Maybe she was treated poorly, but at least she's alive. I would make the same decisions all over again," he said. "When you become Alpha, you'll have to make tough decisions for the sake of the pack also."

I was done listening to my parents' antics. I was completely mortified that they would have even considered ending an innocent child's life. There was only one thing they said that I was curious about. "You said they changed her name, meaning that you must be aware of her having a different name?" I asked. "What was it?"

They looked at each other. "She was wrapped in a blanket with the name Amina Sturges stitched into it," said my mother.

Eliza gasped. "So...my name, my real name is...Amina?" My mother nodded. Both my parents looked embarrassed, and I sensed regret, but there was no way I could forgive them at that moment for stripping Eliza of her identity and self-worth.

"Like I said before, the name change was for the protection of the pack. We couldn't take the risk of anyone coming to look for her," said my father.

"So, someone could have been looking for her? Someone who maybe loved her, but you choose to hide her and treat her like crap instead?" I said to my father. I was fuming with anger.

"It could also have been someone who wanted to harm her, Ethan. You're missing the point," said my father.

"You took away the only thing she had left in the whole world, and you never intended to tell her. No one ever intended to tell her," I said. "That's cruel." I pulled Eliza close to me and kissed her forehead. I couldn't bear to have my mate suffer anymore. I realized that Eliza was right. She couldn't stay. There was too much pain to erase.

"Come on, Eliza. Let's go," I said. We turned to leave the house.

"Where are we going?" she asked quietly.

"Anywhere but here," I said. We walked to my car as my parents called my name, demanding to know where I was going. In truth, I didn't know where we were going. I just wanted to get Eliza far away from all the people that hurt her.

The first ten minutes of the car ride were quiet. Eliza looked out the window as we drove. I could see that she was crying in her reflection in the window. I wanted to comfort her, but I didn't know what to say. I was looking at a woman who had been hurt by everyone around her for her entire life. I didn't understand how she was still going after all the abuse and mistreatment. I began to understand that Eliza was strong, probably stronger than she even realized. *She'll make a great Luna,* I thought.

Eliza snapped her head around to look at me. "I'll never be your Luna," she said. "I'm sorry Ethan, but there is no way I'll stay in this pack."

"I know, I know," I said. "After what we just heard, I understand why you don't want to stay. It's just...I don't want to lose you. I can't lose you."

There were a few more minutes of awkward silence as I drove. Eliza was thinking something and trying to block it from me, but I caught a few words of it. *"...reject him before it goes too far."*

I slammed on brakes and Eliza stretched out her arms as if she were trying to stop an accident with her bare hands. "What they hell, Ethan," she exclaimed.

"No, Eliza, you can't," I said.

"Oh my God, does this mating thing mean I can't have one thought to myself?" she asked. I almost answered, then I realized she was asking that rhetorically.

"Eliza, I know I have been a source of some of your pain, but I'm try-ing to make it right. I want to make it right. We could be good together. We just have to figure some things out."

"Figure some things out?" she said. "Ugh, Ethan...there's nothing to figure out." She unbuckled her seatbelt and proceeded to get out of the car. I got out and met her on the other side.

"Eliza, please get back in," I said.

"Why? You don't even know where to take me. There is nowhere for you to take me. I don't belong anywhere," she said. She tried to dart around me, but I blocked her path.

"You belong with me," I said. "Eliza, you're my mate. As long as I'm okay, so are you."

"Do I look okay to you?" she asked. "You have a home to go to. A family who loves you. A bright future ahead of you as Alpha of the pack. Maybe even college. I don't have any of that. I mean I'm not even wearing my own clothes for Goddess's sake! Ethan, it's not going to work between us. We're too different. That's why I have to re—"

"Don't!" I shouted. I covered her mouth with my hand. "Eliza, don't. Please don't push me away. I love you and I know you love me."

She pushed my hand away. "I don't know how I feel about you Ethan. I love you and I hate you! I want to be with you, but I want to go far away from you and your family. I don't know how I can want two things at once like this, but it's driving me crazy." She tried to push me out of her way, but I wasn't budging. I was determined to fight for Eliza.

"Listen to me. Eliza, listen! I'm sorry about everything. Words can't describe how sorry I am. I can't change the past, but I can change the future. You don't want to stay in the pack? Okay, fine. We'll both go, but we're going together. I'm not losing you," I said.

Eliza stopped struggling. "What do you mean...we'll both go? Ethan, you can't leave. You're—"

"—the future Alpha, yeah, I know. Everyone's been telling me that my whole life and I thought that's what I wanted. Now I know that there's only one thing in this entire world that I want. That's you. If you aren't going to be the Luna, then I don't want to be the Alpha."

"You can't just give that up," she said.

"I can and I will, but I will never leave you Eliza. You don't have to be out in the world alone," I said. "You can leave the pack, but don't leave me."

She looked down as tears streamed from her puffy, swollen eyes. "I...don't know how to be with someone. I don't know how to love," she said.

"Then let me show you," I said. I lifted her face up to mine and I kissed her gently. I kissed her lips, then her cheeks. I ran my fingers through her soft, curly hair, then embraced her and pulled her close to me. *It's time, Eliza*, I projected to her. *We need to make this official.*

I can't. I'm scared, she projected back. *I can't take any more betrayal. I don't...I want to be alone, so I won't be hurt anymore.*

"You've been alone your entire life, Eliza. That's the problem. Think about it." I said. She frowned, then raised her eyebrows as she considered what I said. "I'll never betray you. I'll never hurt you again. I'll do everything in my power to protect you. I'll give my life for yours before I let anyone hurt you again. Plus, you can still..." I shuddered as I was about to make the statement, "...reject me later if you truly want to, but if you don't at least give it a shot, you'll never know how much better things can be."

She took a few moments to think. Then she wiped the tears from her cheeks, looked at me, and nodded. I could see the fear in her eyes and all I could think about was eradicating it away from her forever. "At this point, what do I have to lose?" she asked.

I held her hands. We took our time finding the perfect place on each other's necks, then we bit each other. There was a rush of pure excitement. The feeling was phenomenal, like being pulled through space and time quickly, falling into eternal ecstasy. It took my breath away momentarily, but I kept biting her anyway. Her taste was inebriating ...addictive.

Suddenly I felt all of her in a way I hadn't before. I felt every part of her body as if it were my own without having to touch her. I felt her emotions—her doubts, fears, sadness, and confusion. I felt her love for me. It was infinite, intense, and unconditional. I thought her scent drove me wild before, but now it was simply intoxicating. As I stood there with my teeth in her delicate neck, savoring all the feelings and emotions that were surging through me, there was one thing that I was sure of beyond a shadow of a doubt. Eliza was mine and there was no force in the universe that would ever come between us.

When we finally came out of our states of ecstasy, we licked our marks to seal them, then I had the primal urge to rip her clothes off and make love to her right there on the side of the road. I didn't, but I suddenly knew what my next move was.

"Come with me," I said. I pulled her back to the car. We got inside and I drove. Once we got to our destination, she looked at me and smiled. It was the first smile I'd seen on her face all day. She knew exactly what was about to happen.

We walked to the spot where we'd made love for the first time. I kissed her, then kissed her mark. She looked beautiful as the light from the sunset illuminated her cocoa-colored skin. We started undressing each other, then Eliza stopped.

"Ethan, wait," she said.

"What is it?" I asked, hoping she hadn't changed her mind. I was rock-hard and being that close to her, it would've taken an act of the Goddess to stop me from taking her.

"From now on, call me Amina," she said.

I smiled and kissed her. "Amina, my love," I said. It felt right coming out of my mouth. We finished undressing, laid down in the grass, and made love to each other over and over for hours. Then we fell asleep in each other's arms under the moonlight where it seemed our dreams, like everything else, were intertwined.

...

I betrayed myself. I'd always had plans to go rogue, but I let Ethan mark me, and I marked him. Marking him and being marked by him was unbelievable. I'd never imagined it would feel that way and although I was skeptical before, it gave me strength and comfort that I never imagined I would ever have. Still, I was scared. I'd just committed to loving Ethan for a lifetime, and I wondered how I could show love when I'd never experienced it. Plus, the desire to leave didn't go away.

What did I do? Am I obligated to stay in the pack now? I wondered as I sat there playing with the beautiful bracelet he bought me while looking at the sunrise.

Ethan wasn't awake yet. I wanted to let him sleep since we both had a pretty exhausting ordeal the day before. Plus, I didn't really have anywhere to go anyway because we still hadn't solved that problem. I was homeless and mated to the richest guy in town. Talk about irony.

I thought about my name. *Amina Sturges.* I was a member of the Sturges family. The name sounded strange. I'd never heard of any Sturges' in the area. I had no idea who they were or where they were, or if there were any other remaining family members. I could be the last, which is what I always thought anyway.

Ethan woke up as I was pondering my family situation. "Wha...what time is it," he asked.

"I'm not sure, but the sun is rising so it's probably around six," I said.

"Oh man, I'm starving," he said. "We need to get some food."

"Yeah, I agree," I said. "What's for breakfast?"

"You if we don't get dressed quickly," he said as he stared at me. I smiled at him, and he kissed me.

"No, but seriously, we have a lot to figure out today so let's get some fuel in our systems," he said. "Starbucks?"

"Sounds great," I said. "I've never been there."

"You've never been—" he started. Then he shook his head. "I'm not even going to think about it. It will just make me mad. C'mon, let's have a good day."

We got dressed and headed to the car. On the way, Ethan turned on his radio and started singing. "C'mon, let's hear it," he said as he nudged me. I felt myself blushing.

"I don't sing," I said. "Well, not in front of people."

"Please, I really want to hear your voice," he said. "I won't judge."

"Yes you will," I said, "but fine. Okay." We sang together all the way to Starbucks and, while neither of us were going to win any awards, we didn't sound too bad. It was a good start to the morning.

Considering the fact that we had just spent the night in the woods, we looked a mess and probably smelled like animals so we decided to go through the drive-thru line. *The life of being homeless,* I thought, *and here I am dragging Ethan into it.*

"We're not homeless," he suddenly said with a mouth full of food.

I was annoyed. "Am I ever going to be able to have a thought to myself?" I asked. "I mean, it's not that I want to keep things from you, but I'm kind of a private person...usually."

"I don't know," he said. "I'm new at this too, remember?"

"Yeah," I replied. There was silence for a few moments as I sipped on my iced coffee and ate my turkey and gouda sandwich. They both tasted so good. I knew I'd be eating at Starbucks a lot going forward.

"Where are we going," I asked Ethan as I realized we were heading out of town. Then it hit me. We were heading out of the pack's territory! "Ethan, isn't it forbidden to leave the pack lands without permission?"

"Yes, well, sort of. I mean, we're just going out of town on a little trip. Now, how long the trip will be, that remains to be seen," he said.

"You could get in trouble," I said. "Ethan, you don't need to—"

"—yes I do, Amina. You need to get out of here and I'm going to provide you with everything you need from now on. Your well-being is my top priority. Now sit back and enjoy having someone take care of you for once, okay?" He smiled at me and rubbed my leg.

"Okay, well if you're providing me with everything I need, I need another one of these sandwiches," I said. Ethan laughed and we had a good car ride to the next Starbucks.

We reached the next town about an hour later. It was still early, so we rode around and did some sightseeing. It was the first time I'd ever been out of the pack's territory, and I was amazed. We stopped by a big fountain and Ethan gave me a quarter.

"Wait, before I make a wish, can I do it privately? Like, maybe you don't listen to my thoughts?" I asked.

"We could try," he said. "I have no idea how to do it, but I'll give it a shot. Maybe I'll think about something else instead."

"Okay, great," I said. Just as I was about to make my wish, I heard Ethan's thoughts. *I can't wait to be inside of her on a bed. It's going to feel great.* I turned around and looked at him.

"That's not how you do it," I said.

"Oh, did you hear that?" he asked. His cheeks started turning red.

"Yes, I did," I said. I smiled and pecked him on the cheek. Then I turned and flipped the quarter into the fountain. I made my wish, and I turned to Ethan. "Did you hear it?"

"Actually, no," he said. "I didn't do anything. Did you?"

"Yeah, I kind of put up a mental block as I thought about it," I said. "I just imagined...like a brick wall."

"Okay, a mental block. Interesting," he said. "So, what was the wish?"

"I'm not going to tell you," I said as I chuckled. "There would be no point of putting up the mental block if I did."

"Aww, baby, I don't want any secrets between us," he said as he embraced me.

"It's not a secret, it's just personal. Plus, if I tell the wish, it won't come true," I said.

"Okay, fine. You can have that one thought to yourself," he said. We kissed each other and it felt romantic locking lips with him in front of such a beautiful fountain. He let me go and looked at his phone.

"Check in isn't until three, so we have a few hours to go shopping," he said.

"Shopping? Like this? Ethan, we're a mess," I said.

"Yeah we are, but we need clothes and other stuff," he said. "Otherwise, we're going to stay a mess. Don't worry so much. We're a mess together."

We spent the next few hours going to several different stores and taking a bunch of selfies. Ethan bought me anything I wanted. If I even looked at it with a smile, he bought it. I'd never had so many clothes and shoes in my life. He even bought me accessories to go with them. We had a great lunch at a little café and by the time we made it to the hotel, Ethan was out of close to a thousand dollars. It didn't seem to faze him one bit. *Must be nice to have that kind of money,* I thought.

"It has it's perks sometimes," he projected back.

He paid for an entire week at the hotel. "A whole week?" I asked. "We're staying here for a week?"

"Maybe more," he said. We took the elevator to our room. I took a shower while he brought up all my bags. Then he took a shower, and we made good on that thought he had at the fountain. It was so much better on a soft bed. I didn't want him to stop.

"A whole week of this," he said. "Every day. I can get used to this." He pulled me close to him and kissed me.

"Ethan, we need to have a serious talk," I said.

"What did I do?" he asked.

"No, nothing. It's just, umm, I don't want to make things awkward, but...aren't you worried about me getting pregnant? We haven't been using protection and it's probably not a good time for a baby," I said.

"Yeah, about that..." he started. He gulped. "I was kinda hoping you would get pregnant."

"What? Why?" I asked as I sat up and pulled away from him.

"So that you would stay with me," he said. "I mean, we're marked but you never really said that you were planning to stay. I was worried that I might wake up and you'd be gone."

"So, basically you wanted to obligate me to the pack with a baby? That's a little underhanded, Ethan." I got out of bed. "That's...manipulative."

"No, no, not the pack. I wanted to obligate you to me," he said as if that were any better.

"That's dishonest," I said, "and an absolutely horrible reason to have a baby." I started getting dressed.

"Where are you going?" he asked.

"For a walk," I said. "I need to clear my head."

"Do you want me to come with you?" he asked.

"No, I want to be alone right now." I said. I could feel Ethan feeling uncomfortable. "Don't worry, I'm not going to run away," I said. "I just need some space for a while. I need to think about...me. This new me. Amina."

"Okay," he said. "Just please, don't go far. I'm already going crazy, and you haven't even left the room yet." I turned to go, and he said, "wait! Amina, I love you and I'm sorry."

"I love you too. I'll be back soon," I said. I left the room and tried to block out Ethan's feelings of anxiety.

9

Groove Nightlife

I wasn't mad at Ethan. I was disappointed. We'd just started building our trust and his dishonesty basically put him right back to square one in my eyes. I was back to feeling alone again, and on top of that I might be pregnant. *This is not how things are supposed to be right now*, I thought to myself while making sure to keep up my mental block.

I decided that I needed to make a plan and I knew I couldn't make that plan with Ethan no matter how much I loved him. In fact, it's because I loved him that I had to make the plan without him. He was expected to take the helm of a pack that I didn't belong in. I would never fit into the Moon Valley Pack, nor did I want to. No matter how close I'd gotten with Ethan, that fact hadn't changed.

I walked around for about half an hour and came across a bar. I'd never been to a bar, and I'd heard stories about how some of them could be rough, but I was curious. I decided to go in. There weren't a lot of people, probably because the night was just getting started. The music was loud, and the cigarette smoke was thick. I started coughing as the scent filled my lungs. *Not my scene*, I thought. I left the bar and relished the fresh air outside. *I'm never smoking a cigarette*, I thought to myself as I continued walking.

I came to a little club with some good dance music floating from inside. I looked up at the sign. It said *Groove Nightlife*. There was a sandwich board sign at the door that said *Ladies Free Before 10.* I liked to groove, mostly when I was alone, but I was up for a new experience. I looked at the phone Ethan had bought me earlier. The time was 9:17.

Perfect, I thought. What was not perfect was that I had a missed call and two text messages from Ethan. *Ugh, can't that man give me an hour to myself?*

I ignored his messages and got in line for the club. I definitely was not dressed appropriately. I had on jeans and a t-shirt while most of the girls were barely covered in tiny pieces of fabric that were supposed to be dresses. I wondered if Ethan would like the way I looked in a dress like that. *No! Stop it. Don't think about Ethan,* I thought to myself. *It's about you right now. Keep blocking him out and enjoy yourself for once.*

Inside the club, the music was even louder than the bar. It was dark and people had glow in the dark lights. There were hundreds of people dancing and other people sitting at tables or standing on the walls. I suddenly felt completely out of my element. Not that I had an element.

I found an unoccupied space on the wall and stood there, taking in the whole scene. A few minutes later I was tapping my foot and bobbing along to the music. I was starting to have a good time.

"Hey, would you like to dance?" someone shouted in my ear. It startled me and I jumped. It was some guy with a circle of glow in the dark lights around his head. He lifted his hands and started grinding in my direction.

"No, ugh ugh!" I shouted. I backed away quickly and walked to the bar. As I waited for the bartender, I looked at the menu. I wasn't familiar with any of the drinks at all. I also wasn't sure if I could get one. I wasn't old enough to drink and I didn't know if the bartender would ask for ID. I saw something called Rum and Coke. It was one of the cheapest drinks, and I liked Coke, so I decided to go with it.

To my surprise, the bartender did not ask for my ID. She whipped it up for me and I took a big sip. That was a mistake. The alcohol burned down my throat and I started coughing up a lung. Everyone nearby stared at me, and I saw some people laughing. A guy approached me, a different one this time.

"It's obviously your first time drinking," he shouted in my ear. "Probably should have gone with something softer like a mimosa."

"I'll keep that in mind for the next time," I said while still coughing a little.

"Hey, let me get a mimosa over here," he shouted at the bartender. She gave him a thumbs up.

"Oh, no, no, that's okay," I said. "I'm good, really."

"Hey, no pressure, no strings attached. Just doing a nice deed," he said.

I realized I wasn't sure if Ethan was the jealous type or not. Would he be upset that a guy at a club bought me a drink, even if it was an innocent interaction? I hoped he wouldn't. It wasn't like I was going to sleep with the guy.

He went down the bar and met the bartender halfway. He said something to her, she nodded, and then he came back and handed the drink to me. "I told her to put both your drinks on my tab," he said.

"Thanks, I guess," I said. "I should let you know that I have a mate...I mean a boyfriend." I took a sip of the mimosa. The guy was right, that one was much easier on my throat.

"Oh, where is he? I'm not trying to start anything," he said, looking around.

"He's not here," I said. "Doing the solo thing tonight."

"'Trouble in paradise?" he asked.

I shrugged. "Just needed some me time." I drank more of the mimosa. The DJ suddenly shouted, "alright, I need everyone to put your hands in the air!" The dancers did so and cheered as they kept dancing.

"Do you want to dance?" the man asked.

"Oh, no," I said. "There really will be trouble in paradise if I do that."

"You said he's not here, right? What he doesn't know won't hurt him," the man said.

"Look, I don't want to give the wrong impression here," I said. "I'll pay for my drinks. I don't want to lead you on."

"No, no, don't worry about it. You're very pretty. I had to try. He's a lucky man." *Wow*, I thought. I smiled as the guy walked away. As terrible as it was, I liked the attention. I'd never gotten the attention of any guy except for Ethan and that was only after he discovered I was his true mate.

I finished the mimosa and decided that it was time to leave before I started enjoying myself too much and got into trouble. I started walking towards the door when I felt a wave of lightheadedness hit me. *What the heck?* I thought. *That alcohol must have been a lot stronger than I thought.*

I composed myself made my way out the door. I had this sudden feeling that something wasn't right. I became aware of three guys walking behind me. I could hear them talking.

"...amount should have knocked her right out," said the guy that had bought me the drink.

"How is she still walking straight," said another.

Oh my gosh. Did that guy spike my drink? I realized that there was a moment when he had his back turned to me after he grabbed the drink from the bartender. For only a second he'd turned, and I couldn't see the glass. *One second was all it took to spike a drink. Wow.*

Of course, the guys didn't know I was a werewolf. It would take a lot more to knock me out than a typical human woman. Despite me obviously not passing out, the guys didn't back off. *I'm going to have to fight them off,* I thought as I sensed them getting closer.

When they got close enough to reach out and touch me, I spun around and punched the one in the middle square in the nose. He flew back and landed on the sidewalk with a thud. He was the guy who had bought the drinks. He sat up and blood was spewing from his nose which was now crushed in the middle of his face. This surprised the other two so much, they stopped and looked at me with stretched eyes and open mouths. Unfortunately, they still attacked.

They tried to subdue me, but I was too strong for the two of them despite the fact that I lacked fighting skills. Two humans were no match for one werewolf, even a young, untrained one. I slung them off me easily and kicked them both in the balls as hard as I could. They screamed as if I'd shot them.

One of the guys dropped to his knees and grabbed himself down there. Blood soaked the front of his pants. The one that didn't drop caught a meeting with my fist. I felt the bones crush in his face as I made contact. He flew back and landed on the pavement next to his friend. After that, none of them got up or attempted to attack me again. I turned around and quickly walked away, smiling and feeling good. It was the first time in my life I had ever defended myself. I decided it wouldn't be the last.

When I got back to the hotel, Ethan was waiting out front. When he saw me, he dashed over to me and hugged me tight. "Amina, where were you! You didn't answer my calls or texts. I thought you left me."

"Left you? Ethan no…" Before I could get my statement out, Ethan let me go and looked at me strangely. "What?" I asked.

"Your scent, it's tainted. I smell…" he sniffed, "…cigarettes and…other men."

You've gotta be freaking kidding me, I thought. *Even when I block him out, he still gets in.* "Amina, please tell me you didn't cheat on me!"

"Cheat on you?" I scoffed. "Ethan, seriously? You think I cheated on you? I think you would have sensed that from miles away. Our marks, remember?"

He let out a sigh of relief. "You're right, I forgot…but where were you? What happened?"

"I went to a bar, but I didn't like it," I said. "So, I left and went to a club. A guy bought me a drink." Ethan frowned and I could sense jealousy. *Yep, jealous type. Now I know.* "It was innocent, I swear. Or at least I thought it was. He spiked my drink and when I left, he and two of his buddies attacked me."

"Holy shit, Amina, are you okay? Did they hurt you? Show me where they are. I'm gonna rip them to shreds!" Ethan shouted.

"I'm okay, really!" I said. "It was human guys, and I beat them up. I beat them up really bad. Can you believe it? I defended myself and won!" I was ecstatic, but Ethan clearly was not.

"This is not a good thing Amina! How can you stand there and be happy that you got attacked?"

I sighed. "You don't get it." I walked past Ethan and into the hotel. He followed me, speaking quietly so people couldn't hear us.

"What you did was dangerous. What if it were wolves that attacked you? You wouldn't have been able to beat them," he said.

"But it wasn't wolves. It was humans and I'm fine," I said. I was getting annoyed that Ethan didn't understand my position.

"Amina, stop!" He grabbed my arm and swung me around. "You can't do this. I understand that you need some independence to figure out...whatever you're trying to figure out, but what you did tonight was reckless."

I shook my arm from him and pressed the button on the elevator. "This is the first time I've gotten to do something on my own terms. The very first time! I had fun. So, I got into a little trouble. That's what normal people do!"

We stepped into the elevator and other people joined us, so we didn't talk anymore until we got into the room. Once we got in, Ethan didn't waste time resuming the argument. "Amina, normal women don't take drinks from strange guys in the club! They also don't ignore texts and calls from their mate, or block them out! Nothing about what you did tonight was normal...or safe!"

"Well maybe I don't want to be normal," I shouted back.

"So what? You're back to wanting to be a rogue now?" he asked.

"I never left that idea," I yelled back at him. "Maybe I don't want to do this whole relationship thing. Maybe I just want to be left alone!" Ethan recoiled at that statement so suddenly that I instantly felt like a jackass. I could tell I hurt his feelings and that was not my intention. "Ethan, I'm sorry. I didn't mean that."

He sat on the bed. "You're going to leave me, aren't you?" he asked quietly.

I sat next to him. "No, I'm not," I said. "I'm just scared of this. Of us. I've protected myself all my life by not getting close to anyone."

"I love you," he said as he looked at me. "I'm not going to hurt you."

"I know you won't. Just be patient with me. Please," I said, "and in return, I won't block you out if I go out again. Deal?"

He perked up and that made me feel better. "Deal," he said. "We should kiss on it," he said, "but after you take a shower. I love you, but you stink." We both laughed and I went to the bathroom to wash away my night.

10

A Proposal

The rest of the week went by smoothly. Ethan and I didn't argue anymore. We spent lots of time together doing all kinds of fun activities. We went to an amusement park, a museum, and we went to see a play. He took me shopping and bought me any and everything I wanted. Best of all, we ate lots of good food, including several trips to Starbucks. He was even confident enough to give me time to myself without panicking and trying to track me down. It was a week that I might have only dreamed about in the past, but Ethan assured me we would have many more weeks like that.

We decided it was best if we used protection during sex so I wouldn't get pregnant, that is, if I wasn't already. I was glad Ethan saw things from my point of view, although I had to continuously reassure him that I wasn't going to leave him. It seemed that with each passing day, our bond grew stronger and by the end of the week, I couldn't imagine being without him.

We were walking to the car from Starbucks, laughing at a really bad joke that Ethan had just told when his mother stepped right in front of us. She startled me so badly that I almost dropped my cake pop.

"What are you doing here?" Ethan asked. His tone had gone from lighthearted to heavy in an instant.

"You haven't been returning any of our calls, so someone had to come find you and drag you back to your senses," she said. She was talking directly to Ethan and behaving as if I weren't standing there.

"Mom, I'm not doing this with you right now," he said. He grabbed my hand and attempted to circle around her, but she stepped right back in front of him.

"Ethan, you've missed an entire week of school, and you have responsibilities. You've had enough galivanting around with..." she looked at me and I could see her distaste for me on her face, "this...girl long enough now. It's time for you to come home."

"I'll come home when and *if* I'm ready to. Now excuse us, mother," he said.

I had to almost run to keep up with Ethan's pace towards the car. His mother yelled out, "if you don't come with me now, your father will be back to get you and we both know how that will go." Ethan opened the door for me and almost shoved me in. He closed it, got in on the other side, and pulled off.

We rode in silence back to the hotel. Ethan's mood had obviously been soured by the appearance of his mother and I had no idea how to fix that. When we got into the room, Ethan sat quietly on the bed.

"Umm, do you want to talk about it?" I asked.

"No, but I guess we have to," he said.

"What did you mean by *if* you go back? You're going back, right? You have to," I said.

"What if I don't want to," he asked.

"Ethan, you have to. You're the next Alpha. The pack needs you," I said.

"*I* need *you*," he replied. There was a moment of silence between us. Then he said, "listen, I need you to know that no matter what happens, I love you."

"What I that supposed to mean? Ethan, you're scaring me. What's going to happen when your father gets here?" I asked.

"Nothing for you to be afraid of," he said. "Nothing like that. Just forget about that for now. We have a movie to catch. I want you to wear that blue dress you bought today," he said. "I love the way it looks on you." He smiled in an attempt to redirect me, but I could still feel the heaviness in his heart.

"Amina, please let's forget all of this mess with my mom. I want us to have a good last evening of our trip. Now go on, get dressed." He kissed me gently. I wanted to pry more, but I didn't want to end up in an argument, so I got ready to go.

By the time we were leaving out, the air wasn't so heavy anymore. We were back to laughing and joking, and I had forgotten all about the situation with his mom. The movie we saw was a comedy and we both laughed so loud that people around us gave us dirty looks. I didn't care what they thought. I was carefree for the first time in my life, and I was enjoying it.

We ended up starting a popcorn fight which really set people off, then we got kicked out of the movie theater. Before we left out of the theater, Ethan shouted, "he dies at the end and his girl marries his best friend!" I gasped. Everyone in the theater either groaned or shouted expletives at us for ruining the ending. I almost died from laughter.

"I thought you never saw that movie before?" I struggled to ask through my giggles.

"I haven't," he said. "I don't know what happens at the end." That made us double over with laughter. I couldn't stop the tears from trickling down my face. "C'mon," he said, "let's get out of here."

We hopped in the car and Ethan took me to a really fancy French restaurant for dinner. "So that's why you suggested this dress," I said. He smiled at me and nodded.

At the restaurant, I ordered something called Boeuf Bourguignon. I didn't know how to pronounce it, so I just pointed at it on the menu. It tasted heavenly! I'd never eaten anything so savory and scrumptious in my life. "I think I have a new favorite meal," I said to Ethan as I ate a big forkful.

Ethan stared at me, and I could tell he was thinking about something, but he was blocking me. I cocked my head to the side and tried really hard to tune in. He must have noticed because he said, "I was just thinking about how this has been the best week of my life."

That surprised me. I didn't expect that at all. I thought his life was great. *Surely this can't be the best week of his amazing life,* I thought. Then I realized I forgot to block him *Crap, this is going to take some getting used to,* I thought.

"It really is. You're more than I could have asked for in a mate. Your beautiful, smart, funny, and such a strong woman. I don't mean physically, not like buff or anything." He almost looked embarrassed. "I mean yeah, you're strong. You kicked those guys asses, but that's not what I meant."

I chuckled. It was cute when he stumbled over his words.

He took a deep breath and pulled a box out of his pocket. I immediately knew what it was. The smile left my face, and I felt frozen in the chair. Ethan got up and came over to me and knelt. People around us stared and murmured to each other.

"Amina Sturges, I know you're already my mate, and that's stronger than any proposal, but I would like to ask that you do me the honors of being my wife."

His wife? This proposal came out of left field. But had it? Is that what this whole trip was about? Was he proposing to me simply to ensure that I stay with him, or did he really want to marry me?

"I...I...we're already mates," I said. I looked around at all the eyes on us and then I looked at Ethan.

"I still want to marry you," he said. He seemed genuine in the proposal, and I could see the nervousness in his eyes, but I just wasn't sure. Still, the pressure of all those stares was too much for me to let him down in public.

"Yes," I said. "I'll marry you." Everyone in the restaurant cheered and Ethan put the ring on my finger. He kissed me passionately and whispered, "I love you so much." I whispered back to him, "I love you too."

He stood up and yelled, "she said yes!" People stood up and everyone cheered. He pulled me up to him, picked me up and spun me around.

I was feeling a slew of mixed emotions. I wanted to be happy. My wolf was definitely happy. She was jumping for joy. However, we still had so much to work out in our lives and the next day, reality was going to hit us in the face hard.

"You've made me the happiest man alive," said Ethan. "I'm going to be sure to make you happy. You'll see."

I smiled and we sat back down. I looked at the ring that was perched on my finger. I didn't know enough about diamonds to know how many carats there were, but the biggest diamond on the ring was almost the width of my finger. There were also smaller diamonds around the band. They sparkled brilliantly even though the lights in the restaurant were dim. *This must have cost a fortune,* I thought. Then I thought, *shit, did you hear that?* I gave Ethan a guilty look and he smiled.

"Yep, I heard it. I'm glad you're impressed," he thought.

"I am. It's beautiful," I thought back.

Ethan started talking out loud. "Your body language isn't telling me that you're happy," he said.

"What? No, I'm happy," I said. "This is wonderful. I love you."

"I believe you, but there's something bothering you. I can feel it," he said.

I sighed. There was no use hiding it. "This trip has been great. I really appreciate everything, and I know you've done all you can to try to make me happy. It's just..."

"Just what?" he asked.

"You don't think we're a little young to get married? We don't even have a life plan," I said. "You have a home and a family to go back to. What am I going to do tomorrow? This trip hasn't fixed anything. I'm still an outcast. I'm still a rogue and you're still the future Alpha. It's just so hard to completely give in to all of this when I don't even know where I'm staying tomorrow or how I'll take care of myself."

"Tell me what you want," he said.

"What I want? What do you mean?" I asked.

"Tomorrow, what do you want to happen? Tell me. Be honest," he said. "In an ideal situation, what do you want to happen?"

"Well...in an ideal situation, I would finish school, then leave to try to find out where I came from," I said, "but I know you don't want me to leave, so we have a problem."

"What if I go with you?" he said. "Two heads are better than one. I can help you find...whatever it is you're looking for."

"You would do that for me?" I asked. "What about the pack?"

"I have siblings. My father can choose one of them to lead the pack," he said.

"Ethan, do you realize what you're saying?" I asked. "You're talking about giving up your Alpha position. You're talking about...abandoning the pack for a rogue. Your parents would never allow you to do that. You'd be exiled for life."

His expression changed to sadness, only for a split second. I know he tried to hide it, but I caught it. "I mean, I can only hope I'm not exiled, but they can't stop me and if they do exile me, then so be it," he said. "I've told you already, your happiness is my priority. If that's what you want, then that's what we'll do. We'll finish school, then we'll leave."

I couldn't believe what I was hearing. Ethan was going to give it all up for *me*? In that moment, I understood just how deeply he loved me, but more importantly I understood that I loved him just as deeply. I felt tears threatening to drop from my eyes.

"As for where you'll go, I'll rent an apartment," he said. "We'll stay there until we graduate. Everything will be alright Amina. I promise you. Just trust me." I nodded and wiped my eyes. "I'll never leave you," he said.

Trust him, I thought. I was pretty sure that thought came completely from my inner wolf. I was tired of fighting our connection. I wanted to give in to Ethan and believe in our relationship. I wanted to believe that I wasn't alone in this world, which was ironic considering that a week ago, all I wanted was to be alone. Now that I was bonded to Ethan, I wanted to stay with him. I decided that I was going to take the plunge. After all, what did I have to lose?

"And I'll never leave you either," I said. I touched my mark, then my ring. "We're going to be together forever, Ethan Rohe. I love you." I was surprised that I could feel the relief that my statement gave him. It was as if a weight was lifted from Ethan. All the stress he was feeling about me disappearing on him suddenly melted away. I didn't realize how heavily it weighed on him, but I was glad the burden was gone.

"It's time to go, Amina. Let's make the most of our last night on this trip," he said. I knew that what he was really saying was let's go back to the hotel room and have sex. I was all for it. He paid our bill, and we left.

11

Lift the Ban

Crash!

Amina and I both screamed as we were frightened out of our slumber by the sound of our hotel door crashing open. Amina slid so close to me we could have been attached to each other. I put my arm in front of her to shield her from whatever might be coming at us. Just as I had started shifting, I realized I was staring into the eyes of my father.

"What the hell, Dad!" I half-yelled, half-growled as I stopped shifting. Amina and I quickly covered our naked bodies with the blanket. "What the fuck are you doing?"

"This has gone on long enough, Ethan. You've had your fun. It's time for you to come home now!" he said. He stood there with an angry look on his face like he was scolding me for some silly thing I'd done when I was twelve.

"Are you crazy? How dare you disrespect my mate like this," I yelled at him. "This is unforgivable! Get the hell out of our room right now!"

"I won't say it again," he said.

"Get out!" I shouted. I knew how ruthless my father could be when he was angry and I didn't want Amina to get hurt, especially since he seemed to not like her very much, but I was livid that he would go to such lengths to bring me home. "I don't want to fight you Dad, but this is a new low, even for you! How would you feel if someone did this to you and mom?"

We stared each other down for a few moments. My father would never admit that he was wrong, but he at least backed down in this instance.

"We both know I would rip you to shreds, but I didn't come here to fight. I'll leave long enough for you to get dressed, get your things, and join me," he said. "Don't make me have to come back in here." He turned and left through what was supposed to be a door but was now a gaping hole in the wall.

I looked at Amina and tears were streaming from her eyes. She was terrified. My father had scared her tremendously.

"Baby, I'm sorry about my dad. He can be—"

"—I know," she said. "He's the Alpha." She looked down and a tear dripped onto the blanket. "He hates me so much. You're going to have to leave me, aren't you? He's never going to let you go."

"I'll never leave you. I told you already," I said, "but we need to get dressed. We're already going to have trouble with the hotel because of the damned door."

We got up and quickly put on some clothes. We had already packed most of our things since we were planning to check out anyway, so we packed the last few items and headed out to my car. My father was waiting.

"We're not doing this," I said as we tried to walk past him. "I have nothing to say to you."

"We don't have to talk. All that matters is that you're going home," he said.

"Get in the car, Amina," I said. She looked at me questioningly. "Everything's alright," I said. I kissed her and pushed her towards the car. Then I turned back to my father.

"We're going back to the pack lands, but I'm not going home," I said. "Amina and I are going to look for our own place."

Dad started laughing. "Your own place? Boy, don't be silly—"

"—I'm not a boy. I'll be eighteen in a couple of weeks and I'm sure I can rent an apartment now. Amina will be eighteen in a couple of days. We'll be fine on our own."

"You'll do no such thing. You're going to take that girl back to wherever you got her from, and you'll return home immediately." He shook his head. "Not even a couple weeks after shifting and you're already making bad decisions. You have so much to learn before becoming an Alpha. Keep this up, and you might never hold the position."

"I don't want the position," I said. "Give it to Lennox." I turned to get into the car.

"Don't be silly. Lennox doesn't have what it takes to be Alpha—"

I turned back to him and shouted, "—well give it to Stacey then! I don't care. I'm done!" I turned around and tuned out his shouting as I got in my car. I cranked up and sped off.

I was furious. Amina and I had such a great week and it all literally came crashing down at the end. I was sick and tired of her being scared and hurt all the time. I wanted to do anything I could to protect her. If it weren't for her desire to finish school, I'd be driving in the other direction.

I looked over at her and she was silently crying and looking down at her hands. "Everything is going to be alright," I said. "I know it doesn't seem like it, but it will."

"It won't," she said. "Your family isn't going to let us be together. We're right back where we started."

She wasn't wrong. I could see that my father was going to be a problem. I could only hope that I'd get us to a safe place. I reached over and grabbed Amina's hand. We rode silently the rest of the way.

A couple of hours later we were crossing back into the Moon Valley Pack's territory. The place that I'd grown up in my entire life suddenly seemed foreign and uncomfortable to me. We pulled into a dinner on the edge of town for breakfast just as the sun was coming up.

We sat down at the booth on the same side. Amina leaned on me, still not talking. She looked tired despite the fact that we had just come from a vacation. We sat quietly until our server, Misty came over.

"Hi, welcome to...oh, Ethan. Hi," said the server. She was my best friend's older sister. "Everyone's been wondering where you were. Gabe said you kinda disappeared from school." She noticed Amina and paused. "Hi...aren't you Eliza—"

"—her name is Amina," I said as I glared at Misty. She looked confused, but she said, "oh...okay, sorry. Amina." Misty cleared her throat. "Are you guys ready to order?"

"Yeah. I'll take two eggs and bacon. Oh, and an orange juice," said Amina quietly.

"Okay, got it...and you, Ethan?" she asked.

"Same, but make mine three eggs. And toast."

"Got it." Misty went off to put our order in. I kissed Amina. "We have plans to make," I said. I smiled at her. She didn't smile back.

"We're going apartment hunting today," I said. "There are plenty of places available and we'll get one easily. You should be excited."

"I want to be," said Amina. "I'm just...not feeling very confident. It seems too easy. I haven't had it easy, ever," she said.

"I won't lie to you," I said, "I don't think things are going to be easy for us, baby, but we'll be fine. We have each other, no matter what, and that's the most important thing. Now relax and let's enjoy breakfast."

We made small talk about the diner and what school would be like when we went back until breakfast came. We ate, laughed, joked, and wasted time until offices started opening, then we started our apartment hunting.

Three hours and six apartment offices later, we sat in the car feeling defeated. "Why won't they rent to us?" Amina asked. "I mean, I know we're young, but you're Ethan Rohe. No one tells you no, ever."

"It's not money," I said. "I'm rich. It's not age because your birthday is tomorrow and mine is in a couple of weeks—"

"—it's me," said Amina. "I'm the reason. They look at me, at the rogue, and they want nothing to do with me." She sighed.

"I don't think that's it either," I said. "I have an idea." We drove to the next apartment building. I had Amina stay in the car while I went in and filled out the application. Only ten minutes later I came out to give her the bad news.

"I was still denied," I said, "but I got some answers this time."

"What is it?" she asked.

"My father. He told the entire pack not to rent to us," I said.

"Seriously!" exclaimed Amina. "I can't believe he's doing this to us." I could see the tears coming back to her eyes. I couldn't bear to see Amina cry again. She'd cried so much already.

"I'm going to fix this right now," I said as I cranked up the car and drove off.

"How?" she asked. "Where are we going?"

"To my...the Alpha's house."

"What! Ethan, no, no, no! That's the last place we should go!" Amina yelled.

"Trust me, baby. Trust me," I said.

I drove straight to my parents' house. When we got there, I almost had to pull Amina out of the car. She really did not want to go in.

"It's us, together," I said. "Come on."

We walked into the house where my family was waiting. I had already texted them to let them know I was coming because I wanted this to be as fast as possible.

"Ethan, I hope you've come to your senses—" started my mother.

I held my hand up. "Dad, lift the ban," I said.

"Ban? What ban?" asked my mother.

"No," said my father.

"Lift it," I growled.

"I will not," he said. "You need to reject this rogue, come home, and start training for your position."

I felt my anger surging. "Don't call her that," I said. I instinctively pushed Amina out of the way.

"I think he's ready for his first lesson," said my father. My mother and siblings started backing up. They knew what was about to happen. Both of us started changing and I lunged first. That was a mistake because he swiped me out of the air fast.

I flew into the wall and felt a surge of pain float through my side. I briefly heard screaming, although I didn't know who it was, and I had to shake my head to focus. I looked at Amina standing on the side of the room by herself. She was scared and crying. That was all the focus I needed.

I returned my attention to my father. This time my attack landed. I knocked him back and then leapt on top of him. We fought as everyone, including Amina, yelled for us to stop. I finally got my father pinned down and, through mind link, I demanded that he lift the ban.

"What ban?" screamed my mother again.

He won't let anyone rent an apartment to us, I projected to her. *Lift the ban or I will reject the pack!*

"No, oh my Goddess! Roland, lift the ban!" shouted my mother. "I'm not losing my baby because you have a complex!"

I let my father up, not yet processing the fact that I had just beat him.

"Dammit, Roland, lift the ban!" my mother shouted again.

Fine, I projected. *I, Ethan Rohe, hereby re—*

"—stop it, Ethan! Stop it!" yelled my mother. I looked at her and saw that she was crying. "He'll lift the ban. I'll make sure of it," she said. My father started to protest. "Shut up, Roland!" she screamed. "Ethan, he'll lift it. Just stay with the pack. Please, don't leave us," she said.

I turned around and motioned for Amina to come with me. We went out to the car where I changed back to my human form. I put on some clothes, and we left to go find a place to live.

...

My heart was fluttering as Ethan unlocked the door. We stepped inside and I couldn't help but smile as I stared at the empty apartment and took in the scent of the new apartment smell. *This is real*, I thought as I stared at the bare, white walls. *I'm moving into a nice place with...my mate. My mate.* I let that sink in for a few moments as I watched Ethan walk around and check stuff out. A few weeks ago, I would never have believed this would happen. In fact, I wouldn't have wanted it to happen, especially not with Ethan Rohe. Now I couldn't imagine being without him. *It's crazy how things can change in such a short amount of time,* I thought. Ethan smiled at me. I guess he heard that thought.

"It's small and plain, but it will do for now," Ethan said as he finished his inspection. "We'll only be here for six months." He seemed as if he didn't really like the apartment.

"It's perfect," I said. "I've never lived in a place this nice before." To my surprise, Ethan shook his head. "It gets better than this. I promise."

"I mean, you can't compare this to where you grew up. You lived in a mansion. This is a downgrade for you," I said.

"Yeah, I guess it is," he said unenthusiastically.

I walked over to him and gave him a kiss. "I still can't believe you gave up your perfect life for me," I said. "I don't think I've said it before but thank you for everything."

"My life is only perfect with you in it," he said. He stepped back and pulled a box out of his pocket. "Happy birthday, baby."

"My birthday isn't until tomorrow," I said, but I took the box anyway. I lit up with excitement as I opened it. It was a gold bracelet with diamonds and a wolf charm on it. Ethan took the box and put the bracelet on me on the arm opposite of the other bracelet.

"I wanted to give it to you early," he said. "I couldn't wait."

"It's beautiful," I said. I felt tears coming to my eyes. It was the first time anyone had ever bought me a gift for my birthday.

"Now let's go shopping for our new home," said Ethan.

We made multiple trips for supplies. We were able to find some cheap, boxed furniture that was easy to put together and would fit into

Ethan's car. There was no point in spending a lot of money since we'd only be there for a couple of months. We went out once more to order a bed. We made it to the furniture store just a few minutes before they closed. We had to hurry, so we chose the first bed we saw and did the paperwork.

Once we finally got back home, I made dinner for Ethan for the first time—chicken, rice, and broccoli. I was thrilled that he liked my cooking. "We're already like a married couple," I said. "It's just the first night here and I'm already making you dinner."

"I'll make dinner tomorrow night. Deal?" he said.

"Deal," I agreed.

Later, we made pallets on the floor since we didn't have our bed yet. It felt good lying on the plush, sand-colored carpet in our place. We may not have had the fanciest things, but we had something that was a lot better. We had peace of mind.

Ethan and I stared at the ceiling fan, just enjoying the peace and calm of the place that would be our home until we graduated. I looked at Ethan and smiled.

"There's that smile I like to see on your face," he said.

"It's nice that we're settled until we graduate, but what's going to happen after that? We need to make a plan," I said, "because I don't think your family will let you go so easily. Plus, there's the fact that we don't know where we're going."

"Don't worry about that right now, Amina," he said. "Just enjoy the moment. Enjoy your birthday. Take the win."

"You're right," I said. "I don't want to jinx this." We laid in silence for a few moments, then I said, "you know, we need to christen this place before we clutter it up with a lot of stuff."

"I guess you're right," he said with a smile. Ethan pulled me on top of him. We kissed. One thing led to another and eventually we were making love to each other for the first time in our new home. Later, when I was lying on Ethan's chest and trying to fall asleep, I thought about how everything seemed perfect now that the ban was lifted and we were settled, but I couldn't help but wonder what other hurdles were ahead of us.

12

It's My Birthday

The next morning was what I had been dreading. Ethan and I were going to return to school—together. I wondered how many people knew we were mates. *Will they stare at us? Will they still bully me?* I wondered. My nervousness grew with each thought.

"Don't worry about it so much, birthday girl" said Ethan as he walked me to the car. "You're about to find out what it's like to be popular."

I looked at him with trepidation on my face. "I don't want to be popular. I want to be invisible."

"Being popular is a good thing, Amina," he said with a chuckle. "You'll see."

We arrived at school, and I was on the verge of an anxiety attack. Ethan calmed me down by giving me kisses on my neck around my mark. It helped a little, but only a little because people could see us. I could feel their eyes burning question marks into us as they watched us making out. *I'm glad we have first period together,* I projected. *I don't think I'd make it out of the car if I had to go in alone.*

"I promise, everything will be fine," he said aloud. "You'll see. Now let's go."

I took a deep breath, said a prayer to the Moon Goddess, and forced myself to get out of the car. As soon as I stood up, I met eyes staring at us as people walked by. If I were white, I would have been as red as a tomato. I looked at Ethan. Nope, no redness. He was used to being stared at.

Okay, Amina, I thought as I gave myself a quick pep talk. *You're mated to the most popular guy in school. Nothing bad is going to happen. What could go wrong?*

Ethan took my bag, and we walked inside, hand in hand. As soon as we hit the hallway, Ethan's three best buddies bounded over to him. I instantly froze. Usually when those guys were coming my way, they were about to do something horrible to me like pull my hair, knock my books out my hand, or push me against a locker. I prepared for any of those things to happen, but to my surprise they basically ignored me.

"Ethan," said Gabe. "Welcome back. Where the hell did you go?"

"We thought you weren't coming back," said Jabari.

"I just took my mate on a vacation," he said as he pulled me close to him. I could see the surprised expression on the guys' faces. I wanted to run away and hide.

"My sister was serious," said Gabe.

"Eliza Wilton is your mate?" asked Tyler in amazement.

Ethan tensed up. *They don't know,* I projected to him. *Don't get mad.*

"Her name is Amina Sturges now. No one is ever to call her the other name again," he said sternly. The guys all sort of shrank back a little. "Okay, man, it's cool," said Jabari. "Amina, we got it." Then to me he said, "congratulations Amina."

"Uh, thanks," I said. *That's it? No teasing? No name-calling?*

"I'll catch up with you later," Ethan said to the guys. "I need to get Amina to class." They all bumped fists, and the three guys headed off to their classes. I finally relaxed a little.

"See, nothing to worry about," he said with a smile. We headed to Mr. Jamison's class. As we walked in, Caroline Bancroft and her two little groupies froze as they watched us walk to my desk.

"Beat it," Ethan said to Samuel. Samuel grabbed his books and scurried away.

You don't have to be so mean, I projected to Ethan. *You're supposed to be different now, remember?*

That was mean? he asked. I shook my head and started to sit down but he stopped me and pointed at Samuel's desk. *I want to be able to keep my eye on you*, he said.

I sat down in Samuel's desk. *Why? Do you think something will happen?* I asked.

No, of course not, he said. *It's just, you know, I don't like the idea of you sitting behind me...it's a protective thing I guess.* He smiled at me and I nodded.

I turned around and although people were trying not to stare, I could see the awkward glances they gave us. Caroline and her friends looked like jealousy was eating them alive. I smiled. I kinda liked the fact that they were jealous of me for once.

Emily and Justin came over to us. *Oh my God, the project! Did they get a bad grade because of us?* I knew things were going too smoothly. There had to be a hiccup somewhere.

"What happened to you two?" asked Emily. "You disappeared on us."

"We're sorry," Ethan said. "Things...happened. I hope you guys didn't get a bad grade."

"Actually, no. Mr. Jamison let us do the project on our own since you two went missing, so it's all good," Jason said.

"We were just really worried about you," said Emily, but she was looking at Ethan. I don't know where it came from, but a sudden burst of jealousy sparked in me.

"My *mate* and I..." I made sure to put extra emphasis on the word mate, "...went on a vacation."

If Emily's face could have fallen off, it would have at that moment. "Your...mate?" She looked back and forth between Ethan and me. "Oh, congratulations," she said, but I could hear the disappointment in her voice.

"Mates, huh? Great. Now some of us might actually have a chance with the other girls. Congrats guys," said Justin. "Glad to see you're okay." They both went to their desks. I looked at Ethan and he smiled at me. *Your jealousy is cute,* he projected. *Glad to see you asserting yourself,* he said.

I have a feeling I'll be asserting myself all day, I said as I nodded towards some of the girls in the class who couldn't keep their eyes off of us.

Ethan suddenly got up and went to Mr. Jamison. They had a quick conversation with each other. I saw Mr. Jamison look at me once. *Are they talking about me?*

Ethan came and sat back down. I turned to him. "What was that about?" I asked, but he just smiled at me.

"Good morning, class," said Mr. Jamison. "Let's welcome back our future Alpha and his new mate, Amina. It's her birthday today, so let's give her a warm birthday welcome."

Oh my Goddess, I thought as the class applauded. The ones who weren't looking at us before were all looking at us now. I hated the attention and all I could wonder was how much more we would get.

School was a foreign country to me that day. Word spread fast that I was Ethan's mate, and no one bothered me. Well, at least not physically. I got plenty of stares from curious and jealous faces. I was also told "happy birthday" by at least three dozen people. I could hear whispers from people as they passed by—*"Eliza Wilton is the future alpha's mate? No way. She's a rogue."*

"This has to be a joke." "Her name isn't Eliza anymore. It's Amina." "Since when is her birthday in March? That makes her a Pisces, right?" "I think it's cute. It's like a fairytale love story." "Do you think she'll make it as the Luna? She doesn't talk much." I might have been off limits from physical bullying, but not even being Ethan's mate could make people like me.

Word about my new name must have spread even faster than word about us being mates because my second period math teacher also called me Amina. *I love that he's looking out for me,* I thought as I realized I missed him after only a half hour away from him. As I was sitting in class not really listening to Mrs. Roswell go over the binomial theorem, I realized that we hadn't been apart from each other since we'd mated, other than my few solo trips that I took when we were on vacation. *Will it be like this forever?* I wondered. *Together forever? Will we ever do anything apart from each other?* It's not that I wanted to be away from Ethan, I just didn't want to completely lose myself to him. I would have to figure out a way to balance my life against our lives together.

"Amina!" yelled Mrs. Roswell. She jerked me out of my daydream, and I realized all eyes were on me. *Crap, still the mutie,* I thought. I cringed at my own self-loathing, vowing to dispose of that name permanently.

"Uh, sorry Mrs. Roswell," I said. "What was the question?"

"Can you tell me what the binomial coefficient is in this equation?" she asked as she pointed to the equation on the board. I had no idea what she was talking about. I couldn't even fake it. I stared at her like a deer in headlights.

"Um, I'm sorry. I haven't had a chance to catch up since I got back," I said as I felt like I was dying from embarrassment.

"Okay," she said. *Phew, that's the end of it,* I thought, but I was wrong. "Amina, I need you to see me after class," she said. None of the students said anything, but I could see the amusement on some of their faces.

After class, I slowly approached Mrs. Roswell's desk, preparing to be scolded for my flop in class. Mrs. Roswell waited until all the students had left before she addressed me.

"Congratulations on being mated to the future Alpha and happy birthday," she said. I was surprised. I wasn't expecting that at all.

"Umm, thanks," I said.

"I'm sure it's a lot to deal with, given your particular...social status around here," she said. Her statement could be interpreted as being mean, but I didn't think she meant it that way. Plus, she was right, but she had no idea how right she was.

"Amina, you've always been one of my best students. I don't want you to put that in jeopardy because of your new relationship. A lot of the teachers here are often bullied into giving the Alpha's family members good grades. I'm not one of those teachers," she said.

"Oh, I don't expect that. No special treatment," I said.

"Good. You were only gone for a week, but in math, one week can be detrimental to your work going forward. You're only three months away from graduation and you have to pass this class to graduate. Here," She handed me a stack of worksheets. "These are handouts for the concepts you missed last week, plus two graded assignments that you need to turn in to me by the end of the week. I wouldn't suggest you spend the whole week on this because you also have to keep up with this week's assignments. That means you may have to...cool things with Ethan a bit until you catch up." She smiled at me, a smile that said she knew exactly what I had been doing with Ethan. I could feel my cheeks grow hot with embarrassment yet again.

"Yes ma'am," I squeaked out. "Thanks for letting me make up this work."

I took the papers and headed to lunch, grateful that at least Mrs. Roswell seemed to care about me a little. I headed towards the cafeteria, preparing to grab my tray and sit in my usual corner by myself, but before I made it there, I saw Ethan and his buddies heading my way. Usually, I would try to shrink myself as close to the wall as possible to get away from them and I almost instinctively did that, but Ethan must have sensed my nervousness because he broke away from the guys and came over to me.

I couldn't help but smile as he approached. To my surprise, he stooped down in front of me, wrapped his arms around my legs, and lifted me up. I was so startled that I dropped my books, and my arms instinctively went around his neck to steady myself. Everyone passing by in the hallway was looking at us. I was embarrassed for the...well, by that point I had lost count of how many times I had been embarrassed since we got to school.

Ethan started walking towards the cafeteria, still carrying me. His friends scrambled to pick up my books and they followed behind us. "You don't have to carry me," I said. "I can walk."

"I know, but I missed you," he said. "I couldn't wait to have you in my arms again."

"It's only been like an hour and a half since we saw each other," I said with a chuckle.

"So, you're telling me you didn't miss me?"

"You know I did." I leaned in and gave him a kiss. I could hear murmurs of people as they passed by. Then, a teacher said, "put her down, Ethan. You guys know better."

Ethan put me back on my feet gently. He grabbed my books from his friends and as I turned to face the direction of the cafeteria, my eyes locked with Caroline Bancroft. I almost looked away...almost. What kept me staring at her was the look of murderous jealousy on her face. Maybe it wasn't one of my moral high points, but I was ecstatic to see her like that.

Caroline...jealous of me? This is such perfect karma, I thought. I smiled my best bitchy smile at her as Ethan and I walked hand in hand to the cafeteria.

The next few events were pretty standard for lunch. We went through the lines and got our lunches. There was more staring as people took in the fact that Ethan and I were really mates. The next thing, however, was not standard. Instead of me retreating to my safe, private corner alone in the cafeteria, Ethan pulled me over to sit with him and his friends.

I felt completely out of place sitting in the middle of the cafeteria with a table full of football jocks. They were loud and crude as always, and I felt too awkward to eat. *Are you okay?* Ethan projected to me.

This is kind of a lot, I projected back, *but you can stay with your friends. I'll go to my usual spot. It's okay.*

No way, he projected. He suddenly stood up and grabbed both of our trays. Then he nodded for me to follow him to the table in the corner. I loved how Ethan was suddenly so protective of me. He wasn't embarrassed of me in front of his friends at all and that made me feel really good.

We sat down right next to each other, and I could still see curious eyes staring at us from across the room. "You didn't have to do this," I said. "The loner thing is my gig, not yours."

"You're not a loner anymore," he said, "but I don't want to overwhelm you. Baby steps. The kiss was a big leap for you." He leaned in and kissed me again.

"How long do you think we'll be the center of attention around here?" I asked.

"I'm sure it will blow over by next week," he said. "You know how it is...some new challenge will come along and get everyone's attention, or some new, more popular couple, or a fight, or something." I actually didn't know how it was. I'd spent my entire school career trying to not know how it was.

"Has your day been good so far?" he asked. I detected a slight seriousness in the question. What he was asking was if anyone had messed with me. *Geesh, how many people did he threaten*, I wondered.

"Yeah, it's been great," I said. "Well, maybe not math class. Mrs. Rowell gave me a lot of work to make up. That means we'll probably need to, you know, cool it a bit so I can study."

"I could just pay her to pass you," he said.

"What? No," I said. "That's cheating." He shrugged. "No Ethan. I'm going to study and earn it. Plus, I like studying."

He laughed. "No one likes studying," he said. "Especially math."

"I do," I said. We talked more about the first half of school as we finished our lunch. Towards the end, his friends brought my books over. I knew that Ethan usually walked with them to third period, so I encouraged him to go. He was reluctant, not wanting to leave my side, but I convinced him I'd be fine.

"If you need me, I can hear you even if we're not in the same room," he said as he grabbed my lunch tray.

"I know. Now go. I'll be okay," I said. I picked up my books and headed to my third period class.

On the way, I was flanked on both sides by Caroline and her friends. I got nervous. What were they about to do to me?

"I heard that you and Ethan got an apartment together. Is that true?" she asked as if it were any of her business.

"Yes, why?" I asked as I tried not to shrink in her presence. It was hard. All I wanted to do was scurry away like I would usually do.

"My parents would lose their shit if I moved in with my boyfriend," she said. "I guess it's a good thing that you don't have parents." There it was. A backhanded compliment. It was so Caroline.

"Well, that's probably because he's your boyfriend. Ethan's my *mate*," I said, "and my fiancée," I added, raising my hand to show my ring. I was hoping it would sting her ego. It did. I could see it all over her and her awful friends' faces. "Now excuse me, I have to get to class."

I sped up walking to get away from them, but for the first time in my life, it wasn't because I wanted to get away from them. It was because I wanted to leave them in my dust. It felt so good to be on top for once.

13 |

Broke

Fourth period was a drag. Mrs. Snyder was gabbing on and on about how the government affects the country's economy and I was doing my best to stay awake. My best wasn't very good. Even thinking about Amina wouldn't keep me up. I woke up to the sound of the bell ringing and to Mrs. Snyder's icy stare. "Sorry," I said. "I was moving all day yesterday." She shook her head as I left the classroom.

Meet me outside, I projected to Amina, hoping we weren't too far away from each other to send and receive thoughts. As I was walking, Gabe and Jabari caught up with me.

"Hey, you're coming to the party this weekend, right?" asked Jabari.

"What party?" I asked unenthusiastically as the weariness from my interrupted nap followed me.

"For real?" asked Jabari. He shook his head. "The party I have every year towards the end of the school year. You know...with the college girls—"

"—oh shit, I forgot, bro," I said. "I've had a lot going on. Yeah, I'm down for it."

"Good. I was thinking you might be too busy playing house with Amina," joked Gabe. "I can't believe y'all moved in together now. Like before you even graduate. That's wild."

"My parents would never agree to that," said Jabari, "but then again my parents aren't rich and the heads of the pack."

"Actually, my parents didn't exactly agree to it," I said.

"Bucking against the Alpha?" said Gabe. "I like it." They both laughed.

"I gotta catch up with Amina guys, but I'll text you later," I said.

"Okay. I'll be expecting an invite to the new place soon," Jabari said as they walked off.

I waited for Amina and was pleased when I saw her walking out the door with a smile on her face. That wasn't something I'd seen very often. My mind almost wandered to all the times that I was the reason she didn't smile much, but before I could go there, she was throwing her arms around me and planting a kiss on my lips in front of everyone. I was surprised that she did it, but I loved it when she showed me public affection.

"Not that I'm complaining, but what was that for?" I asked.

"Just because," she said.

"Great. A nice, juicy, public kiss...just because." *I can get used to this,* I thought. I leaned in for another kiss and she obliged. Then she gave me a quick peck on my cheek. I smiled at her then realized I was starting to aroused. *Wrong place,* I thought as I fought back the feeling. *Time to go,* I projected to her.

I grabbed her hand and we started walking to the car. We were almost there when I heard Lennox shouting my name from behind me. *Shit,* I thought while hiding my thoughts from Amina. *Not now. I don't want drama to ruin a perfectly good moment.*

"Hey Ethan, wait up," he said as he jogged over to me. "We need to talk."

I felt Amina's sudden change in temperament. I'm sure she was wondering what was about to happen. "Do you want me to wait in the car," she asked as she eyed Lennox.

"No," I said. I grabbed her hand and pulled her close to me. "This won't take long and whatever he has to say, he can say it in front of you." I turned to Lennox. "What do you want," I asked with obvious annoyance in my voice.

"You basically ignored me all day today. I know you're beefing with Mom and Dad, but why are you ignoring me?" he said as he huffed to catch his breath.

"Lennox, I don't have time for this," I said. I tried to turn to go, but Lennox grabbed my arm. I snatched it out of his hand and glared at him.

"Ethan, wait! Geesh, just give me a minute," he said. "What did I do to you? We're brothers. Are you going to just cut me off like you did the rest of the family?"

I took a deep breath, not wanting to get into an argument with Lennox in front of everyone in the parking lot. "You didn't do anything to *me*. It's your disrespect of Amina that I won't tolerate. If you can't accept my mate, then yeah, I'm cutting you off," I said.

"Disrespect? I haven't done anything to her," he said.

"Oh really," I said. "You haven't even spoken to her since you got over here and you're talking about her like she's not standing right here."

Lennox's eyebrows shot up and he looked as if he were about to say something. Then he sighed. "Hi Amina," he said quietly. "Sorry."

"It's okay," said Amina.

"No, it's not. Ethan's right. If he disrespected my mate, I'd beat his ass," said Lennox. "I get it."

A group of girls walked by. "Hi Lennox," said one of them as she smiled at him. None of them said anything to me for a change. *I'm off the market,* I thought. *He's the next best thing.*

Lennox spoke to them and waved, then there was an awkward pause between the three of us. Lennox broke the silence. "Look, I'm on your side. I know Mom and Dad don't approve, but I don't feel that way. Neither does Stacey. I mean, we can't openly go against Mom and Dad, but whenever they're not around, we're cool. Also, I'll be mindful of how I treat you, Amina."

Amina's discomfort eased up and so did mine. I was relieved we weren't about to have a showdown, and it was good to hear my brother say that. At least I had one person in my corner. "That's good to know," I said. "I guess Dad is pretty pissed at me, huh?"

Lennox laughed. "After you beat him in a fight? I don't think pissed quite describes what Dad is feeling towards you."

Whoa! I did beat him! I honestly hadn't thought about the fact that I won a fight against my father. That meant I was stronger than him. I was coming into my Alpha strength fast. *Of course, it won't matter because I'm not going to be the Alpha now,* I thought.

Lennox continued. "Pissed is like cutting off just one of your credit cards. But to cut your whole inheritance? I think Dad's gonna disown you," he said.

That statement slapped me in the face. Lennox must have seen the shock, because he suddenly stopped laughing. I looked at Amina and she had the same kind of expression on her face.

"Wait...you didn't know? Shit," he said.

"Dad cut off my whole inheritance?" I asked. "He said that?"

Lennox looked at me with pity. I'd never been looked at like that before, especially not from a family member. "He forbade us to give you any money," he said, but I'm going to do it anyway. Lennox pulled out a wad of cash from his pocket and held it out to me.

"I'm not taking your money," I said.

"Now is not the time for pride. You just got an apartment, which you haven't even invited me to yet by the way, and you have bills and shit. It's between us. I swear I won't tell anyone," he said. He shoved the money towards me. I didn't want to take it, but I had to take care of Amina somehow, so I swallowed my pride and took it.

"Thanks, bro," I said sullenly.

"I'll see you around," he said. He turned and left.

My stress level skyrocketed. I thought football was stressful, but as I stood there taking in the reality that I was broke, I realized I was experiencing real stress for the first time in my life.

"Ethan, I'm so sorry," said Amina as she cut through my thoughts. "This is all my fault. I'm causing you so much trouble."

"Not at all, baby. Don't ever think that. We'll be fine," I said.

"How," she asked weakly.

"Don't worry, I have a plan," I said. She smiled a little and I was hoping she didn't sense my lie. I had no plan. Nothing at all.

On the way home I stopped by the ATM to confirm what Lennox had said. My card was inactive. There was no need to go into the bank to confirm that my name had been taken off the main account.

I was angry, but not about the money. I was angry because Amina had just had her first good day at school, and it had to be ruined in the end by this. I got to see happiness on her face for only five minutes. *Will she ever catch a break*, I wondered. Then the answer came to me. *Not as long as she's in this town.*

"Two months," I said. "Two months until graduation, then I can take you away from here forever."

"Yeah," she said, but it didn't sound like an agreement. It sounded like an empty response. I tried to sense what she was thinking, but she was blocking me.

"Amina, what's on your mind? You can talk to me," I said.

"Are you happy?" she asked. I don't know what I expected her to ask me, but it wasn't that.

"Why would you ask me that? Of course I'm happy. You make me happy," I said.

"That's not exactly what I mean," she said. "You're giving up so much for me and I love you for it and I appreciate it, but it's not fair for you," she said. "I mean, your home, your parents, your perfect life. That's a lot to sacrifice. I would understand if your inheritance were one thing too many. You shouldn't have to live like—an omega or worse, a rogue."

"You're all I need," I said. "I'll fix this. You don't have to worry."

"Ethan, I'm not worried about the money," she said. "I've been poor my entire life. It's nothing new for me. I just can't...I don't want to be the reason you're unhappy, so don't lie to me, are you unhappy? And you know that I'll know if you're lying."

I sighed. "Do I wish everything were easier? Do I wish my parents would just accept you? Do I wish I could take back all those years I hurt you? The answer to all of that is yes. Yes, I wish I could somehow just make everything alright, but..."

"Just say it," Amina said.

"Okay, fine. I don't know what to do," I said with a sigh. "I don't have any answers. This is all...happening fast."

Amina took in a deep breath and turned her head to look out the window.

"Amina, I owe you so much—"

"—I don't want you to love me because you think you owe me," she said.

"I don't!" I exclaimed. "I mean...I love you, but not just because I owe you, but I do owe you and I just want to make things right. Just, let me think. I'll figure something out."

We rode in silence the rest of the way home. I wasn't sure what was worse—the uncertainty of our financial future or the fact that I felt, once again, that Amina was starting to pull away from me.

...

I don't know what made me think that taking Amina to Jabari's party was a good idea. We both needed to relieve some stress, so I thought that hanging out with friends would be a great way to do that. What I hadn't considered was that none of these people were Amina's friends.

I could feel her insecurities and awkwardness as she basically glued herself to me. She was quiet like always, but her quietness was paired with a slight nervousness and an acute sense of awareness that I'd never noticed before. She was behaving as if she were in a room full of predators and needed to be prepared to flee at any moment.

Jabari, Gabe, and Tyler came over to us and Amina sort of fell back behind me a bit. I instantly felt bad. Usually when the four of us came near her, it wasn't good. I'm sure her reaction was because of some flashback of some awful thing we'd done to her in the past.

The guys were going on about how epic the party was, but I was different than usual. I wasn't as excited as they were. Only a few weeks ago, I would have been the life of the party. I would have probably been drunk already and would have made out with at least one of the college girls by then. I'd be playing beer pong, tearing up the dance floor, or pranking one of the neighbors. As I stood there listening to my boys talk, I realized that I didn't want to do any of those things. I wondered if I'd ever want to do any of those things again. *Maybe I'm just depressed,* I thought.

I tuned back to Amina and I caught the tail-end of one of her thoughts. *"—dressed all sexy and I'm in this ugly crap."* That made me feel even worse because I didn't have the money to let her go shopping for something decent to wear to the party. I liked what she was wearing, but what mattered is that she didn't.

I realized that neither of us were having a very good time at Jabari's party. I just couldn't have a good time when I knew Amina was so uncomfortable. *Do you want to leave,* I projected to Amina.

You don't have to leave. You should have fun with your friends, she projected back. *I can go home. You stay.*

Absolutely not, I projected to her. *I'm not staying without you.*

I've already taken you from your family. I don't want to take you from your friends also. Ethan, please stay. I'll stay also. I'll be fine. Just enjoy yourself.

I turned to her. "We're leaving together. We can go hang out, just the two of us. C'mon." I grabbed her hand and led her out of the party. She was reluctant to go and continued to try to convince me to stay all the way to the car. I understood why—she didn't want me to feel like I was giving up my entire life for her even though it was my choice to do so, but what I didn't understand at the time was how much guilt she was developing or how soon I would find out.

14

She's My Everything

As I watched Ethan sleep, all I could think about was wanting to protect him from my mess. I wiped a tear away from my cheek, then gently stroked his soft brown hair and thought about how much I loved when he stared at me with his piercing green eyes. I breathed in deeply, inhaling his scent, trying to catalog it deep into the depths of my brain so when my nose could no longer smell him my brain could fill the void.

He was sleeping deeply, no doubt tired from all the stress of the day. I was thankful for that. It would make what I was about to do easier. No fussing, no fighting. I kissed his forehead and snuck out of bed. I grabbed the note that I wrote when he first fell asleep and put it on the bed beside Ethan along with my ring. I wiped a few more tears away, then I grabbed a bag that I'd packed while Ethan wasn't paying attention and snuck out of the door as tears flooded my vision.

I didn't need Ethan to verbally tell me how much the rift in his family hurt him. I could feel it. He tried so hard to hide it for my sake, to put on a front that he only needed me, but I knew better. There is no hiding true, deep feelings from your mate. Ethan was suffering for me, and I loved him too much to let it continue. I had watched his life go up in flames and he was still willing to continue sacrificing until nothing was left. If I removed myself from the equation, he would gain everything back. It was a simple solution.

I snuck outside and gently pulled the door behind me as softly as I could. I waited for a moment, hoping that Ethan didn't hear me. He didn't.

I took off my clothes and put them in my bag. I shifted quickly and quietly, picked up my bag in my mouth, and took off running. My wolf was protesting wildly, and my heart was breaking into little pieces with every step, but I knew that leaving was for the best. I ran wildly, as fast as I could because I wanted to get far away from Ethan so he couldn't smell me when he woke up. I knew better than to go to the mountains again, so I ran towards the next town where we'd had our vacation.

Once I got there, I didn't stop. I ran for hours, straight through and past the next three towns. The pain in my mark grew as I got further and further away from Ethan, but I didn't think it was the distance that was causing the pain. It was the thought of never seeing him again that was causing it.

Finally, as the sun began to rise, I stopped just outside of the edge of the last town I'd passed through and collapsed behind the edge of the woods so I was out of sight. I was exhausted and devastated, and I felt a pain more intense on my mark than any pain I'd ever felt. I cried profusely. I knew it would hurt to leave Ethan, but I could never have imagined the intensity of the depression and pain that was consuming me. Suddenly, all my energy faded away and I floated off into darkness.

...

"I can't smell her anywhere!" I shouted into the phone. "She was gone when I woke up. We have to find her. I need your help," I pleaded. "Please, I know you don't like her but—"

"—just try to calm down," said Lennox. "You won't be able to find her if you're too emotional. I'm on the way." He hung up and I tried to calm down like he said, but I couldn't. *What if she tried to go through the mountains again? She could be in danger while I'm pacing the living room,* I thought.

I sat down and read the note she left for the hundredth time as I felt an immense pain growing in my heart. I looked at the ring in my palm and squeezed it in my fist. The note said she was leaving for my sake. She didn't want me to give up everything for her. That when she was gone, I'd get my life back.

Doesn't she understand? She is everything to me. She's my everything. Tears littered the note. I tried to call her again and just like the last eleven times, my call went straight to voicemail. I tried to project to her even though I was sure she was out of range. *Amina, please come home. Just come home and we can work this out.*

I paced the apartment, praying that my brother would hurry because I was growing restless. I knew Amina was getting further and further away with every passing minute. Just as I was about to leave to start the search alone, there was a knock at the door.

I opened the door and to my surprise, Stacey and my mother was with him. "What are you all doing here," I asked with a shaky voice. "I'm really not in any condition to argue—"

"—we're not here to argue," Mom said. "We're here to help."

I was completely shocked. "You want to help me find Amina?" I stepped aside to let them come in. "Why? I thought you hated her?"

Stacey gave me a hug, followed by my mother. "I don't hate her," Mom said. "I just don't like her for you. That's two different things."

"Mom!" said Lennox.

"Relax," she said. "I'm not starting any drama. Ethan, you're my son. I can see how much you're hurting right now and it's breaking my heart. I know things haven't been good between us, and I'm not saying I approve of her, but you'll be in so much pain without her because you didn't reject each other. I don't want you to suffer."

"I guess Dad doesn't feel the same since he's not here," I said. No one said anything and that gave me the answer.

"How are we going to find her," asked Stacey. "Do you have any idea where she could have gone?"

"No. Not a clue," I sat down and put my head in my hands. "How could I not hear her leaving last night? Why didn't I sense it?"

"Stress," said my mother. I could detect guilt in her voice. After a beat, she said, "I have an idea. There are four of us, so we could each go in a different direction. Give us something that has her scent on it, like unwashed clothes or maybe a hair brush. We can use that to search for her. If one of us falls upon her scent, we can call for the others to join us."

"That's a great idea, Mom," I said feeling a shred of hope for the first time since I woke up that morning. "We haven't done laundry yet." I ran to the hamper and pulled out some of Amina's shirts. I gave each of them one. "I'll take the west side," I said. "That's the mountains and I don't want any of you near that area."

"Do you really think she went that way?" asked Stacey. "It's forbidden."

"She's done it before," I said with a sigh. "Lennox, you go north. Mom, you go south. Stacey, that leaves east for you. Let's go."

We all flew out of the house, shifted, and ran. *Amina, I hope you at least didn't go into the forbidden mountains again. Please tell me you didn't make that stupid decision*, I projected as I ran towards the place that I'd seen her in her wolf form for the first time.

I reached the edge of the pack's territory and paused for a moment. I didn't smell her, and I wanted to believe she wouldn't have come in that direction, but I had to check for myself. I gathered my courage and made my way into the forbidden mountains.

I wanted to run as fast as I possibly could, but I knew I needed to keep an eye and nose out for any dangerous wolves, so I chose to run slow so I could concentrate.

As the light of my territory faded behind me, the darkness of the valley closed in. The trees were demented and looked almost as if they had been screaming as they twisted their way into unnatural shapes. Thick vines hung low and made visibility difficult. I couldn't run in a straight line because the trees and bushes weren't growing in any particular pattern. They seemed to be placed haphazardly requiring me to dodge branches, and vines with every step. Tree roots stuck up from the ground everywhere as if they were waiting to grab someone by the ankles and trap them. It was truly scary being in those woods, but I summoned every ounce of courage I had and pushed on. Suddenly, I smelled a scent that I was familiar with. It was not Amina's.

I stopped as the scent and the danger got closer. I couldn't see the dark wolf, but I knew he was lurking. I also knew that this time he wouldn't run away.

I prepared myself for battle, trying to figure out which direction the dark wolf was coming from. I heard a twig snap to my left. I turned just in time to see him attack.

I can't die. That's all I could think as the dark wolf knocked me into a nearby tree. Pain exploded in my side, and I fell to the ground. I quickly got up and dodged another attack from the wolf. I forced myself to ignore the pain and took the offense. I lunged towards the dark wolf.

He went down. *I can't let him get the advantage back.* I dived on him, swiping for dear life. I was happy when I saw my claws shred his side. Blood trickled out and he howled in pain. He kicked my injured side with his back leg and that time I howled in pain. It caused me to pause my attack long enough for the dark wolf to get away from me.

We faced off, both of us giving our fiercest snarls. *I have to get to Amina. I have to end this*, I thought. The dark wolf lunged for me. I evaded him, spun around, and latched onto his throat. I bit down with all my might, shaking my head left and right to make the bite sink in even more. He struggled to get loose, but I wasn't going to let up. I felt the bone in his throat crack, then crush under the weight of my jaw. The dark wolf let out a sick-sounding howl, then collapsed to the ground. He panted for air but couldn't get any. I saw the panic in his eyes as he slipped away. Then, suddenly the panic was gone and was replaced with a blank stare. He was dead.

I sat for a moment, trying to get my breath. My side was on fire, and I was pretty sure at least one of my ribs was broken. It didn't matter. Nothing was going to stop me from finding Amina. After I caught my breath, I forced myself to get up and continued on through the valley.

The trees and vines got thicker and thicker as I limped on. I could hear ominous noises all around me and I kept detecting wafts of scents from other wolves. Their scents were…off somehow, letting me know that they weren't good wolves. They were wolves I'd want to stay away from. Plus, I had no doubt they could smell me also which sent waves of dread through me. Something was telling me that this wasn't going to end well, but I tried to push the thoughts out of my mind and concentrate.

These woods are too thick. I'm having to crawl through them. Amina wouldn't have come through here if she was trying to get away quickly. I sighed. Get away quickly. Would she have been trying to get away from danger, or from me?

I decided to turn around and go back the way I came. I kept walking, but the area I was going through didn't seem familiar. I couldn't see any tracks from when I'd come through the first time. A sinking feeling hit me as I realized I was lost in the most dangerous woods I could be in.

I kept walking faster and faster as the trees and vines thinned out and eventually I was able to run slowly, but despite that I still didn't see the peep of light from the pack's territory that would have put my mind at ease. I tried to use my keen sense of smell to get me back home, but it seemed the scents in the woods were overpowering everything.

I stopped in my tracks. Three sickening scents were suddenly too close to me. I turned to see I was facing three angry, hungry-looking wolves who were looking at me like I was the only meal they'd seen in months. I might have been able to fight one off, but with my injury there was no way I'd be able to fight all three of them.

I started backing up, preparing to run but I knew I couldn't outrun them with a broken rib. I mentally prepared myself for the worst. I felt that this was about to be the end of my short life and all I could think about was Amina. I just hoped she hadn't tried to escape through these woods and suffered the same fate. *I love you, Amina,* I projected as the wolves crept closer to me.

Suddenly a giant wolf with thick, black fur came out of nowhere and jumped in between me and the three hungry wolves. He was easily the largest wolf I'd ever seen, even larger than my father. He towered over the four of us and his light-brown eyes were sharp and focused. He bared his teeth, and I was thankful it wasn't at me. I instantly understood that whoever this mysterious wolf was, he was there to defend me.

Thank you for this blessing Goddess, I thought as I got ready to fight. The three wolves attacked. Two of them went for my ally while one went for me. The mysterious wolf and I fought as hard as we could, and I wasn't surprised that he easily overpowered his two attackers. I, however, struggled a lot more with my one. He dealt serious blows. The pain was immense. I felt bones snap in different places on my body. Eventually I could only lay on the ground and wait for the final blow. It didn't come. I looked up and saw the mysterious wolf snatch my attacker back. He slammed him down hard. I heard the snap of his spine just before I passed out.

...

I woke up and immediately winced from the dryness in my throat. *Water*, I thought. I shifted to my human form long enough to drink a bottle of water. I looked at the watch I'd brought with me since I ditched my cell phone. I'd been asleep for five hours. *Ethan's probably awake right now and going crazy.* I felt horrible, but I tried to convince myself again that I was doing the right thing.

I knew I had to move. There was a twenty-five percent chance that Ethan had come in that direction looking for me and I had to make sure to stay far ahead of him so he couldn't track my scent. Just as I was about to shift back to my wolf form, a wave of lightheadedness hit me, forcing me to have to sit for a moment. *I'm probably still tired from running at such a high speed for so long yesterday,* I thought. *Maybe the water hasn't made it through my body yet. Maybe I just need to eat.*

Once the wave went away, I shifted and continued on my journey at a fast trot rather than a run so I wouldn't trigger the lightheaded feeling again. As I walked, something happened that I didn't expect. I got bored. It made me laugh at myself. *Here I am, on the run from my mate and I'm suddenly bored?*

I decided that I'd drop into the current town I was passing through and grab some hot lunch, just for a little while. I shifted to my human form, got dressed, and headed into town.

I walked along a quiet road, making my way to what I hoped would be a shopping district of some sort. I came across a sign that said, "Welcome to Meadsville". *I hope it's a nice place,* I thought.

It took half an hour before I came to a little stretch of town with quaint shops and nice-looking people. I strolled past the shops, enjoying the views of all the products displayed in their windows. I came across a little bakery and the scents that emanated from it were heavenly. I went inside and the smell of all the treats surrounded me like a delicious air freshener. I browsed the bakery and laid eyes on confections that I'd never even imagined existed.

"Hi," said a woman with a gleeful disposition. I turned to face a woman with bright red hair pulled back into a ponytail and a smile that would brighten any gloomy day. *I'd be gleeful too if I worked here,* I thought. I felt like a kid in a literal candy store.

"We have free macaron samples today. Would you like to try one?"

I had no idea what a macaron was, but I said, "sure."

She walked me over to a display case where there was a glass dish on top that looked like a fancy cake plate. Inside of it were rows of brightly colored, circular treats. She opened it and I picked out a pink one. It smelled delightful. I popped the little round treat into my mouth, and I instantly felt like I'd taken a trip to a romantic, floral-filled retreat. As I chewed the soft, perfectly gooey round cookie-like dessert, my hungry body yearned for more.

"Wow, this is so good!" I said as I looked at the woman with delight.

"That flavor is rose," she said. "It's one of my personal favorites. Do you like chocolate?" I nodded my head eagerly. "Try one. They're to die for."

I tried one of the little brown macarons and it was so good I had to do a little dance. Those two samples were all I needed. I was sold. I left the bakery with a dozen macarons and two chocolate chip cookies to top them off.

I continued exploring the town as I enjoyed my treats. I explored an art gallery, visited a pet shop where I played with puppies, and found a pair of earrings I liked at a local artisan's shop. It was nice to be in a place where no one knew who I was. There was no stress, no bullying, and no judgmental eyes. I was essentially a tourist.

When I was done exploring the town, I was a bit sad that I was leaving. It had been a pleasant couple of hours and the idea of going back on the road alone again left me to deal with the pain of leaving Ethan. I walked back down the quiet road I'd come down and brushed away tears as my mind was invaded by thoughts of my abandoned mate.

15

Follow the Lead

I woke up in the area just inside of my territory. Everything seemed too bright as my eyes slowly opened. I lifted my arm to shield my eyes from the light and realized that my entire body was hurting. I sat up, groaning as I did, and all the memories of the forbidden woods came flooding back. I was wondering how I'd made it out when I remembered the mysterious wolf who came to my aid.

I looked around and spotted a large man sitting in the grass about three yards away from me. *The wolf?* He was watching me intensely with those same sharp, focused light-brown eyes. *Yes, it's him.*

"Thank you," I said. "You saved my life."

"Repayment for saving Amina's life," he said in a deep, booming voice.

That shocked me. How does this man know Amina? I had so many questions.

"How do you know Amina?" I asked.

"That doesn't matter," he replied. "Only one question matters. Is Amina somewhere in the valley?"

"I don't think so," I said. "I was looking for her, but I couldn't sense here anywhere. She ran away—"

"—that's all I need to know," he said. Then he got up to leave.

"Wait!" I shouted. I tried to stand up. It was hard because my injuries weren't fully healed yet. "Who are you, please. Amina's been looking for answers—"

"—you will not tell Amina about me!" he suddenly yelled as he turned and walked back towards me. "Is that clear?"

"I...I don't understand—"

"—telling her about me will put her life in danger and I haven't gone through all of this for..." he paused, and I saw a shred of emotion in his eyes, something other than anger. They suddenly flickered back to the sharpness that was there before. "Do not tell her about me. Make sure she never comes into these woods again. Wherever she's run off to, she's far better there than in these woods. Don't make me regret saving your life. I can easily finish the job those wolves started."

I nodded even though I still didn't understand. I desperately wanted to press him for more information, but I knew I couldn't beat him if he decided to attack me. He turned and headed back towards the forbidden mountains. He shifted, ran, and disappeared into the valley. I was completely confused, but I didn't have time to worry about him. I had to get back to finding Amina.

Luckily the mysterious man had returned my backpack along with me. I put on my clothes and took out my phone. There were several missed messages from my family. The messages went from things like *nothing yet* and *no luck* to things like *check in Ethan* and *Ethan, you okay?*

That's when the phone calls had started. They were no doubt worried about me since they knew I was searching the forbidden mountains alone. However, there was one message that really got my attention. It was from Lennox. It said *Ethan, bro, I think I found a lead.*

I started heading back to town as I called him. He picked up halfway through the second ring. "Ethan, you had us all worried. Where have you been?" he asked.

"Bad reception in the valley," I lied. "Plus, I got in a fight."

"Shit, are you okay?" he asked.

"I'm fine now. Forget that. You said you had a lead? Did you find her?"

"I *had* a lead," but when we couldn't get in touch with you, we all started heading back to the territory.

"No!" I shouted. "No, you can't let the lead go cold," I said. "Go back, Lennox. Please. I can head your way now."

"Okay, I'll turn back. You should call Mom and Stacey and let them know you're okay. They were headed back also."

"Okay, I will. Where are you? Or...I mean, where were you?"

"Just outside of a town called Bromfort. Do you know it?" he asked.

"Yes," I said with disappointment. "That's where we took our vacation. You're probably picking up on her scent from when we were there before," I said.

"No, you don't understand. I'm outside of Bromfort, as in on the other side of it heading into the next town. So, I think she came this way," he said.

"Oh. Great," I said. "It's a start. Listen, keep following the trail. I'll catch up. Just don't lose it, Lennox."

He hung up. I sent Mom and Stacey a text because I didn't want to waste time with phone calls. I didn't have time to have two more full conversations. They responded that they would head towards Lennox. I knew I couldn't run at my top speed yet, so I went home and got my car. I drove as fast as I could, hoping Lennox wasn't running at his top speed because I might not have caught up to him in the car. He wasn't, and a few hours later he was sitting in the car with me.

"You look like shit, bro. Did you lose the fight?"

"I don't want to talk about it," I said. "Tell me about the lead."

"Straight to business. Okay. I picked up her scent. It's very, very light. I might even be wrong about it, but I figured you would be able to discern it if you get close enough. I just hope I haven't wasted your time."

"Any lead is a good lead," I said. "It's more than what we had earlier."

"Cool. I picked the scent up a few miles ahead. It may be a little further than that now if she's on the move," he said.

"Okay. Let's check it out." I put the car into gear and hit the gas. *Please let it be her,* I thought. *Please.*

...

I was so tired. I'd been walking for hours. I decided to find a place to camp for the night. I came upon a group of trees that had a clearing right in the middle of them. It seemed like a good spot to make my camp for the night. I shifted to my human form, sat down, got comfortable, and pulled out my treat box that had my four remaining macarons and my two cookies in it. I thought about the last time I'd been in the same situation. I remembered how I had been cold and how the Moon Goddess granted me my first shift, giving me the warmth I needed to survive in situations like that.

I also started thinking about my first night out in the wild with Ethan, and how our bodies kept each other warm as we made love and slept with each other. Tears flooded my eyes as I thought about how happy I'd been with him. For some reason, it we just weren't meant to be. I would have to find a way to let go going forward. I couldn't survive with a broken heart. I knew what I was going to have to do, and I was dreading it. *Not tonight,* I thought. *I can't do it tonight.* I drank a bottle of water, shifted to my wolf form, and forced myself to go to sleep.

A noise woke me up. It startled me so much I was fully alert as I sat up and looked around. There was a bear staring straight at me. *Oh my gosh,* I thought. I started panicking. I knew you weren't supposed to run from bears, but I was pretty sure he was about to make me his dinner. *I can't fight a bear, but I can outrun it,* I thought.

I slowly stood up, grabbed my pack, and backed away from the bear. The bear just stood there, and I felt a bit of relief, thinking that he was going to peacefully go away. The bear suddenly roared at me, and I took off. *Don't fall,* I thought. *Don't fall.*

I ran as fast as I could. I looked back and was happy that I was putting considerable distance between myself and the bear. Eventually, it gave up. *Whew. That was close,* I thought as I slowed down to a trot. I realized that sleeping in the woods wouldn't be very safe for me. *It seemed like such a great idea when I left home,* I thought. *Of course it did. There aren't bears in the pack's territory.*

I decided to shift to my human form and see if there were any shelters in the town I was near. As soon as I put my clothes on, I began feeling sick. I got hit with a wave of lightheadedness and nausea. Next thing I knew, I was puking up my cookies and macarons.

I sat for a while, slowly sipping on water until my sickness went away. *There's no way this could be happening*, I thought. I rarely got sick. I had only ever puked once and that was because I ate some bad chicken. There was only one reason I could think of that I'd be lightheaded and throwing up and I prayed to the Goddess that it was anything but that. I grabbed my bag and headed into town to find a twenty-four hour pharmacy and a possible shelter to stay in for the night.

16

Back to the Pack

I sat on the park bench crying as I looked at the plus sign on the stick. This was definitely the worst case scenario. I was homeless, broke, and pregnant. I was carrying Ethan's child.

I felt horrible in so many ways. I'd left behind the only person in the world who loved me and he would never know he was a father. It was cruel, especially because I knew what it felt like not to know my parents. *Should I go back? Should I call him? What would I say to him? He probably hates me now.* I turned the situation over in my head, each time coming to the same conclusion that Ethan would hate me for leaving him. I broke a promise. It would serve me right if he rejected me after what I'd done.

I had nowhere to go. The local shelter was full for the night, and I didn't have enough money for a hotel room. *This was such a horrible idea,* I thought as I picked up my bag and started walking. I wiped my tears and went back to the pharmacy to buy chips and juice. I was starving.

I put my items on the counter. The cashier was the same one who had checked me out before. "You don't seem like you liked the results," he said. I tried to hold back the tears, but they insisted on running down my cheeks.

"No, not really," I said. I handed the cashier the money.

"Hey, I don't mean to pry," he said, "but it's late. Do you have anywhere to go?" I was surprised at his question. He noticed my expression and held his hands up. "I'm not trying to get in your business. It's just that if you're wandering around alone at this time, I mean…look. It can be dangerous out there. You're more than welcome to hang out in our break room for a while if you need to. There's a couch in there. A little lumpy, but you could at least take a nap.

"I don't know if that's a good idea," I said but I didn't really mean it. I was exhausted and I just wanted to rest.

"No one will bother you. You can sleep for a few hours," he said. "Just trying to do a good deed, here."

I took a deep breath and accepted the favor. After all, I didn't have anywhere else to go and I would be able to think better when I was rested. I thought about the fact that if Ethan were looking for me, he might catch up to me if I stopped, but considering what I'd just found out, that might not be such a bad idea, even if he did hate me. The cashier showed me to the break room, and I collapsed onto the couch. I gobbled down my chips and juice and laid down. The couch was itchy, and it smelled weird, but those two things quickly faded out of my mind as I went to sleep.

I woke up to the sound of yelling. I sat straight up as my brain immediately identified the voice. *Ethan. He found me.*

I walked towards the front of the pharmacy and saw Ethan holding the poor cashier up in the air by his neck, no doubt threatening him in order to force the cashier to tell him where I was. I couldn't help but show a little smile. Angry Ethan was a hot Ethan.

He stopped threatening the cashier and looked at me. Our eyes locked and for a moment, no one else was in the room with us. All the pain, fear, anxiety, and loss I had been feeling oozed away instantly and just like that, I knew that leaving him was the biggest mistake I'd ever made in my life.

He tossed the cashier aside like a ragdoll and ran to me. He embraced me tightly and planted a kiss on me that was so passionate that it literally made my knees weak. If he hadn't been holding me up, I surely would have hit the floor.

I realized we were both crying. "Why do you keep running away from me," he said in a breathy voice. He cupped my face in his hands. "Why, Amina? Tell me."

"I wanted to protect you," I said. "I'm the cause of all the problems in your life. If I was gone, you'd get your family, your money, and your future back."

"We've already discussed this. I don't care about all the shit. My life is nothing if you're not in it," he said. Then he pulled me close and hugged me for dear life. "I was so worried about you, baby. Don't do this again, please."

"I can't believe you came this far to find me," I said. "I thought you would—"

"—what? Stop looking for you? Amina, I would search this entire planet for you," he said. "I would look for you in space if I had to." He kissed me again. "You're mine. I'm never letting you go. Do you understand that?" He touched my mark, and I felt shivers run down my spine. I touched his, and that caused a fresh new round of kisses from him.

"Are you mad at me?" I asked.

"Hell yeah, I am," he said, "but I'll get over it. Just come home, baby. Please tell me you'll come home."

"What is your family doing here?" I asked, trying to avoid the question. We both looked at them and the three of them waved at me. I waved back.

"They helped me find you," he said.

I was shocked. "They did? Are you serious? Even your mother?"

"Yeah," he said.

I couldn't believe they all came looking for me. Could it be that they cared, just a little bit? I was scared to let myself think that because I didn't want to get hurt.

"Of course they care," he said. *Crap, back to sensing my thoughts.* "They care about you because they care about me. I know my family can be harsh and even downright cruel, but they won't harm you, Amina."

"We won't," said his mother, "and I apologize for my behavior towards you before. You have to understand, I'm a mother—I just want what's best for my children. I can see there's no swaying my son to choose another mate, so I'll accept you as my daughter-in-law," she said.

It wasn't exactly a compliment, but it was the nicest thing she'd ever said to me. I was a crying, blubbering mess at that point. Ethan led me to the front of the store where his mother and siblings all gave me a big hug.

"Great, so this story has a happy ending," said the cashier. I think we had all forgotten about him so when he spoke, we all snapped our heads around to him. He was rubbing his neck where Ethan had strangled him.

"Thank you for being so kind to me," I said. "I'm sorry about the…" I gestured to his neck.

"No problem," he said. Then to Ethan, "sorry man. I just thought maybe she was running from an abusive boyfriend or something. I didn't mean any harm."

"I appreciate you trying to protect her," said Ethan. "That's really decent of you. Sorry about that."

"Ah, don't worry about it," he said. "Just let me get your workout routine and we can call it even."

"I'm glad we found you," Lennox said to me. "I couldn't take too much more of Ethan's crying," he joked.

"Shut up, Lennox," said Ethan. "I didn't cry…that much." We all laughed. I was glad the tension was breaking up. The bell to the pharmacy door rang as a couple walked inside. We all scooted away from the door to let them in .

"Busy tonight," said the man to the cashier. He nodded towards us. We all nodded back.

"It seems I've caused a lot of trouble for all of you," I said. "I'm so embarrassed that you had to go through all of this because of me. Even you, sir," I said to the cashier.

"Uh, Ethan," said his mother.

"Yeah?" he responded.

"I didn't get to ask you in the car...why do you look like you were at the losing end of a fight?" Everyone stopped and looked at Ethan. I was suddenly wondering the same thing.

He smiled. "Because I was at the losing end of a fight," he said.

"What!" we all exclaimed collectively with the exception of Lennox. He must have already known about it.

"Ethan, what happened?" I asked. "Who did you fight? Crap, is that my fault, too?"

"It's a long story, one that I don't really want to go into right now," he said. "The most important thing is that I've found you, so I think we should all go home now."

"Wait, before we go, I just want to make sure you promise to stay this time, Amina. This was pretty exhausting, and I need to hit the gym if chasing you is going to be a regular thing," Stacey said. They all laughed, and I blushed hard.

I looked around at them, then at Ethan. I realized that Ethan would never let me go, even if I was trying to leave for a good reason. It would be worse for him to waste his life away looking for me than to fix our lives together. Plus, now that I knew I was pregnant, it would be unfair to Ethan and our child if they never got to know each other. My dreams of living a rogue life, which wasn't going so well anyway, were over.

"Sorry, guys. I won't run away again. I promise," I said. They all looked at me accusingly like they didn't believe me. "Seriously, I won't. I thought I was doing the right thing. I can see now I wasn't," I said as I touched one of Ethan's bruises.

"I'm glad to hear that," said Ethan. "Come on, let's go home."

As we walked out to the car, Ethan's mother said, "Amina, I know you're Ethan's mate, but I don't ride in the back seat of anyone's car."

"Yes, ma'am," I said. I looked at Lennox and Stacey. They shrugged their shoulders and smiled. "You'll get used to the family dynamic," said Stacey. *The family dynamic,* I thought. *I hope it's better than the family dynamic I had with the Wiltons.*

It will be, Ethan projected. I mentally scolded myself. I just couldn't seem to remember that Ethan could hear my thoughts.

"Wait," said Ethan. He reached into his pocket and pulled out my engagement ring. He grabbed my hand and held the ring to my finger. Then he looked at me questioningly. I nodded and he slipped it back on my finger where it belonged.

"Engaged? Why?" asked Lennox.

Stacey hit him on the shoulder. "It's sweet," she said. "Congratulations!" She gave me a hug, followed by the Luna.

What about your father, I asked as we all got in the car. *Has he changed his mind about me?*

Ethan's smile went away and that gave me the answer to my question. *I'll handle my father,* he said.

You're not going to fight him again, are you? I asked. *Please, no more fighting. Maybe you can patch things up with him somehow.*

Don't worry about it, Amina. I'll handle it. Let's just get home. Let's celebrate this win, he projected.

I sighed. *Okay.* Ethan started the car and proceeded to take me back to the pack territory once again.

17

A Pup on the Way

Everything in me wanted to tie Amina up and lock her away so she wouldn't run away from me again. I wanted to believe she would really stay this time, but my trust in her was broken. Still, I tried not to show it. For two weeks I smiled, kissed her, protected her at school, and made passionate love to her all while hiding how scared I was that she would leave.

Amina surprised me with a small birthday party at our apartment. She'd invited family and close friends that had been curious about our new digs. I tried to behave as if everything were normal, but there was a constant element of fear that I'd wake up and she'd be gone. I tried to keep my eyes on her as much as possible and I even got some of my friends to watch her when I couldn't. She didn't know she was being watched, of course. She would be pissed if she knew.

It was my brother who pointed out that I probably needed a break from my stalker duties. He convinced me to take my eyes off of her and go hang out with him and the guys for a while. I agreed since I realized I could smell Amina's scent from miles away, so if she left again I'd know immediately.

We went out to the mall, a place where everyone goes after school, but for some reason I felt out of place. For starters, I wasn't the center of attention for once. I was used to people staring at me, speaking to me, and trying to get my attention, especially girls. Now, it seemed they were all giving that attention to Lennox. I mean, I never wanted the attention, but now that I didn't have it, I felt awkward. *They're all so fake,* I thought. *When they thought I was going to be Alpha, they all wanted to be my friend or my mate. Now they act like I'm not even here.*

"These would be a flex," said Jabari as he stared at the new Jordans in amazement. "Do you have these in a size ten?" he asked the store clerk. The clerk retreated to the back to find the shoes in the requested size. Normally I'd be requesting a size eleven right along with Jabari's request, but a pair of $180 sneakers wasn't in my budget anymore. Apparently Lennox didn't have that problem because when the clerk came back, he requested them in his size.

"I can't believe you're not getting any," said Gabe. "What's the matter? Wifey got you on a budget already," he said jokingly. "We're not even out of high school yet, Ethan."

"Shut up, Gabe. I still make my own decisions," I said.

"Yeah right. Amina's got you wrapped around her finger," Gabe said. "You're whipped." The other guys nodded their heads in agreement.

"I get it though," said Tyler. "Ever since I mated with Macy—"

"—you mated with Macy? Macy Burrows?" I asked. He nodded and I noticed the mark on his neck. "When did you mate with her?"

"Two days ago," he said, "and it's crazy. Like I can't get her off my mind. It fucking sucks," he said.

"I'm not mating with anyone," said Jabari. "Player for life."

"Yeah," said Gabe as he fist-bumped Jabari.

"Bro, you might not have a choice," said Tyler. "I wasn't looking for a mate. It just happened. It was like, all of a sudden, her scent just—"

"—took over," I finished.

"Yeah," said Tyler. "You can't fight it." He shrugged.

"Cap," Jabari said. "I can fight it just fine. All I have to do is reject her and I'm a free man. Rizz King for life." Lennox and Gabe nodded in agreement.

"Yeah, well, we'll see if you're saying the same thing when you find your mate," said Tyler. The clerk came back with Lennox's shoes. They guys paid and we left the store.

"I'm just curious," said Tyler. "What are you two gonna do? I mean, it's no secret that you've got...issues with the Alpha so is he going to skip over you and pass the mantle to Lennox?"

Everyone stopped and looked at him. "Why the fuck would you bring that up?" asked Gabe.

"What? I mean, it's a legit question. Everybody's been wondering," said Tyler.

"We haven't even discussed it," said Lennox. A group of girls walked by and obviously tried to get Lennox's attention.

"See?" said Tyler. "Everyone thinks Lennox is going to be the new Alpha. Is your father going to make you two fight for the title?"

"What? Tyler, shut up," said Gabe.

"Nobody's fighting anybody," I said. "If Lennox wants it, he can have it."

"Yeah, and I wouldn't fight my brother for that anyway," Lennox said. "I swear people in this pack like drama way too much."

"Well, if you two did fight, who do you think would win?" asked Tyler with innocent curiosity.

"Me, of course," I said with a smile.

"Just because you're older doesn't mean you'll win," said Lennox.

"Please. I've been beating your ass our entire lives. Nothing's changed," I said.

"Really?" said Lennox. "We'll see about that old man." He started fake boxing me as we walked to the food court. We all got some food, sat down and ate it, and made our way to the arcade. By the time we got there, two girls had joined Lennox and were all but throwing themselves at him. We hung out for about an hour, and everything was going well until suddenly my nose commanded my attention.

Something changed with Amina's scent. It was her, but it wasn't her. It was like her scent was tainted. *Is she...cheating on me?* That was my first thought, and I wasn't sure if it made any sense, but something had definitely just changed with Amina. I felt panic rising.

"I have to go," I said to the guys. They all stopped what they were doing, and I could tell from the expressions on their faces that they sensed something was wrong.

"Is it Amina again?" asked Lennox.

"I don't know," I said as I turned to leave. "I'll call you later," I shouted. I made my way to my car as fast as I could and sped off towards home. I started to call Amina on the way, but decided against it. If she was cheating on me, I wanted to catch the culprit in the act so I would know exactly whose throat I needed to rip out. By the time I got home, the scent was overwhelming and invading, and my anger was boiling over.

I burst into the apartment, almost ripping the door off the hinges. I heard Amina in the bathroom, so I ran to it and to my surprise, she was in the bathroom alone, puking her guts out in the toilet.

"Amina, baby, what's wrong," I said as I went over to her and helped her hold her hair back. "Are you sick?" I could smell the strange scent emanating from her. *Did she eat bad food or something*, I wondered.

"No...I didn't eat anything bad," she said. Then she put her face over the toilet and puked again. "It's....ba...eye," she said as she wretched up whatever was inside of her.

"Don't talk right now," I said. "Just get it out."

Amina gave up what was left in her belly, then I helped her clean herself up. She was trembling slightly, so I picked her up and laid her on the bed. Then I got her a glass of water. She sipped it slowly, testing herself to see if she could keep it down. When she saw that she could, she took larger gulps. When she was settled, she was ready to talk.

"Ethan, I...I don't know how to tell you this. You already have so much on you," she started. She didn't have to say another word. I already knew where she was going with this. I felt the blood drain from my face.

"You're pregnant," I said.

She nodded, then a tear ran down her cheek. "It's the last thing we need right now. What are we going to do?"

"I can tell you what you're not going to do," I said. "You're not going to run away from this."

She looked at me with a surprised expression. "I wasn't going to...is that what you think?"

"I never know what you're going to do," I said. "I mean, can you blame me?"

"Ethan, if I wanted to take your child away from you, I would have never let you catch up to me at the pharmacy!" she shouted. She got up from the bed and was about to storm off.

I grabbed her arm and pulled her back. "You knew you were pregnant at the pharmacy?"

"Why do you think I was there? I bought a pregnancy test," she said as she yanked her arm back. "That's when I found out."

"And you're just now telling me this? That was weeks ago! Why would you hide this from me? Were you going to leave and not even tell me about my child?" I asked.

She rolled her eyes and turned around to leave the room. "I wasn't planning to leave! I didn't tell you because...well this! I thought you would be upset," she said as she started to cry. "We're already struggling. Now we're arguing."

"Amina, wait. Wait," I said as I followed her down the hall. "I'm not upset. I'm just surprised. Please don't cry."

"You're upset. You don't trust me. You think I don't know that your goons watch me everywhere I go? I mean, I guess I deserve that..."

I caught up to her and stopped her. I pulled her close to me. "I just don't want to lose you. I'm sorry for yelling. Let's not argue. This is supposed to be a celebration."

"A celebration? So, you're happy that I'm pregnant?" she asked as she pouted.

"Of course I am," I said. "I wanted to get you pregnant, remember?" I smiled at her as she looked up at me with a sparkle in her wet eyes. "I mean, yeah, we said it was a bad idea, but I don't care. The idea of you carrying my pup, it makes me happy."

"I'm not sure how I feel about it yet," she said. "It's just...so much happening. I haven't even figured out my future yet and I'm almost married with a kid on the way." I leaned down and kissed her. "Don't worry, Amina. I'm going to take care of our family, okay? Just trust me. Everything is under control."

She wiped away her tears and gave me a look that melted my heart. I could see in her eyes that she put her trust in me as the head of our little family. She finally fully trusted that I would take care of her and for the first time in weeks, I was confident that she would stay.

...

It wasn't easy getting through the next few weeks of school. It seemed I was sick every morning and I would get tired by the middle of the day. I tried my best to hide the fact that I was pregnant. I didn't want to be the pregnant girl at school, even if it was by my mate and we lived together. It was no one's business and I didn't want people to ask me questions about it.

Ethan got an afterschool job, so we saw less of each other. Between working, studying, and sleeping, he really didn't have a lot of time for me. It made me feel lonely, but I kept reminding myself that school was almost over. Then we'd be on our way to find our new lives outside of the pack.

I was at home studying for my exams when there was a knock at the door. I wasn't expecting company, so I was automatically on edge. To my surprise, it was Stacey.

"Oh, uh, hi," I said. "If you're here for Ethan, he's not home. He's at work."

"Ethan's...working? Wow, that's interesting. Anyway, I'm actually here for you," she said.

"Me?" I asked.

"Yes. Well, are you going to invite me in?"

"Oh, yeah, yeah. Come in," I said. I stood to the side, and she walked in.

"I was wondering," she said as she made herself comfortable on my couch, "if you have any friends at all in the pack?"

"You came all the way over here to ask me if I have friends?" I asked in confusion.

"Well, yes. I mean, we have over 5,000 wolves in the pack. Surely you have at least one friend."

"I don't," I said quietly. "I'm a loner."

"That's pretty sad," she said with obvious pity in her voice. Suddenly, she perked up. "No worries. Now you have one. Me."

I sat on the couch beside her. "Why would you suddenly want to be my friend?"

"Well, we're basically family now. I should get to know my sister-in-law," she said. "C'mon. We're going shopping."

"I can't go shopping, Stacey. I don't have money—"

"—I know that, silly. Don't worry about it. C'mon, let's go. It will be fun," she said as she smiled at me. I didn't know why Stacey suddenly wanted to hang out with me. It seemed a little suspicious, but I was tired of being stuck at home all the time, so I agreed to go shopping with her.

Stacey took me to the mall, a place I usually tried to avoid because I didn't want to run into people from school. She talked for the entire ride there, mostly about pack gossip, but also about celebrity gossip and deals we'd find at the mall. It was hard to make conversation with her. I wasn't used to girl talk...or any talk for that matter.

Once we got to the mall, Stacey started the shopping trip by taking me to her favorite store. "Look at this dress!" she exclaimed. "This color would look so good against your skin. You're a size eight, right?" She grabbed a dress from the rack and handed it to me.

"Umm, Stacey, there's something I should tell you," I said as I looked at the dress. I suddenly felt giddy at the prospect of telling her my secret. After all, I hadn't had anyone to share it with.

"Sure, what is it," she said as she pulled another size eight from the rack.

"I don't know if I'll be able to fit this in a few months," I said.

"Well why wouldn't you?" she asked. "Are you going on a diet or something? You know, size eight isn't really that big," she said.

"No, I'm not going on a diet. I'm pregnant," I blurted out.

Stacey looked shocked. She paused for a moment then she snatched the dress from me and put both dresses back on the rack. "You're pregnant?" she asked with sheer excitement. "I'm going to be an auntie!" She shrieked and hugged me. People in the store looked at us with confused and annoyed looks.

"Does Ethan know?" she asked.

"Yeah, that's why he's working," I said.

"We're doing the wrong shopping," she said. "Come with me."

Stacey led me to a baby store. There were so many cute outfits and accessories. Being in the store really made it sink in that I was going to be someone's mom.

"I don't know the gender yet," I said as I looked at a cute, pink newborn dress.

"Well let's get some gender-neutral stuff," she said. She picked up a mint-green onesie that was the most adorable thing I'd ever seen.

"I love it," I said. She dropped it into my basket. Stacey and I shopped in the baby store for half an hour picking out cute baby items that were mostly shades of green and yellow. After that, we went to several stores including a maternity wear store. Once we were done with shopping, we decided to get something to eat from the food court.

"How do you think the rest of your family is going to react to me being pregnant," I asked.

"*Our* family. You should get used to saying that now. Mom and Lennox will be cool with it. My dad...he's probably going to blow a fuse," she said.

"Great. Something else about me for him to hate," I said. "Do you think your father will ever accept me?"

"Oh, you *want* to be accepted!" exclaimed Stacey as she obviously dodged my question. "That's a good sign that you aren't going to run away from Ethan again."

"I'm not going to," I said.

"Good. There's no point anyway. My little brother would scour the earth until he found you," she said.

"I noticed," I said, and we both laughed. "This has been so much fun. Thank you for being so nice to me."

"Ah, don't mention it," she said.

We finished our food then left. Stacey was as talkative on the ride home as she was when we first went to the mall. You would think we were friends all our lives.

"Graduation is right around the corner," she said. "Are you excited?"

"More like relieved," I said. "I was scared I'd fallen too far behind to catch up, but I made it."

"Do you have plans after high school?" she asked.

"I had a plan, but that was before I knew Ethan was my mate. Now my plans have changed."

"That makes sense," she replied as she pulled into the driveway of my building. "Well, here you are. We should do this again."

"I'd like that," I said. She dropped me off and I headed inside with all my goodies.

I was sitting on the bed marveling over the amazing baby clothes and accessories when Ethan got home. I ran to the living room and planted a big kiss on him. "Did you bring them?" I asked with wide eyes.

"Of course I did," he said as he handed me the bag of macarons. "I mixed up the flavors just for you."

I squealed with delight. Then I snatched the bag from him. "What an exciting day," I said as I popped a whole macaron in my mouth. "Your sister came by and took me shopping." I pointed to the baby stuff on the bed. "Now I'm eating macarons."

"My sister took you shopping? That's weird," he said.

"Yeah, I thought so also but I had fun. She paid for everything! I didn't ask her to, she just volunteered."

"I'm glad you had a good day," he said. He planted a kiss on my forehead since my mouth was working on the second macaron. Then he went to take a shower. When he came back out, I had put all the baby stuff away because I knew he'd want to go straight to bed. To my surprise, he didn't.

Ethan snuggled close to me and kissed my mark, then the rest of my neck. Before I knew it, we were making out and ripping off each other's clothes. He made love to me gently. I was so happy to have his attention, even if it was only for a little while. I'd missed him so much. When we were done, Ethan stared into my eyes, and I could see that he was drifting off to sleep.

"Ethan, are you sure you don't want me to get a job? I can work for a while to help us save money faster," I said.

"Absolutely not. I don't want you to be stressed. You just take care of our pup," he said as sleep took over him. Suddenly he was snoring. I smiled and kissed him gently on the forehead. Then I settled in and went to sleep also.

18

Graduation

I was incredibly nervous. I never thought the day would come when I'd be walking across that stage. *Please don't let me get sick before I make it across,* I thought as the valedictorian was giving her speech. I had already started showing, so I was glad my gown was loose-fitting and no one could tell I was pregnant. Still, I was nervous because waves of nausea seemed to hit me at random times. I didn't realize how tightly I was wringing my hands until I unclasped them, and I felt the ache from the squeezing I had been doing.

Ethan turned and looked at me. He smiled at me warmly and winked. Usually that would make me feel better, but my nerves were strong that day.

"Don't be so nervous," said Felicia Simmons who was sitting right beside me. I was surprised because she had literally never spoken to me before. Not even once.

"This is our time to be happy. We're finally getting out of this hell hole." She giggled and surprisingly I giggled also. "Just don't fall on your face and you'll be fine," she said.

"This is me we're talking about," I said. "Falling on my face was a daily hazard for me in school," I said. As true as it was, it was still funny so we both giggled.

"I'm sorry I never got to know you," she said, "but I wish you well in the future."

"Thanks. Same to you," I said. That made me feel better. It was nice to have someone being...well...nice to me. The valedictorian finished her speech, and we all stood up and applauded. It was time for the most important part of the ceremony—diplomas.

The ceremony was beautiful. There was no bullying, no pettiness, and no cliques. There was just all of us that had worked so hard to make it to this moment. You could see the pride in everyone's eyes as they walked across the stage. Everyone got a general applause from the crowd but many peoples' moments were elevated when their families and friends shouted and celebrated on top of the generic applause.

When Ethan walked across the stage, the entire football team celebrated, plus a plethora of his friends. *He's so popular. I still can't believe he's mine,* I thought as he walked across the stage. *I love you,* I projected to him. He looked directly at me and projected back, *I love you always.*

His family was there also, even his father. They yelled and celebrated almost as loud as the whole football team. I was happy to see that even though Ethan and his father weren't on good terms, Ethan still had his father's support in some way.

When it was my turn to walk across the stage, it dawned on me that I didn't have any friends or family to shout for me. *I'll just have to be happy with the general applause,* I thought. When my name was called, I started walking and to my surprise there was a bunch of shouting and celebrating in the audience. I looked out there and Ethan's family, with the exception of his father, was cheering for me. So were Ethan's closest friends. One of them shouted, "way to go Mrs. Rohe!"

A big smile came across my face and I had the urge to hide my face in my hands. I didn't since I needed to see where I was going, so I just walked over to get my diploma and tried not to do anything stupid. They continued cheering as I walked off the stage. Ethan projected to me, *we did it. We made it.* I looked at him as I walked past his row and nodded.

The rest of the ceremony went by just as smoothly. We got to the end, threw our hats in the air, and finally we were free from the tyranny of high school. I was surprised that I got hugs from people I'd never even really talked to much and several of them wanted selfies with me. I tried to look around for Ethan, but I figured he was being swamped by friends and family.

A couple of guys came over to me and asked to a selfie with me. One guy was Johnathan, whom everyone called John for short, and I didn't know the other guy's name. I posed in between them, feeling a bit awkward. After, John said, "too bad I didn't get to know you more. I always thought you were kind of cute, but now you're spoken for."

My mouth dropped open. I probably should have brushed him off, but I was speechless. I hadn't expected that. Before I could find words to reply, Ethan swooped in and stood between us. *Gosh, where did he come from? I was just looking for him.*

"Yeah, she's spoken for so why don't you move along," he said.

John put his hands up. "Hey, sorry bro. I didn't mean anything by it." He backed away then walked off.

Ethan turned and looked at me. "Sorry, I didn't know what to say. He totally caught me off guard."

"It's fine baby. That's what happens when you're the sexiest woman at graduation," he said. He pulled me close and kissed me. A few people around us said, "aww," and some of them clapped.

"Hey, guys!" I heard Lennox shout from behind me. I turned to see Ethan's family coming over to us. I got nervous as I locked eyes with Ethan's father. He quickly diverted his gaze to Ethan making the situation even more awkward.

"Congratulations," said Ethan's mother as she came over to us. She scooped me up in a big hug. "Even after all you two have been through, you've managed to still graduate, and with honors!"

"Yeah, the two nerds belong together," said Lennox.

"Congratulations, son," said Ethan's father in a cautious tone. It was the first time the two of them had spoken since their fight, so everyone was a little unsure of what Ethan's reaction would be. We all stood quietly as Ethan stepped over to his father.

"Thanks, Dad," he said. Ethan stuck his hand out, but his father grabbed him and pulled him in for a hug. All of us let go of our tension as we watched them bond. You could hear an audible sigh from us collectively. A few people around us were staring at the Alpha and Ethan, probably wondering what was about to happen. It was no secret in the pack that they had been at odds with each other.

"I'm proud of you son, always," he said as he hugged Ethan. "You've grown into the man I always knew you could be."

"Thanks Dad," said Ethan with obvious surprise in his voice. "I'm glad you came."

"Wouldn't miss it for the world," said his father. His father suddenly turned his attention to me. "Congratulations Amina." The statement was slightly less enthusiastic than when he said it to Ethan, but it seemed genuine. Everyone, including me, was shocked to hear that coming from the Alpha.

"Th...thanks," I said. That's all I could manage to stutter out.

"Well, I think this occasion calls for a celebration," said Ethan's mother. "Shall we go to our favorite Italian spot or our favorite Mexican spot?" she asked to the family.

"Italian," said Lennox quickly.

"Oh, uh, I'd love to," said Ethan, "but I was going to celebrate with Amina," he said as he stepped back to my side and grabbed my hand. "I mean, you know, since we both graduated."

"Oh," said his mother. The disappointment in her voice was obvious. The statement was followed by pause from everyone. Two seconds isn't a lot of time, but it's enough time to make any conversation awkward.

"Well, uh, okay," she said. "We understand—"

"—Amina can celebrate with us," said Ethan's father suddenly. "I mean, we can all celebrate together, if you want to."

That was my next shock of the evening and apparently Ethan's also because the same look of surprise that was on my face was on his also.

"Are you sure, Dad?" Ethan asked.

"It's okay, Alpha Roland. I don't want to impose into your family's celebration." Then to Ethan I said, "you should celebrate with your family. We can go out later."

"Nonsense," boomed the Alpha. "You aren't imposing at all. You're invited."

I wasn't sure what was causing Alpha Roland to be so nice to me, but I could see that his decision made everyone happy. They all looked at me with bright eyes, hoping I'd say yes to the invite. I looked at Ethan, and he had the same bright look.

"Okay," I said. "If you insist."

"Well let's go," said Ethan's mother enthusiastically.

Ethan grabbed my hand, and we smiled at each other as we followed his family out of the auditorium. *What's gotten into your father?* I projected to him.

I have no idea, he projected back, *but let's take the W while we can.* I nodded in agreement. We got into Ethan's car and followed his family to their favorite Italian restaurant.

...

"Oh, my Goddess!" screamed my mother as she dropped her fork onto her plate. "My first grandchild! I'm so excited," she exclaimed as Amina and I told the family the news. I was amused at how excited my mother was that Amina was pregnant, especially since the first time they met each other, my mother was less than pleased at the mere idea of Amina being pregnant.

"Congratulations," said Lennox.

"I can't believe you didn't tell them," I said to Stacey. "You? Keeping a secret? Unbelievable," I joked.

"You knew and you didn't tell us?" asked my mom. "Stacey, how could you hold out on me?"

"It wasn't my news to tell," she shrugged. "Plus, I didn't know whether...you know, you'd be—"

"—I get it," said my mother quickly in an attempt to field the obvious negative statement that Stacey was about to make. "But no, this is great news. We're going to have a baby in the family again." She smiled at my father. He didn't smile back.

I was suspicious of my father's motives for inviting Amina along to celebrate with the family, but despite my apprehension, everything went well. They all treated Amina with grace and respect. My father was nice to her although he didn't talk to her much. I wanted to relax and believe that this is how things would be from then on, but I couldn't shake the feeling that my father had some ulterior motive for his behavior.

"You don't think it's a little soon to have a child," said my father in a serious tone. "How are you going to take care of a wife and a baby while you're in college?" *Leave it to him to put a damper on the celebration*, I thought. I knew the positivity couldn't last.

"I'm not sure that I'm going to college," I said.

"What?" exclaimed everyone collectively.

"What do you mean you aren't going to college," said my mother. "You've graduated with honors. You worked so hard. You had a whole plan, Ethan. Now you're not going to go?"

I looked at Amina and her gaze was down to her hands. I could feel her discomfort. She was feeling as if it were her fault I wasn't going to college.

"Before you all jump to conclusions, just know this is my decision and mine alone. I have to be responsible now and my family needs me to provide for them. Maybe I can go in the future, but right now I have to do what I have to do," I said.

"Ethan, that's nonsense. If you don't go now, chances are you'll never go," said my father.

"Well, Dad, with all due respect," I said, "I had planned to go to college when I had my inheritance, and I didn't have to worry about money. That's clearly not the case anymore, so my plan has changed."

There was an awkward silence at the table. Lennox silently mouthed the word "wow".

My mother cleared her throat. "Let's change the subject," she said. "We can talk about this another time." No one said anything. I could feel Amina's discomfort growing by the minute and suddenly all I wanted to do was leave.

"How far along are you, Amina," asked my mother.

"Maybe two months. I'm not quite sure," she said. "I haven't been to the doctor yet."

"Oh my," said my mother. "You haven't had any type of check-up? We need to fix that immediately. We can get together about it this week," she said with a smile. Amina smiled and nodded. I admired the turn around my mother had made. She was really trying to accept Amina even though I'm sure it caused some tension between her and my father.

"We can go shopping again also if you'd like," said Stacey.

Amina smiled and nodded. "Sure. We had fun the last time," she said quietly.

My father grunted and everyone turned to look at him. "Seems you've found a way to spend my money indirectly," he said, "so not having an inheritance shouldn't really be a problem."

"Oh, for Goddess's sake, Roland," said my mother as she put her napkin down. My anger suddenly started surging.

"Is that why you invited us to dinner? So, you could put us down and make my mate feel uncomfortable?" I asked trying my best to control my temper.

"No, I was just saying—" he started.

"—you know what? We don't need this. We don't need your pity, and we don't need your handouts," I said. I pulled out my wallet and put seventy dollars on the table. "C'mon Amina. Let's go."

"Wait. Wait, Ethan!" said my mother. "Don't go, please." Then to my father she said, "Roland, apologize!"

"No, Mom, I'm sorry. I love you very much, but I have to protect Amina. I know you understand," I said as I stood up.

"Sit down, Ethan," commanded my father but I ignored him. I helped Amina up and we began to walk away. I heard my father stand up. "Ethan!" he yelled in his Alpha voice. Everyone in the restaurant stopped immediately and stared at all of us. Amina almost jumped into my arms and the sound of my father's voice. I turned around, prepared to argue or possibly fight with my father, but when I looked at him, I knew neither of those things were about to happen. For the first time in my life, I saw embarrassment on his face. I was shocked.

He took in a deep breath. "I apologize for my behavior, Amina. Now will you please rejoin us to finish dinner?"

Holy shit! Did my father just apologize to us in public, in front of pack members? Somewhere outside, pigs had to be flying.

I looked at Amina. *If you want to leave, we can leave,* I projected to her.

We can stay, she said. *If he can try, we can try.* She smiled at me to indicate she was okay, so we rejoined the table. Slowly, the restaurant came back to life and the customers returned back to their conversations although many of them threw glances our way occasionally.

The mood had obviously been ruined and no one really knew what to say, so we all just resumed eating. However, my mother seemed determined to put things back on the right track. She was always the token of hope and positivity in the room, two qualities that had served her well as the pack's Luna.

"Have you thought about whether you want a girl or a boy?" she asked Amina.

"Not really," Amina said. "I just want a healthy baby."

"It could be cool to have a nephew," said Lennox. "I could teach him to play baseball."

"You could also teach a girl," said Stacey.

The server came around and offered dessert, but everyone declined. Then he came back around with the check. My father grabbed it. He looked at my money, which was still sitting on the table. "Put your money away," he said.

"It's fine, Dad. I can cover our part of the—"

"—do not insult me," he said. "Put your money away." I didn't want to start another argument, so I did as he said. He handed the waiter his credit card.

"While we're waiting for him to come back, maybe you can answer a question," said my father, "and it's just a question. No arguing." I nodded and waited for whatever bullshit he was about to drop.

"If you're not going to college, what's your plan?" he asked.

"Roland—" started my mom.

"—relax, Rose," he said, "I'm just being a curious father here."

That question reminded me of something. I hadn't mentioned the mysterious wolf in the woods to Amina. Up until that point, I wasn't sure if I would or not, but in that moment I made my decision. "Our plan was to leave and try to find out anything about Amina's past."

Amina looked at me with wide eyes. "Was?" she said. I could detect a bit of panic in her voice.

I held up my hand. "There's something I need to tell you, Amina. We may not have to leave to find out about your past." Amina frowned in confusion. "When we were searching for you, I thought you might have tried to go back into the forbidden mountains—"

"—the forbidden mountains? You went into the forbidden mountains? When was this—" asked my father.

"—so, I went there to look for you first."

"You WHAT?" yelled my father. People in the restaurant turned to look at us again.

"I...got attacked by three wolves," I said. My mother gasped and Lennox and Stacey looked at me in utter shock.

"Actually, I got attacked twice, but that's not the point. The last time, I would have died, but this mysterious wolf came to my aid," I said.

"Ethan! You almost died?" exclaimed Amina.

"I can't believe you went into the forbidden mountains," yelled my father. He was completely missing the point of the story.

"You almost died?" asked my mother. I could see tears in her eyes. "We knew you'd gotten into a fight, but we had no idea it was that bad," she said. "Who is this wolf. We need to thank him."

"Well, that's just it. I don't know who he is, but he knows Amina," I said, "and not from like now, like the present. It seems he knew something about her past."

Amina gasped hard. "He knows me? How?"

"I don't have the answer to that question either," I said. "He told me not to tell you or anyone about him. He said he would kill me if I did."

"So, let me get this straight. He saved your life, only to threaten it afterward?" asked Lennox.

"You're just telling me this?" Amina asked. "Why didn't you tell me before?"

"I knew it would distract you from school," I said.

"Well, I'm out of school now so we need to find this wolf," she said.

"No one is going back into the forbidden mountains," roared my father.

"Roland—" started my mother.

"—Alpha Roland, please," pleaded Amina. "It might be the only chance I have to find out anything about where I came from."

"I am really trying here," my father said, "but I will not tolerate disobedience. No one is to go into the forbidden mountains and that's that. End of discussion."

Amina looked at me with desperation in her eyes. *We have to find him Ethan. We have to! Please!*

We will, I said. *I give you my word.*

The waiter came back and gave my father his receipt and credit card. My father scribbled a tip on the receipt and stood up. He glared at us with a stare that said *dinner is over and so is this discussion.* We all stood up and followed him out of the restaurant.

19

The Night Guardians

The glare from my father felt like hot coals burning into me as we stared at each other on the patio of his house two days after all of us had been out for a graduation dinner. Once, not so long ago, he looked at me with pride. Now, I could see hints of disappointment and anger in his eyes. It hurt me so much to be at odds with the man whom I'd admired my entire life, but I knew I couldn't back down.

"I know you're planning to disobey me," he said. "You've been disobeying me since you mated with that girl...Amina, so it's no surprise that you'll continue to do it."

"Dad, I don't want to argue with you right now," I said, "and if you're planning to attack Amina again, that's exactly what will happen so why don't we end this conversation before it starts." I turned to walk back inside, but he yelled my name in his Alpha voice and it stopped me in my tracks.

I turned to him and gestured to where my mother was peeking curiously out of a window. "I'm only here because Mom said she needed my help, Dad. Then I'll be leaving so we really don't have to do this."

"Your mother asked you to come because I needed to talk to you. I knew you wouldn't come if I asked you to," he said.

I was surprised. I looked at my mother through the window. She gave me a guilty smile and then disappeared behind the curtain. "So, Mom tricked me? Unbelievable," I said.

"Ethan, listen to me son," said my father. "We need to have an important conversation about this mysterious wolf in the woods. Please, have a seat." He gestured to the patio table and chairs. I hesitated. *What could he possibly want to talk about concerning the mystery wolf other than telling me not to look for him,* I wondered. He looked at me as if he wouldn't take no for an answer, so I sat down.

My father sighed as he sat in the chair across from me. He seemed as if he had some heavy thoughts he wanted to get out. His demeanor sparked my curiosity.

"As the Alpha, I'm rarely at a loss for words, but here I am. I don't know where to start," he said.

"The beginning is usually a good place," I said.

"The beginning," he said with a chuckle. "That's complicated." He pulled out his phone and sent a text to someone. Then he put his phone away.

"As an Alpha, I have to make the best decisions I can to ensure the survival of our pack. You have to understand that sometimes these decisions can put you at odds with your morals. This is something that I've been trying to teach you in order to prepare you to take on this massive leadership role."

"If you're about to tell me that your decision to treat Amina like shit was for the good of the pack, save it Dad. That's a load of crap," I said. I was about to stand up and leave, but his next statement struck a nerve.

"As I recall, you spent most of your life treating her like shit also. What was your excuse?" he asked. The shame hit me like a punch to the gut. I had to look away from him.

"You're right," I said. "That's why I'm trying to make up for it."

"So how can you sit there and judge me when you've done the same?" he asked.

"Because I've admitted that I was wrong," I said, "and I've changed my behavior. I'm trying to be better. You aren't."

"The only reason you're trying is because she's your mate," he said, "otherwise you wouldn't have thought twice about her after graduation. That doesn't make you a changed person. That just makes you a man who's in love."

He was right. I had never thought about it like that. I thought about some other people at school I'd bullied, and I didn't bother to make amends with them. *Maybe I really am a shitty person*, I thought.

My father put his hand up. "This is not what I want to talk about. I need you to understand why you must not seek out the man in the woods."

One of the house workers came out with two glasses of lemonade and set one in front me and the other in front of my father. He then set a pitcher of lemonade in the middle of us and went back inside.

"Why Amina can't find out where she comes from you mean," I said as I took a sip of the lemonade. It was cool, flavorful, comforting, and refreshing. The drink was quite a stark contrast to the conversation I was having with my father.

"I still have hope that you'll take my place as Alpha, so I need to tell you this story. I would have told you anyway as it relates to the safety of our pack. Long ago, there was a wolf pack known as the Night Guardians. They were allies of ours, a ferocious pack that were protectors of all things good. Their territory was far away from ours, all the way in Georgia, and they were fighting a raging war against another pack known as the Shadow Walkers." My father took a big gulp of lemonade before proceeding.

"I don't know much about their war or why they were fighting it. I only know that they lost. The Night Guardians were the fiercest warriors known in the Southeast and these Shadow Walkers decimated their entire pack. The Alpha and Luna of the pack, along with their baby and their Beta, Pax, escaped and made their way here, but unfortunately the Alpha and Luna, who were battered from the war, died."

I stared at my father in disbelief. "So, you're telling me that Amina is the daughter of an Alpha?"

"Yes," he said with a nod. "Luke found the four of them on the side of the road. He called me there and Pax begged us to take Amina. According to him, the Shadow Pack wouldn't stop until every single one of the Night Guardians were dead. We didn't want to take Amina because her mere presence would have put our pack in danger. I mean, if the Shadow Pack could destroy a pack as strong as the Night Guardians, our pack wouldn't stand a chance. However, the Beta offered us something we couldn't refuse."

"What's that," I asked.

"Lifetime protection," he said. "He agreed to be our guardian in the forbidden mountains if we took Amina in. He's the reason the dark wolves in the valley don't encroach on our territory. He protects us from them. The dark wolves in the forbidden mountains are no match for a night guardian. They're nothing close to the Shadow Walkers."

"Wait, so he's been alone in the valley fighting wolves for fifteen years?" I asked.

My father nodded and looked down in shame. "The agreement was that he would stay there and remain hidden while we take Amina in and treat her like a rogue, never telling her who she was so that the Shadow Pack would think she was dead."

"So, while we've been living this cushy lifestyle, one, single man has been fighting all of our battles? Meanwhile you've allowed Amina to be mistreated her entire life out of fear?" I couldn't believe what I was hearing. Our pack was over 5,000 strong and my father allowed one lone wolf to be our sole protection for over a decade.

"It's been working," he said. "Our pack has been safe and protected. We don't have attacks from the dark wolves of the mountains and the Shadow Pack has never come for us. You have to understand, I am the Alpha of *this* pack, so I have to make decisions for our well-being. Amina and her uncle were not—are not a part of our pack."

I felt my heart skip a beat. I stood up and yelled, "her uncle! The mysterious wolf, Pax, is her uncle? All this time she had a family member who would have loved and cared for her, but you forced him into some twisted servitude? How could you do that and sleep at night?"

My father stood up also. "I slept well knowing that I protected my pack. I did what I was supposed to do as an Alpha. You'll have to do the same."

"If I were to become the Alpha, and I'm not saying I will, I would never allow one man to fight my pack's battles in exchange for a lifetime of slavery," I said. I had never been more disgusted with my father than at that moment. "I can't believe you would...and mom? Mom agreed to this?"

"No. You're mother doesn't know the full story. She doesn't know about Pax. She thinks we found Amina wrapped up in that blanket, but we didn't. That was a story we made up," he said.

Another shocker. He really had them rolling out one after the other. "So, her name isn't Amina? That was a lie?"

My father sighed and nodded his head. "Pax agreed to the story. We can't let her real name get out. In fact, Pax never told me her real name."

"You're unbelievable," I scoffed. I turned to go.

"Ethan, I know you're angry, but you can't tell Amina the truth. If the Shadow Pack finds out that two of the Night Guardians are alive and we've been hiding them, who knows what hell they'll rain down on us," he said.

I kept walking. I knew my father was right about us not being able to defend against Shadow Pack he spoke of, but I was not going to lie to my mate. Amina, or whoever she was, deserved the truth for once in her life and I was going to give it to her.

...

Ethan slammed the door so hard the entire apartment rattled. I ran to the living room, and I could see that he was extremely angry. "What happened?" I asked. "Did you and your father fight again?"

"No," he said as he walked by me. "I can't talk about it right now. I need to calm down."

"Okay," I said as he disappeared into the bathroom where he slammed the door again. "I'm here when you're ready to talk," I called out to him. I didn't get a response.

I went back into the bedroom to lay down on the bed. I could feel Ethan's anger and pain rolling off of him in waves. I wanted so desperately to comfort him, but I wasn't sure if I should go in the bathroom or just let him be. I decided to go into the bathroom. I went to the door and tried the doorknob. It was unlocked. I opened the door slowly, not knowing if Ethan was going to yell at me for intruding or not. He didn't. He was standing in front of the sink with his head down. I walked over to him and put my hand on his back. He turned and looked at me, and to my surprise, there was pity in his eyes. *What the heck happened over there?* I wondered as the first wave of alarm started washing over me.

Ethan hugged me tightly and kissed my forehead. His arms were strong and warm around me. Usually, I loved being held like that by him, but I knew something was seriously wrong that time. I looked at him, my eyes pleading for answers.

"We need to have a serious talk," he said. "Come. Sit down."

"Okay," I said as I followed him out of the bathroom. I felt goosebumps popping up on my arms. I didn't know what Ethan was about to tell me, but I could tell it was something heavy. We sat on the sofa together and I waited for Ethan to speak.

"We can't go after the wolf in the forbidden mountains," he said. I immediately recoiled at that statement. It felt like all the blood drained from me instantly.

"What? Why? Ethan, you promised—"

"—that was before I knew the truth," he said. "Going after him could put your life in danger. It could put everyone's life in danger."

"In danger from what?" I asked.

"I don't know all the details exactly. My father—"

"—your father knows about me being in danger from something?"

"Yes, but he doesn't know—"

"—so, your father knows a lot more about me than he let on. Of course he does," I said as I shook my head. "Tell me exactly what he said," I demanded of Ethan.

"If you stop cutting me off, I'll tell you," he snapped back.

"I'm sorry," I said. "It's just so frustrating that everyone knows about my past except me, and now you're telling me that the one person who could shed light on it is off limits. I thought you were on my side," I said, unable to mask my disappointment. I scooted away from Ethan and wiped a tear from my eye.

"I'm always on your side," he said. "That's why you can't look for him. I don't want to lose you. Things are so much bigger than either of us could have imagined." He turned to me and grabbed my hands. "Promise me that if I tell you what I know, you won't go after the man in the woods."

"Ethan, don't make me—"

"—promise me!" he said forcefully.

I sighed. "Fine, I promise," I said.

"Okay. To start, you're the daughter of an Alpha, not a rogue," he said.

I gasped. "What? An Alpha? Which Alpha? What pack?"

Ethan held his hand up and I stopped rattling off questions. "You were part of a pack known as the Night Guardians, a powerful pack of protectors. They got involved in a war with an even more powerful pack known as the Shadow Walkers. The Night Guardians were decimated...all except four. Your parents, you, and your uncle, the mysterious man in the forbidden mountains."

I stood up. "My uncle! He's my uncle? Ethan—"

"—I know, Amina. He's the only living family you have, but he's living his life in those woods to protect you because if the Shadow Walkers find out you're still alive, they'll come after you and then start a war with our pack for hiding you," he said.

I shook my head. "That's insane," she said. "My uncle is choosing to live in the dangers of the forbidden mountains to protect me? Why couldn't he live here? Why couldn't we both hide here?" Ethan dropped his head, and I could tell he didn't want to answer. "Why?" I demanded.

He sighed, stood up, and walked to the other side of the room. He seemed to be looking at everything except me. "Why, Ethan!" I yelled.

"My father forced him to...protect our pack from the dark wolves in the valley in exchange for your asylum," he said.

"Protect your pack? Well, for how long?" I asked. I felt I knew the answer already, but I dreaded hearing it come from Ethan's mouth.

Ethan took in a deep breath. "For the rest of his life," he said.

I was mortified. I thought I couldn't dislike Ethan's father any more than I did, but that made me hate him. "So, you're saying that my uncle has been out in that valley fighting wolves all by himself for fifteen years and he has to keep doing it forever? And you're okay with that?"

"I'm not okay with it—" started Ethan.

"—this can't be happening," I said. I felt the tears rolling down my cheeks.

"Amina, I'm not okay with it," he said.

"But you're willing to let it go on so obviously you're okay with it!" I shouted. Suddenly I felt lightheaded. My knees buckled but Ethan was suddenly right there to catch me. He laid me on the couch.

"You have to calm down, baby," he said. "Shh, shh, stop crying."

"Don't tell me to stop crying," I said. "It's not fair."

"I know, but if it's a choice between your life or your uncle's life, it's an easy choice for me," he said.

"It's not for me. Ethan, you're better than this. You're better than your father. There has to be something we can do," I cried.

"*You* can't do anything," he said as he rubbed my protruding stomach. "As for me, well, I'm not the Alpha so I can't end his servitude. I know this is disappointing for you, but your uncle chose his fate to protect you, and we should honor that."

"Do you hear yourself?" I asked as I sat up slowly. "You don't sound like the mate I fell in love with. You're willing to turn your eye to an innocent man's suffering? One who apparently saved your life!"

"What am I supposed to do, Amina? I can't protect the pack from the dark wolves! I couldn't even protect myself, so even if I found a way to free your uncle, how am I supposed to protect the pack from the evil that lurks in the valley?"

"I don't know, but we can't leave him there. Ethan, please," I said weakly as a sobbed. I felt so helpless. If I weren't pregnant, I'd go find my uncle myself, but I couldn't put my baby in danger.

"Amina," he said. He pulled me to him, and I sobbed onto his chest. "Maybe one day we can save him, but today is not that day."

"How can I just go about my life knowing he's out there suffering?" I asked when I got control of my crying.

"Not that there's any high point to a lifetime of servitude, but honestly, your uncle seems to be doing just fine out there," said Ethan with a shrug. "I mean, he's a huge, scary dude. He's the largest wolf I've ever seen in my life. Definitely not missing any meals. He can dominate any wolf out there. Maybe that can give you some type of comfort."

"Only a little," I said. "At least he isn't like, getting beat up every day. It's more than I can say for my own life." I felt Ethan's embarrassment at that statement. "Sorry, I wasn't directing that towards you."

"I know," he said. "Amina, I promise you that I won't forget about your uncle. If I can come up with a solution, we'll save him. I give you my word. In the meantime, you're my priority, okay? I have to keep you safe. Just trust me."

I nodded and wiped my face. I decided to redirect the conversation. "So, I'm not a rogue wolf. My family was the Sturges? The Alpha and Luna of the Night Guardians? At least I know now."

"Well, actually..."

I looked at Ethan. Surely there couldn't be more to the story. "Actually, what?" I asked.

"Your name isn't really Amina Sturges," he said.

I closed my eyes and took in a deep breath. "You're kidding me, right?" I sat back and prepared myself for another emotional rollercoaster ride.

20

The More the Merrier

The next couple of weeks were hard on me. It seemed no matter what I did, I couldn't get my uncle out of my mind. What did he look like? Was he hurt? Was he all alone? Would I ever meet him? Knowing that the key to my past and the only family I had left was right there in the valley haunted me. I had bad dreams. I often felt sick from stress, I was always hot, and it seemed my appetite wasn't what it should be for a pregnant woman.

I finally was able to book a prenatal appointment, and they got me on the schedule fast thanks to Ethan's mom. Anyone in town would pull strings for the Luna, including the most prominent OBGYN in town, and thankfully so because I ballooned in only a couple of weeks and the sudden growth was alarming.

I sat in the waiting room with Ethan's mom who, at that point, insisted I call her either Mom or Rose. Ethan couldn't be there with me because he had to work, and I was incredibly nervous without him.

"What are they going to do?" I asked Rose.

"They're going to do an ultrasound so we can see the little pup and make sure he's healthy," she said. "Of course there's no doubt he is. We wolves are lucky that our pups have regenerative properties even in the womb so it's pretty hard to mess up a pregnancy."

"He?" I asked.

"Yes," she said. "I'm pretty sure. I can tell by the scent. It seems kind of...boyish."

I laughed. "I guess you would know since you've had two."

"Absolutely, " she said with a smile.

"Rose, thank you for this, and for helping me through this. I wouldn't know what to do if it weren't for you," I said.

"Of course," said Rose. "I'm glad I get to do this with you. My first grandchild," she said as she beamed with pride. "From my favorite son. Don't tell them I said that." We both laughed. "You'll have a favorite too when you have more."

"More?" I asked in surprise. "I just want to get through this one before I even think about another one," I said.

"Leave it to my son and you'll have another one as soon as you pop this one out," she said. I gasped and put my hands over my face.

"What? It's not like I don't know what y'all do. I mean...hello!" she said as she pointed to my stomach. "I'm his mother. I *know*," she said with an amused look on her face. "I overhear him talking with his brother and friends sometimes. They're my boys...but at the end of the day, they're men." She shrugged.

A nurse came out and called my name and I was thankful to be saved from that conversation. We made our way to the back where the nurse weighed me.

"One thirty-eight," she said as she wrote it down on my chart.

We went into the exam room and the nurse took my vitals. She said everything looked good, so Rose and I sat quietly and waited for the doctor. She finally came in with a big smile on her face. She was a small lady with wavy brunette hair and cute glasses.

"You're...a human," I said as my surprise got the best of me. I looked at Rose and she wasn't surprised. *Oh, was I not supposed to say that out loud?* I wondered. Some humans knew about us, but not very many.

"Yes, I am," she said. "You're a werewolf." She smiled at me. "It's very nice to meet you." She held her hand out and I shook it.

"I was just expecting—" I started.

"—a wolf doctor. Yes, I get that a lot," she said. "I'm mated to a wolf. That's how I'm in the loop."

"Oh, okay," I said.

"Don't worry. Dr. Marisday knows everything there is to know about wolf pregnancies. You're in the best hands," said Rose.

I nodded and took in a deep breath. "Okay, I'll relax," I said but I couldn't.

"Just lay back and we'll start the ultrasound." I did what she asked, and she put some clear, cold gel on my stomach. The coldness of it shocked me and apparently shocked my baby because I felt it jump which made me jump.

"Oh my gosh, I felt it move!" I said excitedly. "That's the first time I felt that." I suddenly wished Ethan was there so he could have experienced that with me.

"You'll feel a lot more movement from now on, especially since you're only two or three months away from delivery. You're so lucky you don't have to deal with a nine month pregnancy like us humans," she said. "It's miserable." She said it with a smile, so I guessed she was joking.

Dr. Marisday ran the ultrasound wand over my belly, pressing in different places to get a better view. "Oh!" she said. "Oh my."

"What? Oh, what?" asked Rose.

"What is it?" I asked.

"Look at this," said Dr. Marisday as she pointed to three different areas on the screen. "That's three babies. The more the merrier, right?" she asked.

Rose squealed in delight. "I knew it!" she said. "You got so big so fast...sorry, I don't mean you're fat or anything...but I had my suspicions that you were having multiples. This is wonderful. I'm going to have three grandchildren!"

I was feeling the exact opposite. How the hell were we going to take care of three pups? All I could think about was how much stress Ethan was already under. Telling him that we were having triplets might make him cave.

"I can't have triplets," I said as I sat in shock at the news. "We can't afford triplets. We don't even have room for triplets. We live in a one bedroom apartment."

"Time for an upgrade," said the doctor cheerfully. *If only she knew we were flat broke, she wouldn't be so cheerful,* I thought.

"Don't you worry about a thing," said Rose. "I'll make sure you have everything you need for them."

"I know you mean that, but Alpha Roland might not agree," I said.

"You let me worry about that," said Rose.

"Amina, how have your stress levels been?" asked the doctor.

I shook my head. "Not good," I said.

"I can tell," said Dr. Marisday. "You're severely underweight to be three months along with triplets. You haven't been eating much, have you?"

I shook my head. "I just don't have much of an appetite."

"You have to eat," said the doctor. "Your babies need a lot of protein to get them through the short pregnancy cycle that you wolves go through. A *lot* of protein," she emphasized. "If you don't put on some weight, one or all of them could be born too small. They might not survive."

"No!" I said. "I don't want to hurt my babies."

"I know you don't, Amina. Just eat more. Force yourself to eat. You need to put on at least thirty pounds by the time they're born. Preferably at least a month before they're born," she said.

"Thirty pounds!" Rose and I exclaimed at the same time.

"I'm going to be a blimp," I said as I huffed out a breath of air in frustration. "Ethan's not going to be attracted to a fat blimp."

"How can she possibly eat enough to gain thirty pounds in two months?" Rose asked. "Do you know how much food that will take?"

"It's not as hard as you think," said Dr. Marisday. "The pregnancy itself will give you close to half of that—four pounds per baby. So, you just need to eat enough to put on eighteen pounds. I'll print out a nutrition plan for you. I'm also going to prescribe some specially formulated wolf vitamins. These will ensure you and your baby get the vitamins and minerals needed for a healthy pregnancy. I would have liked for you to start these sooner, but better late than never."

I finished up my appointment with Dr. Marisday. When I went to check out, I was shocked at how much the appointment cost. "Two-hundred and thirty-six dollars!" I exclaimed. "I didn't know it cost that much. I don't have that kind of money," I said feeling ashamed of my poor finances.

Rose stepped up to the counter and handed the nurse a credit card. "I'll be taking care of the bill," she said. The nurse blushed.

"Of course, Luna," she said. "I apologize. I didn't know she was with you. I can also give you a discount."

"No discount necessary," said Rose. "I don't mind paying what I owe." *She means what I owe,* I thought as I stood there and felt like a bum.

We finished up with the receptionist and headed to the car.

"I don't know how Ethan is going to react," I said. I paused then the tears started up. "This might kill him," I said. "It might be too much. He's already beyond stressed. What if this the proverbial straw?" I asked.

"Nonsense," said Rose. "We Rohes are always cool under pressure. I have no doubt my son will rise to the occasion and be a wonderful father to these three precious bundles of joy."

"I really hope you're right," I said as I wiped away my tears.

"Of course I am. Now, let's go find you a nice, juicy, steak," she said as we drove out of the parking lot.

...

I was exhausted after working a double shift at the mall, but I was happy that I'd have extra money in my pay the next week. I was thinking about taking Amina out on a date with the extra money. There was a new movie I knew she wanted to see, so a little shopping and then maybe a movie would put her in a good mood.

My excitement of finding out what the doctor said was what kept my adrenaline flowing. I walked into the apartment with a big smile on my face, ready to embrace my beautiful mate and find out what gender our baby was. "There's my gorgeous mate," I said as I laid eyes on her.

When I saw the worried look on her face and the fact that she was chaotically shoving huge chunks of steak into her mouth while looking like it was the most disgusting thing in the world, my excitement quickly morphed into concern and my adrenaline started tanking.

"What's wrong, Amina. Is the baby okay?" I asked as I sat beside her and yawned.

"No," she said with a mouth full of food. My heart sank. *What could be wrong with our child?* I thought in panic. Then Amina said but then she said, "but they will be."

I was confused and too tired to understand. "They? What do you mean *they*?"

Amina swallowed the enormous portion of meat with a huge gulp. I frowned at the sound of it. It wasn't sexy at all. It was kind of gross, actually. *Is this depression eating?* I wondered.

"I'm not depressed," she said as she rolled her eyes at me. "So, I guess now you think I'm a fat slob?"

"Amina, I never said that," I said.

"You were thinking it," she replied.

"No, I wasn't," I said as she took in another huge mouthful of meat. I frowned again. "What happened at the appointment?"

"Apparently, I'm not eating enough," she said as she gulped down the chunk of steak. "The doctor said I need to eat more protein, even if I have to force it down. Hence..." she held up another big chunk of meat and shoved it in her mouth. *Definitely depression eating,* I thought but I made sure to block that thought from her.

"Okay, baby, you need to eat more protein. That's no surprise. I'll make sure to...buy more steak," I said as she gulped down the large chunk of meat. I winced. "What else did the doctor say? What gender is the baby? C'mon, don't keep me in suspense. I've been waiting on this all day."

"Both," she said with a sigh. I didn't feel like playing some cryptic game and I was getting a bit impatient. "Amina, I don't know what you mean. Just be straight with me," I said.

"Two boys and a girl. We're having triplets," she said as she shoved another piece of meat in her mouth. It took me a couple of seconds to process what she said, but it finally hit me, and it felt like all the breath left my body. I plopped back into the sofa.

"You're not kidding, are you?" I said quietly. She shook her head. "Triplets?" I was in utter shock. I knew that with wolves there was a fifty-fifty chance of producing multiples, but I never imagined it would happen to us. I took in a deep breath and let it out loudly. Then I rubbed my hands through my hair.

Amina swallowed and then started crying. "What are we going to do Ethan? We can't afford to take care of three babies. Why is this happening to us?" Looking at my crying mate, I knew my reaction wasn't the right one. She was probably looking for me to be a source of reassurance and I'd displayed the opposite.

"Amina, baby, don't cry. Please don't cry. We're going to be okay, I promise. I've been right about that so far, haven't I?" I pulled her close to me and thought about how I was tired of having to pull her close to me because she was crying. I really wanted to see Amina be happy more often.

"I know, Ethan. You're always so...positive, but we have to face reality. We're broke and we're barely hanging on. I think I'm going to have to get a job," she said.

"We've already discussed this. You aren't getting a job while you're pregnant, especially not while you're carrying triplets," I said.

"Ethan, you already work all the time. You can't possibly work more. We barely see each other now. How are you going to spend time with the babies when they're born?" she asked.

I didn't have an answer to that. The truth is I was tired, overworked, and stressed out. I didn't know what to do, but there was no way I could let Amina know how I was feeling. I didn't want to add stress to the pregnancy.

"I don't have all the answers right now, but don't worry so much babe. I give you my word that we'll be okay. Everything is going to work out just fine." I looked at her and forced a smile. "You should be happy. We're going to have three little pups running around here pretty soon."

"Are you happy?" she asked.

"Of course I am," I said. That seemed to make her feel a little better. She wiped her eyes and gave me a little smile.

"Are you done with your dinner?" I asked.

"I want to be," she said looking at the remaining steak on the plate, "but I have to put on thirty pounds by the time the babies come."

"Thirty pounds!" I exclaimed. "How long do you have to gain the weight?"

"About two months," she said as she resumed eating the steak.

"Okay, yeah. You're not done eating," I said. I went to the kitchen and made myself a microwave dinner. I took my place on the sofa beside Amina and we watched television as we ate together. When we were done, Amina looked exhausted, even more than I was. We both went to bed and snuggled close to each other. I rubbed her belly and to my surprise I felt the baby...well one of them, move.

"Yeah, they've been doing that all day," she said with a smile.

Feeling my pups moving suddenly made everything real. I got hit with a wave of emotions I didn't expect and a felt a couple of tears drop from my eyes. I tried to wipe them away fast, but Amina saw them. She kissed me gently.

"Ethan, I've been thinking about something all day," she said.

"Yeah, what's that?" I asked.

"We have a life together now. We have a home, children on the way, and, I can't believe I'm saying this, but we have family. I mean, your mom and siblings seem to like me, so I guess I can call them family now. Plus, I have an uncle nearby, even if I haven't gotten to meet him yet. Maybe...instead of our plan to leave, we could stay," she said.

I couldn't believe my ears. I sat up and stared at Amina, trying to see if she was joking but she was serious. "You want to stay in the pack?" I asked.

"Yeah, I guess I do," she said. "I don't want my babies to grow up like I did, you know, outsiders, not even knowing who they are or their real names if something happened to us. If they can be accepted in the pack, then I'll stay for their sake. Also...maybe you should consider being Alpha again for the babies' sake. I mean, your dad still doesn't like me, but maybe I can just stay out of his way."

I smiled from ear to ear. "Amina, you don't know how happy that makes me," I said. I leaned over and kissed her. "I don't know about the Alpha position, but I really want our children to be a part of the pack."

Her expression changed. "You do? Why didn't you say that? You kept telling me you were okay with leaving," she said.

"I would do anything to make you happy and leaving seemed to be what made you happy," I said. "Plus, you kept trying to leave me behind and I wasn't having that."

"I'm sorry, Ethan. I should have never convinced you to give up your title and leave," she said. "I would never want you to give up your happiness for mine."

"Hey, don't go back down that road. You didn't convince me of anything. It was my choice, remember?" I stroked her beautiful curls as I stared into the eyes of my mate. I couldn't help but plant a kiss on her lips as I looked at her. I felt my manhood rising. I could see in her eyes that she felt it too.

"By the way, I didn't get a chance to tell you before, but I'm glad you stuck with Amina. That name really suits you," I said. She smiled at me and pulled me down on her. We made love gently and when we were done I held her from behind and rested my hands on her belly. I had my entire family in my arms, and I never wanted to let them go.

21

Alpha Again

It was nice to have a family day at my parents' house as we prepared for the triplets to come. My mother actually cooked, something she didn't do very often since my siblings and I hit our teen years. It seemed the thought of being a grandparent motivated her to get back to her domestic roots and she was all too happy to do it.

Amina smiled as Stacey rubbed her large, round belly. She'd really blown up in these last couple of months. Of course, I'd never say that to her face, and I still thought she was the most beautiful woman in the world, but it was funny to see her waddling around like a penguin as she tried to balance the large bundle on the front of her body. The pregnancy was hard on her, especially being pregnant in the middle of summer, but she never complained, and she handled it like a champ. I knew she was going to be a great mother, and I couldn't be prouder to have her as a mate.

As I stood in the patio doorway watching the two women, my father came up behind me and tapped me on the shoulder. *Here we go*, I thought. Lately, every conversation with him ended in some type of argument or disagreement. I really wasn't in the mood for one at the moment.

I turned to him, and he motioned to me to follow him away from the patio area. *Private argument*, I thought. *At least he has enough decency to not argue in front of Amina.* We went into the library and sat down.

"What did I do now," I said to him with obvious annoyance in my voice.

"I didn't bring you here to argue," he said. "Actually, quite the opposite."

"Oh, okay," I replied. Then I waited to see what my father could possibly want to not argue about.

"I wanted to tell you that I'm proud of you," he said. My mouth dropped open. I don't know what I expect him to say, but it wasn't that. "You've really stepped up to the plate to take care of your mate these last few months no matter what was thrown at you. You've shown that you're at a level of responsibility that I certainly wasn't at when I was your age."

"Wow, thanks Dad," I said. I was completely shocked. I had begun to think my father was disappointed in me and it hurt me so much to think I had let him down. After months of arguing and fighting, I couldn't believe he was giving me such a high compliment.

"I appreciate and admire how you were completely honest with Amina about the man in the woods but still didn't put the pack in danger by going to look for him. You found a way to keep the peace on both fronts, keeping everyone safe. That's what being an Alpha means—keeping your pack safe. Your honesty with Amina is probably what allows her to follow your lead. I see that now," he said.

I nodded in agreement. I had started squirming in my seat because I wasn't sure where this conversation was going, and I was beginning to get anxious.

"Ethan, you've proven that with training, you're more than capable of leading this pack. I want you to resume your position of being my successor," he said.

"Wait, you still want me to be the next Alpha? After all the fighting we've done?" I asked.

"A little fighting amongst men...we all have egos, right?" said my father with a chuckle. "You bested me in a fight. You're stronger than I've ever been, and you haven't even fully developed your Alpha capabilities yet. I can see that you're the right choice. I can't let my pride get in the way of what's best for the pack."

"Dad, I don't know what to say—"

"—say yes," he said. "That's all you have to say."

"Yes," I said quickly. "I want to be Alpha. I've always wanted it."

"Great, it's settled then," he said as he stood up. "You'll begin your training after the pups are born."

I stood up to follow him out of the room. Then I paused, remembering something important. "Uh, Dad?"

"Yeah," he said as he stopped and looked at me.

"I'm not complaining or asking you for anything, but I...I have to work. I don't know if I can do training right after the pups are born," I said. "Maybe after they get a little older I can take some time off—"

"—Ethan, don't be simple," he said. "I wouldn't suggest for you to start training if I didn't plan on reinstating your inheritance. I'm fully aware you can't support three kids and a wife with those mall jobs you're working although I admire the fact that you were willing to work yourself into the ground to do so." He turned and walked out of the library leaving me standing there in shock. Just like that all of our problems were solved.

I went back to the patio where, to my surprise, my father had his hand on Amina's belly, and he was smiling. I wasn't sure how many more pleasant shocks I could handle in a day.

"I can feel them moving," my father said as he looked at me. "Reminds me of you when you were in your mother's womb. You were an active little pup."

"Dinner's ready," my mother called from inside the house. I walked over and helped Amina up and we all made our way to the dinner table where our servants were placing the serving platters.

We took our places, fixed our plates, and began eating and chatting delightfully. It was great to see my father actually smile at Amina and be nice to her instead of simply tolerating her. I don't know what suddenly gave him such a big change of heart, but after so much fighting with him, I was willing to just accept the change without question.

I have a surprise for you, I projected to Amina. She looked at me with raised eyebrows.

I love surprises, she projected back.

No, you don't, I said jokingly.

I like them from you. She winked at me and smiled.

When dinner was over, Amina grew tired, so we said our goodbyes and left. I decided to give Amina the good news on the drive home.

"My father wants me to be the next Alpha again," I said.

Amina smiled so hard I thought her face would break. "Really? Seriously? Ethan, that's such good news. So, you two must be on good terms again?"

I nodded. "He caught me completely by surprise. I guess we are."

"I'm happy for you Ethan. You really deserve it," she said.

"He wants me to start training right after the pups are born," I said.

Amina's smile disappeared promptly. "Right after? What about work? Will I need to get a job?" she asked.

I laughed. "You really want to work, huh? You keep talking about getting a job."

"Actually, yes, I do because I've never had a job before, but that's not why I'm saying that," she said.

"My father also reinstated my inheritance," I said. Amina gasped and put her hand over her mouth, but I could still see the smile on her face. "We don't have to worry about money anymore. We'll have everything we need," I said.

"You're serious?" she asked. She started crying but I knew it was happy tears. "You know what this means, right?" she asked.

"I'm not sure if my answer is going to match yours," I said.

"Two things. First, we can start planning our wedding. Next, it means I'm going shopping tomorrow!" she exclaimed. "There are so many things I want to get for the triplets! Cribs, clothes, toys, a big stroller, you know, the one that can hold multiple babies—"

"—toys? They can't play with toys yet," I said with a chuckle.

"But they will eventually," she said with delight.

"Okay, okay, whatever you want, but maybe we should get a bigger place first. You'll need somewhere to put all of that stuff," I said.

"I guess you're right. We can look at some places tomorrow and I'll go shopping the day af…" Amina suddenly stopped talking and her face developed this long, frightened expression.

"Amina? What's wrong?" I asked.

"We can't go apartment hunting tomorrow," she said.

"Why not?" I asked.

"Because my water just broke," she said as she looked down towards her lap. I slammed on the brakes.

"Like, right now?" I asked. "Like, it just happened now? Oh my…"

"Don't panic, Ethan. Just get me to the hospital," she said. "Remember, Alpha nerves. Calm and in charge." She smiled at me, but I could see her nervousness in the smile. "Call Dr. Marisday on the way."

"Right," I said as I turned the car around. "I'm cool. I'm cool," I said even though I was freaking out inside. I pulled out my phone to call the doctor as I hit the gas and made my way to the hospital as quickly as possible.

...

I'm Ethan Rohe. I was quarterback of my high school football team. I'm the most popular person around town. I'm strong, much stronger than most of the guys around here, maybe even stronger than my father, the Alpha. I've battled evil wolves, and I know how to keep calm under pressure. I'm not afraid of anything. I'd like to think I'm smart—I never had to cheat in school. Well, not very much anyway. I'm the perfect choice to be the next Alpha because I have all the qualities needed. I can handle pressure.

That's why I'm not letting the birth of my kids rattle me. I'm not. I have nerves of steel. Even as I'm listening to Amina scream out in pain and squeeze my hand until I can almost feel the bones snap, I'm not going to let my nerves get to me. Nope, not going to let them rule me. Shit! A head just popped out! Oh my…calm, Ethan. Calm. Sure, I just felt my heart flutter, but that happens, right? My nerves aren't going to get the best of me. Wait...Amina's yelling again. I need to comfort my mate. Nerves in check. Nerves in check. Nerves...holy crap, the baby is out. It's my son! It's...

As I kept trying to convince myself that I had it together, Amina was working so hard to bring our pups into the world. She looked like she was in a lot of pain, and she was a sweaty mess, but she'd never looked more beautiful. My son started crying and my heart did a flip. *I did that,* I thought. *I...no, we created that. Him. Them.*

"You're doing so well, baby," I said to her as she pushed the second baby out. "I'm right here. Squeeze my hand as much as you need to. Breathe. Breathe. In and out—"

"—shut up, Ethan!" she yelled. Then she screamed as she started pushing out the third baby.

"Okay, sorry," I said. "I'm here...I'm—" She frowned at me, and I shut up. She screamed as she pushed the third baby out and finally it was over. Amina slumped back, obviously tired from the activities and the room was filled with the sound of the three crying babies. The nurses quickly got the babies cleaned up while two others got Amina and her bed cleaned up. Then they came over and handed one of the crying babies to Amina and two of them to me. All three of them instantly calmed down and I was in complete shock at the sight of my mate and children right in my view, all together for the first time.

"Ethan, they're here," she said to me with a smile. "Our babies are finally here."

"I'm so happy for you two," said one of the nurses. She was young and looked like she could have been my age, but I'm sure she was a little older. She seemed happy and energetic in her pink scrubs. *Seeing new babies all the time would probably make anyone happy,* I thought as I looked at my son and daughter in my arms.

"My name is Keri and I'll be your nurse while you're here. Think of me as, essentially, your midwife. Anything you need, just let me know," she said. "Mom, I know you're tired, but make sure you give all three of them skin-to-skin contact. You'll also need to breastfeed them in the next half an hour. I'm sure they're very hungry after the ordeal they just went through," she said with a smile.

Two of the nurses came into the room pulling three basinets with them. They lined the bassinets up beside each other. They marveled over the triplets for a couple of minutes then they left the room with Keri.

It was cute watching Amina attempt to get used to breast feeding. It was a clumsy ordeal and apparently it was uncomfortable because Amina let out an "ouch" a couple of times, but eventually she got the hang of it and the three babies got a belly full of milk.

After the newborns had eaten, my family came into the room one at a time for a sneak peek of the babies. My mother cried of course. No surprise there. However, it was my father's reaction that moved me the most. He seemed proud, but not of the babies. He seemed proud of me and that made me feel amazing. It wasn't until that moment that I realized how much his approval meant to me. I wanted to do everything I could to stay on his good side. A little while later the nurses came back for the babies. Amina didn't want to give them up, but she was obviously exhausted and needed rest.

"Where are you taking them?" I asked.

"They're going to the nursery so we can make sure they're okay. Your boys will also be circumcised," she said.

"So you can make sure they're okay?" I asked curiously.

"Nothing to be concerned about," she said. "They were born very healthy. It's just procedure."

They took the babies away and Amina fell asleep almost immediately. I took that opportunity to go see my family. When I entered the waiting room, Lennox and Stacey came over to me and hugged me. "I can't believe you're a father of three," said Lennox. "Damn, you just graduated high school, bro. Your life is over," he joked.

"I can't believe it either," I said. "Everything happened so fast."

My mother hugged me next. "I'm so proud of the man you've become," she said. "Thank you for giving me three beautiful grandbabies. I can't wait to spoil them," she said.

The four of us chatted a little more, then my father nodded for me to come to him for a private conversation. *Always with the private conversations,* I thought in amusement as I walked with him down a hallway.

"How are you feeling?" he asked.

"I'm okay, I guess. A little overwhelmed at the moment, but I can handle it," I said. I had no idea if I could handle it, but I wasn't about to tell my father that.

"I remember when you were first born," he said. "I was nervous as hell."

"Really? You? Nervous?" I was surprised by that. My father always seemed like he had everything under control.

"Yeah. I had no idea how to be a father or what that meant. Plus, I had the weight of the entire pack on my shoulders. It was a lot to handle," he said. "I'm glad your mother and I waited to have kids. I don't think I would have been a very good father when I was eighteen."

"Do you think I'm going to mess it up," I asked.

"Of course. All new fathers mess it up at some point, but I also think you're going to be a better father than I ever was," he said. "No one knows how to be a perfect parent. Not even me."

I couldn't help but smile. That was such a great compliment coming from my father. "Wow, thanks," I said. "I appreciate that. I won't let Amina down. I won't let you down either."

"I know you won't. Listen, Ethan. You have an immense amount of pressure and responsibility ahead of you. Being a new father to one baby is hard enough, but you have three at one time, and their births coincide with your Alpha training. I have full confidence in you, but to say that you're going to really go through a tough time is an understatement." He sighed. "You're going to be gone a lot during the first part of your training. Have you discussed that with Amina?"

"No, I haven't. That means she'll be taking care of the babies by her-self," I said as the realization hit me.

"You know your mother's going to help as much as possible. Lennox and Stacey too, but sometimes the father's absence can…throw a wrench into things. You need to make sure that Amina is fully on board with everything," he said.

I nodded. "I'll talk to her. Amina is reasonable. She's strong. She'll understand."

"Okay, son. Oh, and another thing. You should probably move your family back onto our property. I mean, you don't plan on raising three kids in that tiny box, do you?" he said with a chuckle.

"Uh, no. We were going to look for a bigger place, but the babies came early. Dad, are you sure about us moving home?" I asked.

"Of course. Every Alpha has raised their family there. There's plenty of room. You should be no different. The property….it will be yours eventually anyway," he said.

"Dad, I don't know what to say except thank you," I said. I gave him a big hug.

"Don't get all sappy on me," he said with a smile. He clapped me on the back, and we headed back to the waiting room to rejoin the family.

22

Our New Home

"I feel like a cow," I said as my son took his third fill of the day. "All I do is rotate the babies all day long. When does this get fun?"

Ethan laughed as he taped up a box. "I know we're a team, but I'm glad that's not my job. I'm perfectly fine with doing the heavy lifting." He grabbed the large box, biceps bulging, and headed out to the car. I might not have been enjoying being an all-day buffet, but I loved watching Ethan's muscles flex as he packed and moved our things out of the apartment.

Just as I finished feeding Henry, Hazel started crying. I walked over to her as I was patting Henry on the back to burp him. "Shh, shh," I said as I gently rubbed her tummy. Henry burped and made a mess on the burp cloth as expected. I cleaned him up and put him in his crib. Then I went over to Hazel to begin the process all over again. Luckily Hunter was still sleeping so I didn't have to handle all three at the same time. Taking care of triplets was definitely as hard as everyone said it would be, and I was doing all I could to keep up.

Ethan drove the car load of boxes to his parents' house as I stayed back and handled the babies. I did a little packing whenever I got some free time. We continued the process that way throughout the day and we were able to get everything moved in one afternoon. After all, we didn't have a lot to begin with and Ethan's parents' house had everything we needed anyway. We decided to donate our furniture to some less fortunate Omegas. Ethan's friends handled that part for us. They loaded it all into a truck and carted it away. All that was left to do was get the triplets to their new home.

Ethan and I stood in the empty little apartment for a few moments, reflecting back on our time there. "It wasn't much, but it was home for us," I said. "The first place I ever felt comfortable and safe. The first place I could ever truly call home." I felt tears coming to my eyes. I didn't expect to get emotional over leaving.

"Yeah. A place where we bonded, connected, and grew together. Where we started our family. This apartment will always be special for us," he said. He leaned over and kissed me. Then he wiped a tear from my cheek. "We're going someplace better now where we can make a lot more memories. No more struggling," he said. "I'll be able to give you the life you deserve. C'mon. Let's go to our new life." We pushed the stroller to the car, put the triplets in their car seats, and prepared to leave the apartment behind. I turned and looked at the door one last time before we turned the corner.

When we got to the new place we would call home, I had a moment of disbelief. Only a few months ago, the people in that house despised me. Now they were welcoming me in and calling me family. It felt surreal.

Ethan's mom came out of the house first, in search of the triplets, followed by a servant. "Where are my beautiful grandbabies," she said as she approached the car. Ethan had just gotten the stroller out. Rose started to get Henry out of his car seat but then she stopped. "Where are my manners! I'm so sorry, Amina!" She hugged me. "Welcome home." She turned to Ethan and gave him a hug.

I laughed. "It's okay, Rose. I understand that you've missed them."

"I know you have to keep them close right now...feeding schedule and all, but perhaps I could take them off your hands while you and Ethan settle in? Maybe for an hour?" she asked hopefully.

"Sure," I said. "I'd be happy for a little break.

"Great!" she exclaimed. She proceeded to get the triplets into their strollers. Hazel started crying. "She needs to be changed," said Rose. "I'll handle it." Ethan retrieved their diaper bag from the car and gave it to his mother.

"Do you need help with anything," asked the servant to Ethan.

"No, we moved everything already. Thanks," he said. The servant nodded, turned and headed back inside. Ethan's mother followed, pushing the triplets in their stroller and Ethan and I walked in behind her.

Lennox and Stacey met us in the foyer, excited to see their niece and nephews. Hazel was still crying, so Rose took her to change her. Ethan's father greeted us. "You've been moving all day, so we'll save the extended greeting for later at dinner. For now, you two can get settled into your new place."

He handed Ethan and I each a set of keys. Ethan grabbed my hand and pulled me with him back towards the front door. He had a smile on his face that told me he had some surprise for me. I looked back towards the boys, but Ethan turned my face back to him.

"They're fine, baby. Come with me. You're going to love this," he said. We walked along a path for about fifteen minutes until we got to one of the empty houses on the Alpha's property.

"Welcome home," said Ethan as he smiled at me.

My mouth dropped open as I realized what Ethan was saying. "*This is where we'll live?*" I asked Ethan in amazement. My eyes couldn't stretch any further as I marveled at the beautiful home that apparently belonged to us. I felt like I was dreaming, and I prayed that I wouldn't wake up.

"Yes," he said as he smiled at me. "It's all ours."

I squealed in delight and leapt into his arms. He spun me around then kissed me. "Ethan, this is amazing," I said. "It's so much more than I could have ever asked for."

The beautiful brick home looked almost new. I didn't know the proper terms to describe a house like that, but it looked like a house that would be on the front of a real estate magazine. There were palm trees in the yard and a perfectly paved walkway, lined with freshly trimmed bushes that lead up to a decorative glass door. A two-car garage jutted out from the front.

"Aren't you glad you stayed now?" he asked.

"Yeah, I am," I said. "Can we go inside?"

"Of course we can," he said. I ran up to the door, put the key in and unlocked it. Then I stepped into the house and was overcome with excitement as I looked around at the marvelous place that was now my home. There was so much space. I spotted our boxes in the living room waiting to be unpacked. The master bedroom had a brand new bed in it. Another bedroom had the triplets' cribs in it. Other than the boxes, bed, and cribs, the house was empty and waiting for us to make it ours.

"It's the largest guest house on the property," said Ethan. "There are five bedrooms, three bathrooms, a dining room, kitchen, living room, and bonus room. There is a swimming pool out back just past the patio. It's not a mansion, but it's enough space for our family."

"It's a mansion to me," I said. Even though it was only a guest house, I'd never lived anywhere so luxurious or spacious. The master bedroom alone was the size of the entire apartment we'd just left.

"You know, we won't get the opportunity to be in here alone very often," he said, "and luckily, the bed is already set up."

Ethan took me to our bedroom. The mattress was soft, yet firm. I could tell it was expensive. Ethan began undressing me, then he undressed himself. We made passionate love to each other, expressing ourselves in ways we hadn't been able to since I had gotten pregnant. When we were done, we lay in bed for a few moments, neither of us wanting to rejoin the family.

"We have to go," I said. "They'll be expecting us. Plus, the babies will need to eat soon."

"I know," Ethan said, "but I wish I could hold you like this forever." He squeezed me and pulled me closer. Then he started kissing my neck. I giggled.

"Ethan, we have to go," I repeated. "We'll have more fun later."

Ethan groaned but he let me go. We got up, showered, dressed, and headed back to the main house. When we walked into the family room, Ethan's family stared at us. Lennox and Stacey were smiling.

"What?" I asked. I looked at Ethan and he was blushing. *Oh my gosh, they know what we were doing,* I projected to him.

Yep, he projected back. I could have died.

"Welcome back," said Alpha Roland. "I guess you're pleased with your new home?"

"Yeah, Dad. It's perfect," said Ethan. We both sat down, hoping the situation would pass quickly.

"The triplets behaved well while you were gone," said Rose. She was holding Hunter. His arms were flailing around at nothing in particular. That meant he'd soon be hungry. I'd come to learn that the three of them became active when the first signs of hunger hit them.

"Now that we're all here, we can start dinner," said Alpha Roland. "I'm starving."

"That's a good idea," I said. "I should probably eat before I have to feed the babies."

"The table is set. Let's go," said Rose. "I can have one of the servants take the babies until dinner is over."

"No. I mean, I appreciate it but—"

"—oh, I get it," said Rose. "You're still in the overprotective phase. It'll pass." Everyone laughed as we all moved to the dining room. Alpha Roland stopped us and let everyone else go ahead of us.

"I hope I don't need to say this, but I'm saying it just in case. It's too soon for more pups. Cover up." Alpha Roland gave us a stern look, then he turned and went into the dining room. Ethan and I looked at each other. I knew he was thinking what I was thinking. We hadn't...*covered up* as Alpha Roland put it.

We'll be fine, Ethan projected to me. I nodded and we joined the family for dinner, praying to the Goddess we hadn't just made a big mistake.

...

After a month in our new home, it was nice to be out with the triplets doing something that seemed normal for once, although I still wasn't used to strolling through the mall without a care in the world and shopping until my heart was content. Stacey, who was used to it, insisted on stopping at every single store, even the men's stores.

"This sweater would be nice for Dad," she said as she looked at it. "It's lightweight and soft." She thought for a moment longer. "He's never been much of a shopper. He only has nice things because mom and I buy them for him." She threw the sweater over her arm. "You should grab something for Ethan," she said.

"I don't know if Ethan wants me to buy his clothes," I said. "I mean, that's what old people do." We both laughed.

"Amina, it doesn't matter how young, bright, and active a man is. They're generally helpless," Stacey said. "They wouldn't make it without women looking out for them at every turn. This is especially true for Alphas. While Ethan is training, he's not going to know which way is left or right by the time he gets home."

I spotted a hoodie that I thought Ethan might like. I grabbed it and hung it from the stroller. Stacey smiled and nodded. "Speaking of men, why aren't you mated yet?" I asked. "I mean, you're what, twenty-three years old? It's rare to go that long without mating."

Stacey's face changed from amused to serious. "I'm sorry if I shouldn't have asked that. It's none of my business," I said.

"No, no, it's okay," she said. "It's not a secret. I guess you just...I mean you basically spent your life avoiding everyone so you wouldn't know." She sighed.

"No, I mostly kept to myself. I never participated in gossip," I said.

"That makes you one of the most genuine people I could talk to," she said. "You aren't tainted by the opinions of others." She paused, looked at a pair of pants, and threw them over her arm. "I found my mate shortly after my eighteenth birthday, but he rejected me."

I gasped. "You? You got rejected? I mean, you're Stacey Rohe! What man in their right mind would reject you?"

"One who doesn't really like women," she said. "My true mate...he was in love with a man—his chosen mate. He chose him over me despite how strong our attraction to each other was. Damn near killed me when he did it. I couldn't get out of bed for a week."

"Wow, Stacey, I'm sorry. That really sucks," I said.

"Yeah, well, I'm over it now," she said with a smile. "I mean, it's hard to see my younger siblings finding their mates and being all in love before me. Lennox will be graduating next year, so he'll probably find his mate sometime soon," she said. She trailed off for a moment. "I mean, I'm not jealous of them or anything like that. I'm happy for them, really, but I kinda feel like I'm disappointing my parents. Like, I'm the child that's just going to hang around in their house forever because I got rejected."

"I'm sure your parents don't feel that way about you. From what I can tell, they love you very much," I said.

"Yeah, I don't doubt that. But loving me and being proud of me are two different things," she said as she found a pair of sunglasses. "Dad will like these."

I spotted a pair of jeans that I thought Ethan might like. I hung them on the stroller with the hoodie. "What are you going to do? About a mate?" I asked.

"Nothing, I guess. I mean, I'll just have to find a chosen mate. That means...dating." She shuddered at the thought. "Finding love the hard way."

"Hey, it might be fun," I said. "I've only ever had one boyfriend—Ethan. I'm not complaining or anything because he's perfect for me and I would never, ever want anyone else, but I'll never know what other guys have to offer. You get to test the waters, try out a bunch of different fish."

"A bunch of different fish?" she said with a smile and raised eyebrows. "Amina Sturges, you're naughty." We both laughed heartily and took our items to the register. I thought about the fact that I'd never had a friend before. It felt pretty good to be hanging out with someone as popular as her.

We went on to several other stores in the mall, making purchases from almost all of them. I was glad that I could hang bags from the stroller, otherwise we wouldn't have been able to carry them all. As we came out of one of the boutiques, I noticed a couple of guys looking our way. I was certain they weren't looking at me—the girl with three babies in a stroller. They were looking at Stacey, but she seemed to be oblivious to it.

"Hey, those guys are checking you out," I said to her. She glanced over at them then back at me. "Lots of guys check me out," she said.

"It might be time for you to catch a fish," I said. "You can always throw it back if you don't like it."

Stacey laughed. "Amina, you're funny." Then she sighed. "Okay, in all honesty, I've been a little...apprehensive about dating since my rejection."

"I get it," I said, "but you have to start somewhere, right? Nothing wrong with just saying hello." I couldn't believe that *I* was giving Stacey Rohe dating advice. More importantly, I couldn't believe she might be listening to it.

"Hello, huh? I can do hello." She straightened her dress, fixed her hair, shoved up her boobs, and went over to the guys to say hello.

While Stacey was flirting, Henry started fussing a bit. That lead to Hazel starting up. *Not all at once, please,* I thought. Just as I picked up Henry, Hunter started up. They always seemed to cry in that order—Henry, Hazel, then Hunter. It was like follow the leader and Henry, my youngest by twelve minutes, was always the instigator. I was certain he'd be my problem child.

By the time I got Henry quiet, Hazel and Hunter were crying in full force. People were walking by and giving me looks of pity. Stacey came back over and grabbed Hunter.

"Aww, shhh, shhh," she said to him.

I put Henry down and picked up Hazel to soothe her. "Sorry, I guess I'm not a great wing woman," I said.

"No way, you're the perfect wing woman. I decided to throw them back and the babies gave me a perfect excuse to make my exit," she said. We both giggled.

Stacey helped me get the babies fed from the bottles I had prepared, and we finished our shopping. By the time we left the mall, Stacey had caught two fish that she didn't throw back and we'd bought something for everyone in the family.

By the time I got home and settled with the triplets, I was exhausted. I didn't even bother putting up the stuff I'd bought from the mall. I left the bags sitting in the living room. I looked at the time on my phone. It was late in the evening—after eight. I hadn't heard from Ethan all day. *What are you doing?* I projected to him although I wasn't sure whether or not he was in range to receive my thought.

Ethan had been training for the Alpha position for the last two weeks. I'd seen less and less of him each day. Last night, he didn't come home at all, but he at least called me and told me how much he missed me and the babies.

As I expected, Ethan didn't get my projection. *Or maybe he's ignoring it,* I thought. I wondered what his training consisted of. Was he attending meetings? Doing paperwork? Fighting?

Ethan had told me that his training would take up a lot of time, but I hadn't expected it to take up *all* of his time. I missed him a lot and it was lonely in that big house, especially when the triplets were asleep. *How ironic,* I thought. *I once wanted to live the life of a rogue which was much lonelier than this.* I had changed so much since then. I wasn't the loner I used to be. I'd finally had a taste of what it felt like to be a part of a family—to be loved and I never wanted to give that up.

Ethan's training wouldn't last forever. I just had to be strong and take care of the triplets on my own until Ethan's schedule cleared up. More importantly, I had to fight the sinister thoughts that had been slowly invading my head that Ethan would somehow forget about me in his quest to the top. *He would never do that to me,* I assured myself as I lay in bed. *He loves me. He'll never leave me.* I repeated these things to myself as I drifted off into what would be one of many restless nights of sleep.

23

Fight Training

I was getting my ass kicked. I knew training would be hard, but I had no idea how brutal it would be. I trained for eight hours a day. Four of those hours were straight workouts. "Alphas can't be weak," my father kept saying. "You have to be stronger and faster than anyone here." The other four hours were the hardest—I had to fight until my father felt that I was skilled enough to protect the pack and so far I had lost almost every fight.

When my fight training first began, my father emphasized how important it was to be the top fighter in the pack. "Ethan, being able to fight is extremely important as an Alpha. Not only will you need to protect the pack, but you'll have lower ranking wolves challenge you to try to take your Alpha position. You can't lose—ever," my father said. "If you lose, you lose everything."

"Don't forget, I beat you, Dad," I said with a chuckle. "So, I think I got that part."

"You beat me because I wasn't fighting you like an enemy. I was fighting you like my son," he said. "Had I fought you like an enemy, I would have killed you."

"Oh," I said quietly as I realized he'd basically let me win. My pride took a little bit of a hit. During training, my father showed me just how much he'd held back on me. I fought our packs top warriors, and they'd beat me to a pulp almost every day even though, according to everyone, none of them could beat my father. *If my father is a better fighter than all these warriors, I don't see how I'll ever be able to beat him,* I thought every time I walked away...or was carried away from a fight as a loser.

I suffered broken ribs, a broken cheek bone, a broken collar bone, and more gashes from being clawed than I could count. If it weren't for my rapid healing abilities, I would have surely died within the first few days.

There was one day where I was an observer instead of a fighter. I was incredibly thankful for that break because my body couldn't take a beating that day. I watched my father fight all the warriors for the entire four hours of fight training. Not one of them beat him. Many of them didn't even get in a lick.

Besides physical training, there were a couple of days a week where I had what could be considered as mental or emotional training. On those days I learned the administrative side of things—running meetings, doing paperwork, making decisions. I learned politics and communications skills. I learned how to be a diplomat. I learned how to be a leader. I appreciated those days because it gave me a break from being a punching bag all day.

For the first couple of weeks, I was going home most days, if only to see Amina and the babies for a few minutes before I passed out. However, that changed. My injuries were so bad I didn't want to go home and alarm Amina, so I spent most nights in the infirmary. I missed my family so much and the pain of being away from them for so long was worse than the pain from my broken bones.

One morning when I woke up from a restless night of sleep, my body ached everywhere. I had no idea how I was going to get through the day. I dragged myself out of the infirmary, probably looking more like a zombie than an Alpha. I went to the kitchen where the servants had prepared breakfast for me and the rest of the warriors as usual. I picked at the food on my plate, forcing myself to take a couple of bites when a hand clapped me on the shoulder. Although I tried not to, I couldn't help but wince.

I looked up into the eyes of my father. He was staring down at me with pity in his eyes and I hated that. I felt like I'd been letting him down because I couldn't beat the warriors.

"Maybe you need a day off, son," he said. "Why don't you spend the day with your mate?"

My heart leapt at the thought of holding Amina in my arms, but I knew I had to turn down the offer. I thought about when I was hurt in the valley, and I couldn't defend myself. What if that happened again and the mysterious wolf wasn't there to save me? Worse, what would happen if I had to protect someone else? *Amina,* I thought, thinking about the first time I saved her in the valley. I knew I had to learn to fight through my pain so I could be the protector that my family needed.

"I would love to do that father, but an Alpha can't run when things get hard," I said to him. "I'll finish my training." My father nodded and attempted to keep a stoic look on his face, but I saw a slight twinkle in his eye. I had impressed him and that somehow gave me a little strength.

My morning workout didn't go as well as usual. I wasn't able to do as much due to my body being broken and tired. However, fighting went differently that day. As I faced our top warrior with others cheering us on from the sidelines, I thought about how much my body hurt and how I wanted the day's battles to be over. I thought about being Alpha and how people were counting on me. Mostly I thought about my mate and our children, how I missed them and how I would need to protect them from any and all dangers. I don't know where it came from, but a felt a surge of energy flow through me as the fight started.

The cold autumn air flowed across my skin as I faced my first opponent. I was fighting Kenta in our wolf forms. He was one of our mid-level warriors but still fierce, nonetheless. Kenta was bigger and stronger than me and I knew if I tried to go toe to toe with him, I'd lose. The cold air seemed to increase my alertness allowing me to think through the fight.

Since I had fought him twice before, I knew that two of his weaknesses were speed and focus. I decided to use that knowledge to my advantage. Also, since my stamina wasn't up to par, I knew that I would need to take him out before the fight really got started.

We circled each other slowly and I had no doubt he was making plans of his own. I noticed that Kenta seemed to favor his right side as we circled each other, so if I could take out the right leg quickly, he'd topple over and I'd have the advantage. I attacked quickly before Kenta could finish formulating his plan. To my surprise, it worked! Kenta toppled over and I pounced on him, slashing for dear life. The fight was over in less than fifteen seconds. I had won and Kenta didn't even get in a lick.

At first there was complete silence aside from a few gasps. Then suddenly everyone cheered. I spotted my father, and he was beaming with pride. *Finally, I did it!* I thought. Some of the warriors came and picked Kenta up to take him to the infirmary. For the first time since training, the ground was soaked with someone else's blood besides mine.

Next I had to fight Arias, one of our best warriors. He wasn't as big as Kenta, but he was a merciless warrior, even to the Alpha's son. Rumors had been circulating that he never lost a fight. I had fought him once and he'd beat me so badly that I blacked out. I didn't even remember most of the fight.

For our fight, we shifted to our human forms. I knew that Arias was a very focused warrior, and he would be prepared for almost any attack I'd throw. Because of that, I decided that I wouldn't attack first. We circled each other three times and I finally noticed a bit of confusion on Arias's face. That was his weakness. He was so focused on attacks that he really wasn't much of an instigator. He'd been preparing for every single one of my moves. He did not prepare for me to *not* move. I'd found his weakness.

Arias made a very small, simple mistake, but one that gave me the upper hand. In his confusion, he glanced over towards my father, and I promptly attacked him. I knocked him down and started punching him with everything I had. I bloodied his nose and gave him a black eye. Despite this, he was somehow able to flip me off of him. I knew I couldn't let him gain his composure because if he got his focus back, I was toast.

Arias got to his feet, but by the time he did I was already lunging towards him again. This fight wasn't as easy as the one with Kenta. Arias managed to get in a few licks, but overall, I ended up beating him. I laid him out with a final uppercut. He flew backwards, hit the ground, and didn't move. The warriors all erupted into applause and cheers. I couldn't believe it. I'd just won two in a row.

The rest of fight training went well. I won every single fight, although I still got beat up pretty good. It seemed that somehow all the lessons had clicked, and I was finally the fierce successor that my father had been trying to inspire.

I was tired and in an unfathomable amount of pain at the end of the day's training, but I'd never felt better. I showered, ate, and settled down in the infirmary. After a phone call with Amina, I slept better than I'd slept in months.

24

Surprise

It was my first party, and I was scared. Sure, I'd achieved a lot socially since high school. It seemed that people were nicer to me because I was mated with Ethan and that helped me to come out of my shell a little, but I was far from being a regular party animal. Despite this, it was Stacey's birthday. She planned a huge Thanksgiving-themed bash, and she insisted that I attend.

"It's going to be a big W!" Stacey exclaimed. "You absolutely cannot miss this!"

"What about the babies?" I asked.

"You know mom will watch them," she said. "No excuses. You're coming! Also, we're going shopping for new dresses."

Shortly after that conversation, I found myself walking the mall munching on macarons while looking for the perfect party dress. *What if Ethan comes home tonight and I'm not home,* I thought. I missed him so much. I hadn't seen him in a month at that point and all I could think about was when he'd walk back through the door.

"Ahhh!" Stacey screamed. "That's going to look perfect on you!". Her excitement pulled me out of my daydream about Ethan. I looked at the shop window she was pointing at and there was a fire engine red strapless dress with ruffled fringe across the bosom area as well as asymmetrical ruffled fringe at the bottom. Before I could respond, Stacey pulled me into the shop and requested a size eight.

"I don't know...that's a little much," I said shyly.

"It's hot!" she said. "Just imagine if Ethan saw you in it."

I sighed. "I'd love it if he saw me in it. I don't know when he's coming home."

"Don't worry about that! You know Ethan hasn't forgotten about you, right? He loves you. He's just doing something important. In the meantime, you should have fun."

The clerk came back with the dress and Stacey shuffled me into the dressing room. I put the dress on, and, to my surprise, it looked pretty good on me. I'd never worn anything like it before. It was a fitted dress that hugged my curves and stopped mid-thigh. I wondered if Ethan would like it or if he would be jealous if other guys saw me in it.

I stepped out and Stacey screamed. "You...look...so...good!" she exclaimed.

"I'll admit, it feels pretty good," I said as I smiled and looked back at the mirror. "Okay, I'll take it."

Stacey also found a great dress, one that outshined mine. It was a sexy, gold, diamond sequined halter neck dress that made her look like a goddess. It had sheer diamond panels that were accentuated by beautiful crystals. She was definitely going to be the spotlight of the party. "Going fishing tonight?" I asked.

"Absolutely," she said with a smile. We paid for our dresses and went back to prepare for the party.

When I went home to get ready I almost changed my mind about going. After sitting at home alone for a while, I decided it wouldn't kill me to go. I showed up fashionably late and was surprised at how many people had shown up. There were literally hundreds of people! It was like walking into a night club. Stacey had invited almost everyone she knew, and it seemed they all showed up. Even people who had left and gone off to college were skipping school to come to Stacey's party. *She's so popular*, I thought. *It must be nice to have that many friends.*

The DJ had the party rocking. People were tearing up the dance floor. Others were talking, eating the generous Thanksgiving food, playing games, or making out. As I walked into the room, people stared at me and I suddenly wanted to hide under a rock. Stacey spotted me and luckily came over to save me before I died of embarrassment.

"Amina! You finally came back. I thought I was going to have to come drag you out of the house," she said as she pulled me over towards a group of her friends.

"Everyone's staring at me," I said nervously. "Do I have something on my face?"

Stacey laughed. "They're staring at you because you're a complete baddie. Also, because you're Ethan's mate and the new Luna. Trust me, it's a good stare."

"The new what?" I asked in surprise, but Stacey ignored that question and started introducing me to the three girls she'd been standing with. I didn't even catch their names as I reflected on what she'd just said. Suddenly I heard a lot of gasps coming from behind me. I noticed a lot of people had stopped and were staring at the door. I turned around and I gasped also. I'd never been so surprised in my entire life.

Ethan had just walked in, and he looked hot! I mean, he was hot before, but training had completely buffed him up. He'd gotten a tan and he had muscles bulging in all the right places. He seemed taller. His hair was a little longer and it casually fell around his face making him look like some sexy magazine model. He was wearing a button down shirt that was only buttoned up three-quarters of the way so I could see his chest. It slipped my mind for a few seconds that he was my mate. I was staring at him in heat just like all the other females in the room.

Surprise, he projected to me as he laid eyes on me. I saw his eyes stretch a bit as he looked me up and down. *Fuck, you look hot,* he said. My body finally thawed, and I ran to him and wrapped my arms around him. He picked me up and I planted a kiss on him that I'm sure made everyone jealous. I could feel eyes piercing us, but I didn't care. I was happy to see my mate after being apart from him for so long.

"What are you doing here?" I asked. "I mean, I'm glad you're here, but your training—"

"I got a night off," he said as he smiled at me like I was the only girl in the room. "The whole night." He winked at me, and I understood what he meant. I couldn't wait to leave the party.

Ethan put me down and grabbed my hand. We walked over to Stacey and her friends, and I noticed the sly smile on her face. "Did you know about this?" I asked Stacey.

"Of course I did," she said. "Ethan made me promise to keep it a secret." I should have known something was up when she was pushing me to get the dress.

"This is such a surprise," I said, "and on *your* birthday! Thanks."

"Don't mention it," she said. Just then, a guy came over to Stacey with a small box.

"Hey, Stacey," he said. "I know there's a gift table, but I wanted to give this to you personally." He handed her the box, and all the girls kind went "oooh" and "aww". "You don't have to open it now if you don't want to, but I was kinda hoping the gesture would be enough to get a dance with you."

Stacey looked at me and I shrugged. "Go fish," I said. She smiled, handed one of her friends the box, and took off with the guy.

"C'mon," said Ethan as he pulled me to the dance floor.

"What? Wait, in front of all these people? I can't dance," I said as I tried to resist but there really was no way for me to resist anything from Ethan with him exuding all that sex appeal.

"It will be fine. No one's watching," he said.

"Are you kidding me? Literally everyone is watching!" I said. Ethan just shrugged and pulled me to the dance floor anyway. I felt incredibly shy, but I didn't want to embarrass him, so I decided to try the dancing thing. I moved along to the music cautiously, but Ethan suddenly shook me, then twirled me around.

I gasped. "Get out of your head about it," he said as he wildly danced around me. To my surprise, he was a terrible dancer and that made me feel so much better. I laughed as I watched him, then I relaxed and danced wildly with him. After a few minutes, I'd forgotten about being watched and I was completely enthralled and having fun.

After a few songs, a few drinks, an incident where Ethan shoved a guy for looking at me, and a lot of socializing with Ethan's and Stacey's friends who were apparently also my friends now, Ethan left me to use the bathroom. I went to the bar to get another drink and waited there for Ethan to come back. It seemed to be taking a long time for him to get back, so I scanned the room for him and froze when I spotted him.

There were three girls standing around him in a half-circle. I saw the uncomfortable look on his face as one of the girls attempted to throw her arms around him. He leaned back and pushed her away. When he did, I recognized the face immediately. Caroline Bancroft.

It wasn't until that moment that I became aware of how fast I could really move. Before my mind could catch up, my body had already made its way over to them and I pushed her hard. "Get your crusty hands off my mate!" I shouted as she landed on the floor with a "thud".

People around us stopped in their tracks and stared in surprise and curiosity. Tinsley and Jessica scurried over to help her up off the floor. Ethan grabbed me by the waist and pulled me back.

"Amina, I didn't mean—" Caroline started as she held her arm where she'd landed on it.

"—yes, you did and if you try that again, I'll do a lot more than push you," I yelled.

C'mon, let's go. No need to fight at my sister's party Ethan projected to me as he pulled me away from Caroline and her lackies. I thought he was mad at me, and I was about to apologize, but then he projected to me *that was so fucking sexy. I think it's time for us to go home.*

Ethan led me out of the Alpha's house towards our house. We couldn't help but smile at each other as we both thought about what was going to happen when we got home.

...

I was hard by the time we walked in the house I felt like I was going to burst out of my pants. I closed the door, grabbed Amina, and ripped her dress down the front revealing the black lingerie she was wearing. That was a pleasant surprise, and it ignited me even more.

"Ethan! What—" she started but I planted a tongue-twisting kiss on her to shut her up.

"I'll buy you another one," I said as I planted another kiss on her. I put my fingers in her curls, grabbed her hair, and pulled her head back as I kissed her. She moaned in surprise and excitement. I missed her. I needed her. After being away from her so long, her scent was like a drug that I was having withdrawals from.

When I gave her a moment to take a breath, she looked at me with lust in her eyes. "I don't know what's gotten into you, but I like it," she managed to say before I stuck my tongue in her mouth again. We clumsily made our way to the bedroom while still kissing each other. I pulled the tattered remains of her dress off and I took off my shirt. She stepped back and gasped. *Fuck, do I have scars?*

"Ethan...you've been working out. A lot," she said as she looked at me like I was a side of beef.

"Yeah, training's been intense. Do you like what you see?" I asked.

"I love it," she said in a breathy voice. She looked so sexy standing there in her lingerie and heels. I'd never seen her like that, but I decided I would see her like that a lot more in the future. She walked over to me and put her hands on my chest. She let them trail around my pecs and down my arms. Her touch was almost too much for me to handle. I was about to grab her and throw her on the bed when she stopped me.

"Ethan...I want to..." she trailed off.

"What?" I asked. She gulped and looked down at my crotch. Then she got on her knees and started unbuckling my pants. *Oh...you want to...oh...are you really going to?* I projected to her. She looked up at me with a naughtiness in her eyes that made my heart race.

I've never done it before, but I'm going to try, she projected back. Then she parted her beautiful lips and wrapped them around my manhood. The feeling was immediate and intense and it made me jump. My toes curled as she bobbed her head back and forth. I threw my head back as pleasure swept over my body. "Oh baby, you're a natural," I said as I put my fingers in her hair again. Amina pleased me for almost five minutes which was impressive for her first time.

"My jaws hurt. I'm sorry," she said as she wiped the corners of her mouth.

"No, no, you were great," I said. I helped her off the floor and kissed her. Then I picked her up and took her to the bed. "My turn."

I laid Amina down and slipped off her lace underwear. I could tell she was nervous. I was too but I hoped it didn't show. I'd never done what I was about to do. I parted her legs and kissed her gently down there. Then I attempted to do what I'd seen guys do in porn movies, hoping I was doing it right. Amina moaned. *Is that a good moan or a bad one?*

It's definitely good, she projected. *It's so good. It's better than good.*

I kept going and she kept moaning. Then she started wriggling around a bit and moaning louder. I went faster and she grabbed my hair. "Oh, Ethan, don't stop," she said. Suddenly she yelled out and her body bucked and shivered.

I couldn't wait anymore. I got on top of her and inserted myself into her sweet honeypot, making her whimper in pleasure as I sank as far into her as I could go. The way she wrapped her arms around my neck as I moved inside of her drove me wild. I don't know how long I was inside of her, but I stayed until I couldn't take it anymore. I emptied my seed feeling all the stress of the last few weeks melt away. Then I collapsed on the bed next to her.

"You really missed me," she said.

"You missed me too," I replied. We both laughed. "We definitely took things to the next level. I'm looking forward to more of that," I said.

"Me too." Her tone changed on the next statement. "Ethan, you didn't cover up."

"Are you mad?" I asked.

"No, of course not. I'm just concerned. I can't get pregnant right now," she said.

"You're right, baby. It's just hard to control myself when you're so fucking sexy," I said. "I love feeling you."

"I love it too, but it's just too soon. There are things that we need to do, and I can't be pregnant when we do them," she said.

I sat up and looked at her. I almost got distracted from the conversation as I looked at her boobs. I closed my eyes and tried to focus. "What things? What are you talking about?"

"Well, you'll be Alpha soon and I'm hoping we can find my uncle then," she said. That statement got my full attention.

"Amina, we talked about this—"

"—yes we did, and you agreed that when the time was right, we'd find him," she said as she propped herself up on her elbows. "You're not going back on what you said, are you?"

"No, I'm not but—"

"—but nothing, Ethan. If we're going to find my uncle, I can't be pregnant," she said.

"Amina, you won't be going to look for you uncle," I said. "I'm not letting you anywhere near the forbidden mountains."

"Ethan, I—"

"—you're not going to those mountains, pregnant or not and that's the end of the discussion," I said forcefully as I got up.

"Ethan, that's not fair. This is *my* uncle we're talking about here. You have a whole family here. He's my only family."

I couldn't believe she'd said that. "What are the kids and I? We're not your family?"

"That's not what I meant. You know that's not what I meant," she said. "Ethan, I don't want this to turn into an argument. Please."

"Then let's drop the subject," I said. I sat on the edge of the bed and sighed. "I'm sorry I haven't been here for the four of you. I know it hasn't been easy."

"No, it hasn't," she said quietly.

"Especially when you have to do it alone. I'm sorry about that," I said. "It wasn't supposed to be this way. I appreciate how you're staying positive about this, and I swear I'll make it up to you after training is over."

"I know you will, sweetheart." She'd never called me that before, but I liked the way she said it. I leaned over and kissed her again.

"Your family...I mean, our family has been a big help, so I'm not exactly alone. Speaking of family, maybe we should go get the babies now," she said. "I'm sure they miss their daddy."

As we got up to head to the bathroom, I pulled Amina to me. "Listen to me, baby. I will find your uncle. I promise, okay? I will reunite the two of you. You just have to trust me. Please don't put yourself in danger. Promise me you won't."

She sighed. "Okay. I promise," she said. I hugged her tightly, then we went into the bathroom and showered together. That was a bad idea because we ended up making love in the shower and taking almost 45 more minutes to get the babies. At least that time I didn't finish inside of her.

We finally got ourselves together and headed back to the house. It was late when we got there, and the party was over. The servants were cleaning up and my siblings were nowhere to be found.

"There you are," said my mother as we walked into the room she had turned into a nursery. "I was beginning to wonder if the triplets were spending the night." She looked at her watch. "Hmm, three o'clock. Seems they have spent the night."

"I'm so sorry for being late Rose," said Amina. "I didn't mean to dump them on you like that." Rose waved her hand in a motion that meant *no problem.*

"Thank you for everything, Mom," I said. I gave her a big hug as Amina gently put the triplets in their stroller. Henry woke up and started to cry when Amina picked him up.

"Here, let me," I said. I walked over to them and held my son for the first time in weeks. I prayed that he hadn't forgotten who I was. "I'll carry him home," I said as I rocked him to soothe him. We thanked my mom again, said our goodbyes and headed back to our house to get settled in for the few hours I had left with them before I had to go back to training.

25

He Loves Me

Ethan would be furious if he found out what I was doing. I couldn't help myself. He hired a nanny a week ago to help me with the triplets and Rose and Stacey went on a two-week mother-daughter trip, so I suddenly had all this time on my hands. Perhaps I should have learned a new skill or taken up a new hobby. Instead, I decided to break Ethan's trust by going out to the forbidden mountains. As I approached the place where Ethan had defended me that long night ago, an inner voice told me to go back before it was too late. Unfortunately, another inner voice, a louder one, told me to keep pushing forward, that this was the only way I'd ever meet my uncle.

I knew Ethan loved me and that he would do anything for me. I knew he had every intention of finding my uncle for me one day and ending my uncle's servitude, but he had no idea how long that would take. What if my uncle died before then? I'd never get to know him and I'd never get answers. I just couldn't take that chance any longer.

I stood at the edge of the pack territory as my conscience debated itself. I decided to sit down right at the entrance of the valley and think. I faced the dark woods, suddenly taking in the stark contrast of the color of the pack's territory versus that of the woods. The pack's territory was bright and vibrant. The grass was strikingly green, even in December, and the sky was a magnificent blue. I looked around at the beautiful winter flowers that sprinkled the field and listened to the chorus of insects that called the field their home. Then I looked back at the valley. It was various shades of grey and black. The ground, the trees, and the vegetation were all dark as if the area had been burned, but the trees and plants weren't dead. There was an unnaturally straight line that separated the colors of the valley from those of the pack territory. *Hmm, I* thought. *There should be a gradual shift from the bright colors to the dull, dark colors of the valley. Something's strange about this. How did I not notice this before?*

I decided to worry about that another day. On this day, my priority was my uncle. I stood up and took a couple of steps forward. My shoes were just touching the edge of the woods. *Should I call for him? Maybe that's a safer way to get his attention.*

"Uncle?" I said weakly. *Don't be silly, Amina. He can't hear that.* I decided to get a little louder. "Uncle?" I called out. "It's me...Amina. Well, that's the name I go by."

There was no response, but I suddenly smelled something...something not quite right. Something bad. Something dark. *A bad wolf?* I thought. Panic started rising in me. Suddenly I heard a distant growl. I froze and goosebumps popped up all over my arms. I heard a twig snap, then I heard different growl followed by a lot of twigs snapping. My body finally started moving and I realized I was running back into the pack territory as fast as I could. I kept running until I was completely out of breath then I finally stopped and let myself look back. Nothing was following me. I caught my breath and went home.

As bad as that first experience was, I did the same thing for the next three days. Some days I'd hear the growls and the twigs snapping. Other days I'd hear nothing. On the fourth day, I decided to go into the woods.

I only went in about five yards and stopped. I felt I was still close enough to the pack's territory to make a run for it if I needed to. I gathered my wits and called out for my uncle. A few seconds went by, and I smelled the bad scent again. I was certain by that point it was one of the bad wolves. I started backing up when I suddenly saw a pair of glowing eyes staring at me. That's when I noticed the sharp teeth of the wolf as he bared them at me. *Shit, I'm going to die,* I thought. *Ethan doesn't deserve this. Why didn't I listen?*

Suddenly one of the largest wolves I'd ever seen in my life stepped in between me and the glowing eyes. I was so scared I hadn't even heard the wolf approaching, nor did I smell him. He growled at the other wolf and the wolf retreated back into the woods. He turned to face me and for a second I was scared out of my mind, but as I looked into his eyes, I realized he meant me no harm. I took a deep breath. "Uncle?" I said quietly.

The wolf huffed, walked towards me, and nudged me back towards the field so hard I almost lost my balance. "Okay, okay. I get it!" I turned around and made my way back to the light with the wolf right on my heels. Once we reached the field, the wolf shifted into a very large man.

Before I could say anything, he said, "don't *ever* come back here." I was surprised at his lack of manners. He turned to walk back towards the woods.

"Wait!" I shouted. "Please. Please talk to me." He kept walking and I could see he was about to shift back to his wolf form.

"Uncle, wait! If you don't talk to me, I'll come back here every day until you do," I said. He stopped. "Please, just talk to me. I've waited so long..."

He sighed deeply. Without turning to face me, he asked, "do you realize you're putting your life in danger? I'm trying to protect you."

"I know and I appreciate everything, but...please. You're the only family I have. You're the only connection I have to my parents and my old life."

"You shouldn't worry about your old life," he said. "It's better this way."

I felt tears coming to my eyes. This wasn't the reunion I was hoping for. "Do you know how hard it's been? Being treated like an outcast my entire life? Growing up thinking that no one in the world loved me? Now I find out I have one remaining family member, and you want nothing to do with me. I feel like an outcast all over again." Tears trickled down my cheeks.

"I have to stay here—" he started.

"—I know, the servitude and all. I know, but can't you just talk to me for a few minutes? Please? Just allow me to ask some questions?"

He sighed again, but this time he turned to me. He stood there silently. I assumed he was waiting for my questions.

"Okay. First question. What were my parents' names?" I asked.

"Telling you that could put your life in danger," he responded.

"Well, where am I from?"

"That answer could put your life in danger also," he responded.

"I need to know something about myself!" I shouted. "Anything, please!"

"All you need to know is that...you've never been alone," he said. To my surprise, he walked over to me and hugged me. I don't know what came over me. It was a wave of emotions I'd never felt before, not even with Ethan and Ethan hugged me all the time. Tears fell from my eyes as I squeezed his massive body as tightly as I could. He tried to let me go, but I didn't want to let him go. I used all my strength to hold on to him.

"Don't go," I said through my sobs. "Just stay for a little while."

"I can't," he said. "I need to be in there protecting you." He broke my embrace, and I realized that he was only obliging my hug. My meager strength compared to his was never actually holding him in place.

He backed away from me, turned, shifted, and ran back into the valley. I turned and headed towards home. I eventually found a way to stop crying before I got into town. I didn't want anyone asking me questions. As I got close to home, I could hear Ethan projecting to me. *Where are you? What's wrong, Amina. Talk to me.*

Crap! Did I forget to block him out on my way home? I knew Ethan was going to demand answers. I wouldn't be able to lie to him and he was going to be mad. *I'm coming home,* I projected back. *I just went on a walk.* That wasn't a lie. I just didn't tell him what I did on the walk.

Before I even got all the way to the house, I saw Ethan come out the door. I sighed and prepared for the argument that was coming. To my surprise, when I reached him, he pulled me to him and gave me a big hug, squeezing me almost as tightly as my uncle did. That sent another wave of emotions through me and before I knew it I was sobbing onto Ethan's shirt.

"Amina, I told you not to go into the forbidden mountains," he said sternly, but not stern enough that I felt he was scolding me. "You could have been hurt or killed."

I looked at him in shame, feeling the guilt swirling in me. "How do you know?" I asked.

"I can smell him on you," he said. *Ugh. Freaking wolf senses. I can't hide anything.*

"I know you're mad at me for breaking my promise," I said.

"I'm not mad," he said. He paused. "Okay, maybe I am mad, but I'm more concerned about you right now. What happened?"

"I...he...he hugged me," I said as I sniffled and attempted to get control of my crying. "He loves me. I could feel it."

"Yeah, baby, I know he does," said Ethan. "C'mon. Let's go inside and talk more."

Ethan grabbed my hand and as we walked to the door, it suddenly hit me that Ethan smelled like an animal, and he had a bruise on his cheek. His hair was ruffled, and he was limping. I stopped him. "Ethan, have you been in a fight?" I asked.

He blushed. "I forgot how rough I look right now. It's nothing, really."

I crossed my arms. "What were you doing? I thought you were training," I said.

"I was. I felt your...I don't even know what it was because you were so far away. I just felt that you weren't okay, and it must have been a pretty strong feeling for me to sense it that far away, so I just dashed out to find you."

"You abandoned training? Won't you get in trouble?" I asked.

"Probably, but we can worry about that later. C'mon." He grabbed my arm and attempted to pull me, but I stayed put.

"Ethan, you look like you got your ass kicked. You haven't been honest with me about your training," I said. I narrowed my eyes as I looked at him.

"And you haven't been honest with me about your whereabouts," replied Ethan. "Seems we both have some explaining to do."

"Yeah," I agreed.

"Go inside," he said. "I need to make a quick phone call to let my father know where I am. I'll be right behind you."

I nodded and went inside to wait for him so we could have a talk.

When Ethan came in, we stared at each other for a moment. "I'll start," he said. Then he took off his shirt. I stared at Ethan's body in horror. There were bruises all over his sides and arms. There was a knot protruding from his side. I was pretty sure it was one of his ribs. He looked like he'd been beaten with a bat.

"I have to fight a lot in training. That's why I don't come home more often. I knew you'd react like this. I was trying to protect you," he said. He dropped his head, almost as if he were ashamed of his next statement. "This...was a good day. There were some days that were much, much worse."

I threw my hands up. "My Goddess, you're always trying to protect me from everything! Did you ever stop to think that maybe I would want to be there for you sometimes?"

"No, I didn't," he said.

"Ethan, I've been raising the babies alone because you're keeping secrets from me. That's not okay."

"You're right. I shouldn't have kept this from you, but you were keeping secrets from me also. How many times have you been out there? Were you even going to tell me that you were going into the forbidden mountains?" he yelled back.

"I only went in the woods once," I said. "I mean, I went to the edge of the territory a few times, but I only actually left the territory once."

Ethan scoffed. "Fuck, Amina! You could have been killed. Is that what you want? To leave the babies without their mother? What if I had to come find you? What if I had to fight a bunch of evil wolves and I had gotten killed. Then the babies wouldn't have either of their parents! Is that what you want? For them to go through what you went through?"

That stopped me cold. He was right. I'd never considered that. The thought that my children could have grown up alone like me because I made the selfish decision to go into the forbidden mountains made me cry.

"I'm sorry. I didn't think about that," I said as I sat down. "I didn't mean to…"

Ethan took a deep breath. "I told you to wait. Why do you think I'm doing all of this? Why do you think I'm getting beat to a pulp every day? I'm learning to fight. I'm getting stronger. I'm gaining the power of an Alpha so I can protect you and the babies!"

"You keep saying that Ethan and I'm starting to get the feeling that you're not talking about those mangy wolves in the woods. My uncle said something similar. What are you guys talking about? Are the Shadow Walkers coming?" I demanded. "If you all would stop hiding things from me, I wouldn't need to take matters into my own hands!"

"My father has been teaching me…well, everything, and Amina, for your safety there are some things that can't be answered," he said. That made me furious.

"That's a bunch of bullshit and you know it!" I saw a look of surprise come across Ethan's face and, honestly, I surprised myself. I'd never spoken to anyone that way before. I recoiled a bit, mostly because I had screamed so loud that Hunter started crying in the other room.

"I got him," yelled Eloise. I'd forgotten all about the nanny as Ethan and I were arguing. *Was she listening? Did she hear everything*? I wondered briefly before my attention returned to the argument.

"Stop hiding information about me! This is my life and my past. I deserve to know!" I yelled at him. "Stop treating me like some child!"

"Amina, lower your voice! You're scaring the kids," he demanded. I decided to lower my voice because he was right, but I wasn't yielding my position.

"This conversation is over until you decide to be honest with me," I said as I pushed past him to walk out of the room.

"Where are you going?" he asked. "You better not be going back to the forbidden mountains—"

"—or what?" I snapped back at him. "What are you going to do?" Ethan didn't say anything, so I left the room and walked to the front door. When I opened the door, there were two guys standing outside of it. They turned to face me and quickly stepped in front of it to block my exit.

"What are you doing—" I started.

"—they're here by my command," Ethan said from behind me.

"What are you talking about?" I demanded as I turned to him.

"They're here to ensure you don't go anywhere you're not supposed to," he said. As realization sank in, all I could do was stare at Ethan with my mouth open. "I hate this, Amina. I don't want you to feel...trapped or whatever, but you've broken my trust. I have to finish training which means I can't be here, so these guys are here to make sure you and the babies are safe."

"You mean they're here to make sure I don't go anywhere," I said.

"You can go places. You just can't leave the pack territory," he said.

"Ethan, you're kidding me!" I shouted. "You're...you can't do this! I don't want those guys following me everywhere. What if I want to go out of town or something? You can't just force me to stay here! My Goddess, it's 2023. People don't do that sort of thing anymore."

"Amina, you've left me with no choice. It seems every time I turn my back, you...go somewhere you shouldn't be. You run right into danger. Now, I have to think about our kids. They need you." Then, he said quietly, "I need you."

There was an awkward silence between us for a moment. "Look, I'll tell the guys that you can go out of town if you want, but you absolutely will not go anywhere near the forbidden mountains. That's final," he said. He walked over to me and tried to kiss me, but I turned my face away. I could feel sadness emanating from him. I could feel that doing this to me hurt him, but it hurt me more.

"Your training for the Alpha position seems to be going well. Congratulations," I said. "You're becoming more and more like Alpha Roland every day." I knew that statement hurt him. In fact, that's why I said it. I wiggled away from him, went into the bedroom and slammed the door behind me.

I love you, Amina. I'm sorry it has to be this way, Ethan projected to me before he left. I heard the door close, and a flood of tears dropped out of my eyes as I sobbed on the bed alone. *How will I talk to my uncle now?* I wondered. I was getting the feeling that Ethan had no intention of ever getting my uncle out of the valley. *Surely he wouldn't lie to me, would he? He's my mate. He wouldn't do that.*

I took some time to get myself together. I decided to take a short nap because that's all I could do those days, then play with the babies for a little while as Eloise cleaned up the house. I thought about how only a year ago I was planning a life alone yet here I was—a mate, a mother, and apparently a prisoner. At least, that's how I felt. I was incredibly angry, but more than that I was hurt. I was surrounded by people who loved and cared for me, but I'd never felt more alone. It's like Ethan didn't understand how I felt. He didn't get how this situation with my uncle plagued me and kept me from sleeping. Honestly, how could he? His perfect family was all well and protected.

It was time for Eloise to go home for the evening, so I dismissed her and decided to take the babies out for a short stroll before it got too dark. I opened the door and stepped outside to be greeted by the two prison guards that Ethan had left with me. I paused, gave them my best angry stare, and said, "stay out of my way." Then I pushed the stroller along and they fell in line right behind me.

I walked towards the driveway, intending to head to the park which happened to be in the same direction that the forbidden mountains were. We were nowhere near the mountains of course, being that the Alpha's property was right in the middle of town, but for some reason, one of the guys must have thought that's where I was going because he suddenly said, "you can't go that way, ma'am." I ignored him and kept walking.

He did something that, to my surprise, set me off dramatically. He stepped up beside me and put his hand on the stroller to stop me from walking. "You can't go that way, ma'am. Ethan's orders," he said.

I don't know what happened. I felt a surge of anger I'd never felt before. Not only was he taking away my freedom, but he had the audacity to touch my babies' stroller. The moment the word "orders" left his mouth, my body reacted faster than my mind did. I lifted him up and threw him at least fifteen feet. He crashed into a fence, which was made of wrought iron, and his body broke through it like it was made of toothpicks. When he landed on the other side, he didn't move.

I gasped as I realized what had just happened. I looked at the other guy. He put his hands up indicating he didn't want me to do that to him, then he ran over to the poor guy I'd just possibly killed. "I'm sorry. I don't know what happened. I don't know how I did that," I called to him. I ran over to them. The guy I had thrown was still breathing, but I could tell he was badly injured.

"I'm going to have to report this to Ethan," he said. He seemed nervous as he said it, like I would attack him.

"I'm really sorry," I said as I felt myself starting to cry. "I didn't mean to."

I stood there helplessly as he called Ethan. There was just no way the day could get any worse.

26

Social Media Post

"What did you do!" Alpha Roland roared at me as I sat helplessly at the dining room table. It was less of a question and more of an accusation.

"Dad, stop yelling at her like that!" Ethan screamed at him.

"Ethan, she almost killed one of our fighters! One of our *trained* fighters," he said to Ethan. Then to me, "how the hell did you do that! Tell me right now!"

"I...I don't know! I swear I didn't mean to. Please Alpha—"

"—Dad, stop it right now!" shouted Ethan so loud that both me and the Alpha froze. "Can't you see she's scared? She doesn't know any more than we do!" To my surprise, the Alpha stopped yelling at me. We all took a beat.

Ethan sat beside me and held my hands. "Baby, tell me exactly what happened," he said. I nodded, wiped my face, and took in a deep breath.

"Like I said before, I just wanted to go on a walk. I was so angry after our fight. He put his hand on the stroller and...I don't know, I just didn't want him to touch the stroller," I said.

"And you threw him through the fence?" Ethan asked.

"Through an iron fence," the Alpha added. Ethan gave him a glance that said "silence". The Alpha got quiet again.

"I didn't mean to. I mean, I just wanted him to get away from us. I don't know how I did that. I really don't," I said. "Ethan, you have to believe me."

"I do," he said. He wiped tears from my cheeks and kissed me on my forehead. Then he stood up and faced his father. "I think I know what's going on," he said.

"You do?" both the Alpha and I said in unison.

"Amina is from the Night Guardian pack, right?" Apparently it was a rhetorical question because Ethan kept talking. "Well, you've seen her uncle. He's huge and more powerful than any wolf we've ever met, characteristic of their pack, right? I think Amina shares that strength."

I was speechless. The Alpha was not.

"That uh, makes a lot of sense," Alpha Roland said. "Everyone knows the Night Guardians were excessively strong which is why they were such a revered pack of protectors. If she shares that DNA...but why is it showing up now?" he asked. "Wouldn't we have known about this a long time ago?"

"Not really," said Ethan. "Amina's...never really stood up for herself." He dropped his head. I have no doubt he was recalling all the times he bullied me. Considering what happened, it's good for Ethan that I didn't stand up to him.

"Well, there was that one time..." I said. "I tried to tell you about it, but—"

"—but I didn't listen," he said. He slapped his forehead. "I'm sorry Amina." I just shrugged.

"So, your mate has the strength of a Night Guardian?" The Alpha scoffed. "She needs to be one of our warriors."

I think the Alpha was joking, but Ethan didn't take it as a joke. He glared at his father. "Why? So she can go fight evil wolves in the mountains for the next fifteen years?"

"You know I didn't mean it like that," said Alpha Roland. "Don't start, Ethan."

"Don't tell me not to start when you started this an hour ago," said Ethan.

"Actually, your mate started it when she destroyed my fence with a body," replied the Alpha.

"Guys, please!" I shouted. "Please, no more arguing. How is the guy? Is he going to be okay?"

"You really messed him up," said Alpha Roland. "You broke most of his spine, his hip, and one of his legs. He'll regenerate, but it's going to take a while."

"Stop being so dramatic," Ethan said to his father. "Amina, he'll be fine in about a week. We're done here. I'm taking Amina home."

"No, we aren't done here," said the Alpha but Ethan helped me up anyway.

"Dad, it's over. Amina's strong. We know it now. Now we have to tend to our children." Ethan led me out of the room. We got the babies and went home.

"I was going to the park," I said as we got the babies settled. "I swear, I wasn't going to the forbidden mountains. The guy overreacted. I just needed some fresh air."

"I know you weren't going to the forbidden mountains. You might not care about your safety, but I know you'd never put the babies in danger," he replied.

"I care about my safety," I said.

"Yeah, sure," Ethan responded sarcastically. "Listen, forget about what happened today. Don't tell anyone," he said. "We need to keep this a secret until we can find out more about you and your people. I'll order the men to keep it a secret also."

"Order the men," I repeated. "I didn't get to say it because I was mad before, but you giving orders...it's kinda sexy."

"You think so? Great, come show me how sexy you think it is," he said. We went to bed and enjoyed our night together, making up for our earlier argument. Then I settled into Ethan's warm, strong arms. I missed doing that so much. Being in his arms seemed like the safest place on Earth. I fell asleep feeling happy and stress-free. It was good that we were able to get that quality time together because the next day, all hell broke loose.

We woke up to the sound of both of our phones ringing at the same time. "What time is it?" groaned Ethan as he reached for his phone. I reached for mine and saw that it was Stacey calling me. It was six in the morning.

"Hello," we both said at the same time.

Stacey's shrill voice filled my ears so rapidly I couldn't quite make out everything she was saying. I suddenly heard Ethan loudly say, "what!" There was panic in his voice, and he threw the covers back and hopped out of bed. Stacey was saying something about a video.

"Stacey, wait, wait. Can you start over?" I asked as I sat up.

"The video on social media! It's going viral!" she exclaimed. "Dad is pissed."

"What video? What are you talking about?" I asked.

"Someone recorded you throwing that guy through the fence!" she said.

That dragged me right out of my grogginess. "What! Are you serious. Oh Goddess, please tell me you aren't serious."

Ethan looked at me as he held the phone to his ear. "Dad, slow down," he was saying. "Dad. Dad!" He left the room.

"Amina, I didn't know you were that strong. Holy crap, girl! You've been holding out on me!" said Stacey.

"I didn't know it either. It caught me by surprise," I said. "Stacey, who posted the video?"

"I don't know, but Dad's going to get to the bottom of it," she said.

I could hear Ethan talking to his Dad in the other room and I could tell the conversation wasn't a good one. Then came a knock on our door. I heard Ethan say, "Dad? Is that you?" I already knew the answer to the question, and I wanted to just shoot myself and get it over with before I had to face him.

"Stacey, I'll have to call you back," I said. I hung up before she could say anything else. Then I quickly threw on some clothes and joined Ethan and his father in the living room.

"Do you understand how bad this is? This compromises the pack's safety," yelled his father as I entered the foyer.

"I know, Dad. I'm going to find the person who posted it so they can take it down," said Ethan. He almost sounded defeated as he tried to talk sense into his father. No, he sounded tired.

"It's already viral, Ethan. The wrong people could have seen it by now. I don't think you get it—"

"—I get it, Dad!" yelled Ethan. "You literally beat it into my head every day."

Alpha Roland looked at me and there was so much anger in his eyes. He was about to yell at me, but Ethan stepped in front of him. "Don't direct your anger at Amina. It's not her fault. She didn't post the video," he said.

"She may as well have," Alpha Roland shouted back. He took a beat, then he said, "the person who posted this will pay with their life!"

"Dad, lower your voice," said Ethan. You're going to wake up the babies. Also, stop being so dramatic. We aren't going to kill someone over a social media post."

"Ethan, I'm beginning to think you'll never understand the hard decisions you have to make as an Alpha," said Alpha Roland.

"I understand just fine," said Ethan. He looked at me, then turned back to his father. "Dad, if I'm going to be the Alpha, I have to handle things my way. Let me handle this."

Alpha Roland grunted and gave Ethan a stern look. Then he turned and left out of the front door, slamming the door behind him. When he did that, Hazel and Henry started crying.

"Oh, great," I said as I headed towards the babies' room. I went to comfort the babies, but my mind wasn't on them. All I could think about was how I was no longer invisible in the pack, and maybe in the world. I felt so exposed, and the worst part of the situation was that some inner voice was telling me that things were about to get worse before they got better.

...

"Please, Ethan! I'm sorry! I just needed more followers. I didn't mean to get your mate in trouble," said Samuel. Samuel had always been obsessed with social media ever since I'd known him. In school he was always shooting videos and taking photos. *When he wasn't dodging me and my boys,* I thought to myself as I recalled all the times I'd bullied him.

"I was almost at two million followers, and I knew this video would catapult me over that number. I mean, look. I'm almost at three million now! I didn't think it through. I'm so sorry. Please have mercy on me," he said. "I'm taking it down right now. Look, see? It's gone." Samuel looked up at me with pleading eyes from the spot that Jabari and Gabe had thrown him to when they dragged him into the room. He held his phone up with a shaky hand as he cowered before Amina and me on his knees.

I was furious with Samuel, but I didn't want to fight him over the social media post. I knew that's what my father was expecting, but I didn't want to be that kind of Alpha. After all, no one knew about Amina's secret past, or the dangers of the Shadow Walkers so how could he have known how much trouble that post could bring? Had the pack known the truth, they'd know the dangers, so I felt that ultimately, it was my father's fault. Still, I knew there had to be some type of consequence for his actions. As the up and coming Alpha, I couldn't allow the pack to think I was weak.

"Give me your phone," I said as I snatched it away. I went to each one of his social media accounts and deleted them as well as all the photos and videos in his phone. I handed it back to him and when he realized what I'd done, he looked like he was going to have a heart attack.

"You didn't! Ethan! I've been working on those accounts for years! That's how I was helping my parents with their bills! What are we going to do now?" he started crying and I felt horrible like I was still bullying him.

"You should have thought of that before you posted a video of my mate without my permission," I said. "Be thankful that I'm not punishing you worse than that. Consider your intact bones as mercy." Then to Jabari and Gabe I said, "get him out of here." They each grabbed one of his arms and dragged him out of the room.

I called my father, hoping that he'd calmed down from our earlier encounter. "Dad, it's done. The video has been removed," I said.

My father took a few moments to respond. "Ethan, you need to get over here right away," he said. "I'm in the meeting room." Then he hung up. I looked at the phone in confusion. *I guess he's still angry*, I thought. I prepared myself for a possible fight as I headed towards the meeting room.

A few minutes later, I stepped into the room and froze in absolute shock as I stared into the face of Pax. "What's going on here?" I asked. "What are you doing here?"

"You!" he said. "What did you do?" He suddenly lunged at me. My father as well as our Beta, Luke, jumped in between us to hold Pax back. "All these years Amina has been safe and now her life is in danger because of you Generation Z brats and your social media—"

"—now wait a minute!" shouted my father. "Ethan had nothing to do with this! This happened because your niece threw one of our men through a fence!"

"She wouldn't have had to do that if she weren't being treated like a prisoner," he growled as he stared at me.

"You're kidding, right? You told me to keep her away from you, so that's what I was doing. If you would have just been honest with her in the first place—"

"—so, you're trying to say it's my fault?" he growled.

"Stop it, both of you!" yelled Luke. "This is everyone's fault. The whole thing has been handled...poorly. From the beginning." He glared at Pax.

"Someone tell me what the hell is going on right now!" I yelled. "Pax, why are you here?"

My father took a deep breath. "We're in trouble, Ethan. That video..." he shook his head and turned away.

"It attracted the attention of the wrong people. Now the Shadow Walkers know that we're alive," said Pax. I fought two of them this morning. More will come. I came to warn you and to take my...Amina to safety."

"You can't leave!" shouted my father. "We held up our end of the bargain and you're sworn to protect us for life!"

"Your end of the bargain was to keep her safe. She's no longer safe so the deal is off," growled Pax.

"What are we supposed to do?" asked Luke. I could see the concern in his eyes. "You know we can't stand up to the Shadow Walkers and we wouldn't be in this mess if you hadn't shown up in our territory!"

"You're not taking Amina anywhere," I said. "She's my mate and the mother of my children. She stays with me."

"Weakling. As if you could stop me," said Pax.

"Do you want to find out?" I growled back at him.

"Pax, you will not touch my son," said my father as he stood in his fighter stance.

"Dammit, stop it!" yelled Luke. "I'm a Beta in a room full of Alphas and I'm the only one acting like an Alpha! We can't fight with each other right now and we can't run. We have a serious problem here and we have to handle this together!"

We all stopped and looked at him in confusion. "What do you mean a room full of Alphas?" asked my father. Pax closed his eyes and frowned, and Luke smacked himself on the forehead.

Pax sighed. "I've truly put my trust in the wrong people." He took in a deep breath. "I was the Alpha of the Night Guardians."

That revelation left my father and I speechless. I looked at Luke. He didn't look surprised. "You knew about this?" I asked Luke.

"Yeah, I did. You have to understand—"

"—understand that *my* Beta lied to me!" yelled my father.

"If you're the Alpha of the Night Guardians—" I started.

"—was—" Pax said.

"—does that mean Amina is *your* daughter? Or is she still your niece? Who is she to you," I demanded, "and no more lies! That's what got us here in the first place."

"She's my daughter," said Pax grimly. "The lies were meant to protect her. To keep her identity a secret. Other than me, she's the only remaining member of the Night Guardian pack. She had to survive."

I was furious, but even more than that, I was sad. Amina was going to feel so betrayed when I once again had to tell her that these same people were still lying to her. "All of these lies...do you realize how all of these lies have hurt Amina? Do you realize what you all have put her through all of her life? She lived her entire life thinking her parents were murdered and all this time..." I trailed off because all I could think about at the moment was how hurt Amina might be when she found out Pax was actually her father. It was a pain I would have gladly taken for her.

"It was the only way to protect her," said Pax. "It was my Beta's body that was lying next to my wife's." He dropped his head in shame. "If the Shadow Walkers found out I was still alive, they'd come. I had to make them think I was dead."

"They're coming anyway," I said. "You put her through all that pain for nothing."

"Look, Roland, I know that you're mad," Luke said as he looked at my father, "and I'll take whatever consequences I have coming for what I did, but right now isn't the time to discuss this. Right now, we need to figure out what to do about the Shadow Walkers."

"We aren't strong enough to fight them," said my father. "Our warriors are fierce, but they aren't even close to being as strong as Night Guardians. We couldn't win a war with the Shadow Walkers."

"Wait, I just realized that you said you have children? I have grandchildren?" asked Pax.

"Yes, three of them. Triplets. Not even a year old yet," I said.

"As happy as I am to hear that, it complicates things further. The babies have Night Guardian blood so the Shadow Walkers may target them also," he said.

Just when I thought things couldn't get worse, the hammer drops. Not only was Amina in danger, but now my children were as well. "This can't be happening," I said. I sat down. "I don't know how to protect my family. Some Alpha I'm going to be."

"You have to leave, Ethan," said my father with obvious desolation in his voice. "You, Amina, the babies, and Pax. It's the only chance we all have of surviving this. If they're not here, the Shadow Walkers might not fight us."

"And if they do fight you?" I asked. "Dad, I need to be here to help. And Pax, he's the only one who might actually have a shot at beating them!"

"Your father is right," said Luke. "We'll definitely lose if they attack us. Pax is strong, but he can't defeat all of them by himself. The only chance we have of surviving is talking them down from attacking us. We can't do that if Night Guardians are here."

"So running is the answer?" I asked. "We'll be running forever."

"Maybe. Maybe not, but if we're going to go, we have to go now. They'll be here in only a matter of hours," said Pax. "Go get them now."

"Get them, Ethan, and I'll meet you out front before you leave," said my father. "We won't tell your mother, brother, and sister. They'll be hysterical and Rose will hold you up."

I nodded feeling my heart break as I realized I wouldn't even be able to say goodbye to my family. However, that was not the time for me to get emotional. My mate and children would be depending on me to get them to safety, and I'd have to keep a clear head. I pushed my emotions down as best I could and jumped into action.

I took off running towards the house. I burst into the door, apparently scaring Amina because she let out a little cry when I came in.

"Ethan, what's wrong?" she asked. She was in the middle of feeding Henry.

"Baby, we have to leave now," I said.

"Leave? To go where?" she asked.

"Amina, I don't have time to answer questions. We need to pack a few things quickly, whatever we can pack in five minutes. We need to get the babies in the car, and we need to leave."

"Okay," she said. I could see the fear in her eyes. As much as I wanted to comfort her, it was good for her to be afraid. That would make her move faster. We got our bags packed and got the babies in the car. As we were putting the last of our things in the trunk, my father, Luke, and Pax met us. Amina gasped when she saw Pax. Tears welled up in her eyes as they embraced each other.

"What are you doing here?" she asked.

"We don't have time to talk," he said. "We have to leave."

"We? You're coming with us?" she asked. I could see a little hope in her eyes.

"Yes, well, maybe not *with* you. There's no room in your car. I'll run," he said. "I can probably run faster than the car anyway."

My father approached me with a box. "You'll need this. You shouldn't use any of your debit or credit cards. You need to stay off the grid. Give me your wallet and your phone. Amina's also."

I took the box and handed him our phones. I looked inside the box. There was money—a lot of money. I had no idea how much money was in the box, but looking at all the stacks of hundreds, I was certain it was at least one hundred thousand dollars. I looked at my father in disbelief.

"It's expensive to be on the run," he said with a chuckle. "There is a paper with an address on it. Go there. Tell him who you are. He'll give you new identities. Ethan, no matter what happens, stay off the grid and do not call. I'll send for you when it's safe."

"How will you know where I am?" I asked.

"I'll find you son. Don't worry about that. Now go."

I was about to get in the car, but I turned back and gave my father the tightest hug I'd ever given him. *I will not cry, I will not cry*, I thought. *Alphas do not cry.* I got in the car, cranked up, and started driving away as I thought about how ironic it was that we were leaving the pack after

I'd done everything I could to convince Amina to stay. It would seem that fate had other things in store for us.

27

The Night Guardians Live

Ethan finally got a chance to tell me how fucked we were. I should have known things were going too well. Someone like me doesn't get a perfect life, but it seemingly happened, and I fell for it. A beautiful home, a family, a brave and loving mate, three beautiful children, and more money than I'd ever need just landed in my lap at the ripe old age of eighteen. *Geesh, I'm a sucker,* I thought. Ethan glanced at me questioningly. *The universe apparently thinks my life should suck,* I thought. He didn't respond.

Despite the fact that my uncle was now with me, I felt nothing but sadness. Our lives had just been uprooted and I didn't have a clue what we were going to do. Some freakishly strong pack wanted me dead, but I wasn't sure why. My babies were in danger and there was a chance that Ethan would never see his family again. The guilt consumed me, and I silently cried all the way to wherever we were going. This time, Ethan didn't...or maybe couldn't...do much to console me. He was pretty upset and trying to keep himself together.

After over two hours of driving, we finally crossed the North Carolina border. We stopped at a rest stop so I could feed the babies. Ethan went to get us some snacks from the antique-looking, caged machines near the bathrooms.

As I started feeding Hazel, I saw my uncle come out of the woods. He was only wearing pants and was carrying a burlap sack. He looked almost like some poor, transient traveler that might have been camping back there. His thick afro was uncombed and had leaves stuck in it. His pants were dirty and tattered. His beard was long and unkempt. However, none of that was the strangest part of his appearance. The strange part was that he was incredibly large and muscular like a giant body builder. He didn't have a shred of fat on him. I never imagined I would see a health-conscious bum, but that's exactly what my uncle looked like walking over to us. As other people at the rest stop gave him curious and suspicious glances, it occurred to me that he looked that way the first time I met him, but at the time, I was too emotionally occupied to focus on that.

"Uncle," I said as he approached me. "I'm glad you're here."

He sat on the bench beside me and glanced at the babies. I saw a gentleness in his eyes as he smiled at them.

"My legacies," he said as he looked at them. *That's a strange thing to say,* I thought. "May I?" he asked.

"Yeah, sure," I said. He picked up Henry just as Ethan came back over with three bags of chips and three sodas.

"There is so much we need to talk about," said my uncle, "but we should wait until we're safe," he said. He put Henry down and picked up Hunter. "We can't stay here too long," he said.

"Well, we can make it quicker if you help me feed them." I pointed at a bag. "There are bottles in there. Each of you grab one."

"Are you sure?" My uncle looked back and forth between Ethan and I with uncertainty. "I mean, I haven't taken care of a baby since..." he glanced at me then he dropped his head.

Ethan nodded as he grabbed Henry and went for a bottle. I said, "I'm sure uncle. You're one of their protectors now so you should bond with them. Food is a great motivator for bonding," I said with a chuckle.

My uncle grabbed a bottle from the bag and nervously started feeding Hunter. Hunter gulped the milk down hungrily while keeping eye contact with my uncle. It was amusing to see this giant man get nervous from the stare of such a tiny creature.

"Why is he staring at me like that. Am I doing something wrong?" he asked.

"No, you're doing something right," I said. "He likes you."

We fed the babies, got them settled back into their car seats, and hit the road again. My uncle continued the journey on foot.

"My uncle called them his legacies," I said to Ethan. "I wonder what he meant by that."

Ethan chuckled and I could tell it was his nervous chuckle. "I don't know," he said, "but I'm sure he'll tell you soon."

I gave Ethan a cold stare. "You're lying Ethan Rohe."

"Ouch, my whole name, huh?" he said.

"We're on the run because of secrets and lies that have been kept and told by both of our families. I think it's time to stop with the secrets," I said. "Now tell me what he meant by that."

"I'm not keeping a secret from you. It just might be better if we discuss this later," he said.

"No! Tell me now, Ethan. I'm not some child who needs to be protected," I said.

Ethan sighed. "Fine. Pax wanted to tell you himself, but...he's not your uncle. He's your father."

I wasn't prepared for that. I was completely stunned and speechless. All I could do was turn my head and look out of the window, into the woods where my unc...father was running. I thought about the sacrifices he made to keep me safe, and I understood because I would do the same for my kids. However, I was still angry. My...father...had lied to me and left me alone my entire life. That part I could forgive, but when I finally met him he lied to me again. What else was he going to lie to me about? How could I trust him when he seemed to be able to lie so easily? I should have been happy that one of my parents was alive and with me, but all I felt was distrust.

We rode in silence for a while and Ethan finally asked me if I was okay. I lied and said that I was and decided to take a nap. I wasn't sure if I could, but the next thing I knew, I was waking up and Ethan was parking the car.

"How long have I been asleep?" I asked.

"A little over an hour. Stay here with the babies. I'm going to make sure it's safe before we take them in." Ethan got out just as my father met him at the car. *My father,* I thought. *I can't bring myself to call him that now.* They said a couple things to each other then they disappeared into the old brick building.

I looked around at the area. I had no idea what town we were in, but the area was an old looking downtown shopping district. Many of the buildings were abandoned and dilapidated. Of the ones that weren't abandoned, there was a little diner with a few patrons inside, a local pharmacy, a comic book shop, and an antique store. A little further down the street, I spotted a sign that said, "Find it For Five". I assumed it was a bargain department store.

I looked across the street from us and there were two suspicious-looking guys staring at me from beside a little bakery. I felt panic take over me as one guy threw his cigarette to the side and they began crossing the street to the car. Somehow, I instinctually knew these guys were trouble. *My babies! They're gonna hurt our babies! Ethan!* I screamed to him. I knew I only had seconds to act.

Before my mind caught up, my body was already in action. I was out of the car and shifting to my wolf form and so we're the two men, but something weird happened. This time when I shifted, I became larger than before. I literally felt my bones and muscles stretching. It didn't hurt, but it scared me. Suddenly I was towering over the two wolves before me. I could hear Ethan and my...Pax run out onto the sidewalk.

"Oh, shit," said Ethan. I didn't need to look at him to know his face was frozen in disbelief.

"The Night Guardians live on," shouted Pax happily as I lunged towards the two wolves. I heard people on the streets gasp and scream as I pinned the first wolf down and bit into his side.

Pax was almost instantly at my side fighting the second wolf. To my surprise, I was larger than him. That realization distracted me momentarily and the wolf scurried out my grip. *Don't let him get away,* said Ethan. *He'll tell the others where we are.*

I chased the wolf down, pounced on him and ripped him to shreds easily. It was like ripping apart a newspaper. When I looked back, Pax had done the same with the other wolf. Ethan had shifted to his wolf form and was standing on top of the car to protect the babies. He looked like a puppy compared to us.

I shifted back to my human form and I was suddenly very tired. I realized I was standing naked in the middle of the street, so I hopped into the car quickly and leaned back. Ethan, also naked, hopped in next to me.

"We have to get out of here now," he said as he put the car into gear.

"But Pax–"

"—he'll find us, Amina. Don't worry, we aren't leaving him behind," he said. Ethan hit the gas, and we sped off. After about twenty minutes, when we were confident we weren't being followed we finally relaxed enough to talk.

"I don't know what happened. I just needed to protect the babies," I said as reflected on my latest shift.

"Baby, you were like this kick ass female! I've never seen anything like it. You were so big!"

"Yeah, that's exactly what every woman wants to hear," I said sarcastically. "Hey, maybe you could slow down now." I was worried about Pax keeping up with us. We sped off so fast from the fight that we didn't have time to discuss where we were going with him, and none of us had a phone so I couldn't call or text him. Ethan ignored that request and went on talking about the fight.

"I thought *I* was becoming some big-time warrior, but I can't do what you and your father did. I mean, you tore that wolf into pieces, and you made it look easy! I didn't know you could fight like that...and without training! You're a natural. It was flawless. He didn't even get a lick in—"

"—maybe we should go back," I said.

"Amina, I already told you your father is going to keep up with us. In fact, he's probably ahead of us—"

"—that's not what I'm talking about," I said. "I mean back home." That statement made Ethan stop and pull over.

"Back home? But my father said—"

"—I know what Alpha Roland said, Ethan, and I agreed with his decision at the time. That was before I knew what I could do and before we were out here on the run. What are we going to do out here? We have nowhere to go, and it seems like the Shadow Walkers are finding us anyway." I sighed. "There aren't any good solutions here, but…I miss home. Ethan, Pax and I…I don't know, there was this connection when we both shifted. There was power there. Strength. I could even feel it emanating from the triplets. They have whatever gene I have, and it seems like with all five of us there, we were somehow stronger. I know I have a lot to learn about my past and my people, but I think Pax and I, along with the trained warriors we already have, can protect the pack. Without us, they don't stand a chance."

As I was looking at Ethan there was a tap on the window. I jumped but calmed down when I saw it was Pax. Ethan rolled down the window.

"Everything okay?" he asked.

"Yeah, Pax. Amina and I were just talking," Ethan said.

"I think we should go back," I said. "That's our home. All of us. You wouldn't have to live in the mountains anymore, right Ethan?" Ethan nodded.

Pax took in a deep breath. "Before the war, the Night Guardians were protectors. It's in our nature to protect others. The Moon Goddess blessed us with our with amazing strength and size to defeat our enemies. I don't know why we lost favor with her, and why she allowed our pack to be decimated, but maybe this is how we get it back."

"How are we going to protect the babies?" asked Ethan.

"They'll be safer with a whole village protecting them than just the three of us," I said.

Ethan sighed. "I guess you're right. Plus, leaving my pack behind didn't feel like the right thing to do in the first place. I was just following my father's orders."

"Your father..." scoffed Pax. "Your father has always been a coward, Ethan."

"What? You take that back right now," Ethan growled.

"I don't mean to offend you, but I'm speaking truth. That's why he had me protecting the pack from the dark wolves in the valley. I truly hope you're a better Alpha than he is. Your pack needs real leadership. Real strength. I can already see, despite your youth and lack of maturity, that you're smarter than your father is. Remember that when you take the helm."

My father tapped the car. "Back to the Moon Valley Pack territory." He turned, shifted, and ran back into the woods. Ethan turned the car around and we started heading back home. I could sense he was still angry about what Pax said.

"Ethan, I don't think Pax meant—"

"Yes, he did," Ethan said. He was frowning and his nostrils were flaring. "I have a lot of respect for your father, and I know I could never beat him in a fight, but he shouldn't have disrespected my father that way."

"You're right," I said. "Our fathers don't have the best relationship with each other, but maybe we can change that in the future." I put my hand on his and that seemed to calm him down just a little.

We started the long journey back home. An hour into it, we had to stop so Ethan could take a nap. I felt bad that I didn't know how to dive. Ethan had been driving the entire time with no rest and he was exhausted. My father and I took that time to feed and change the babies.

"You haven't had any rest either," I said. "You've been running for almost an entire day. Aren't you tired?"

"Yes, I am, but I've been trained to go days without sleep," said my father. Our genetic makeup...well, we're designed to be the ultimate machine. There are a lot of things we can do that a typical wolf can't. Perhaps I should have been training you all these years. I truly thought that the time of the Night Guardians was over. You...Amina, I've never seen a Night Guardian with your size or strength. It's almost like you have the collective strength of our pack. Perhaps the Moon Goddess didn't abandon us after all."

"There is so much for me to learn," I said.

"Yes, there is. I promise you I will teach you everything," said Pax.

We finished taking care of the babies, then we woke Ethan up and got back on the road. We only had to stop once more for gas, and we got back to the Moon Valley Pack territory early the next morning. However, once we got there, we immediately knew something was wrong. Ethan floored the gas, and we sped to the Alpha's house where there was a battle happening.

There was total chaos going on. I was in shock as I stared at the largest and most vicious wolves I'd ever seen besides Pax and myself. The myths were true about the Shadow Walkers. They were huge, evil, and ruthless. Servants were running for their lives. Children were hiding. There were at least two dozen dead wolf and human bodies strewn about, many of them ripped to pieces. There was blood everywhere.

Shadow Walkers, I projected to Ethan. *We have to do something now!* He nodded. Just as the car came to a halt, Stacey and Rose came running over to the car. Pax came running from the woods.

"You have to get the babies out of here," Stacey screamed. "They're murdering everyone, even children!" Rose was bleeding profusely. It looked as though her arm had almost been ripped from its socket.

"Mom! Oh my...what happened?" Ethan asked as he ran to her.

"No...time...must get them to safety," she panted.

Ethan handed Stacey the keys. "Get them out of here, now," he yelled.

"Okay. C'mon mom and Amina. Let's go!" said Stacey. She grabbed the Luna by her good arm and started helping her into the car.

"Not me," I said as I shook my head. "I'm fighting."

"Amina, they'll rip you to shreds!" said Stacey.

I smiled. "We have a lot to talk about, but not now. Just get them all to safety. I'll be fine."

I watched as the two women got into the car with my children. Stacey looked at me questioningly as they backed out. She spun the car around and sped away as fast as the car would go. I heard Ethan yell, "Lennox!"

I turned and Lennox was running with a group of children towards the side gate. "Why are there children here?" I asked Ethan as we ran towards them. He shrugged. I spotted Cam and Cass. They ran to me with tears in their eyes.

"Eliza! I thought we'd never see you again," said Cass. I squeezed them tightly and wanted to ask where their parents where, but I didn't dare.

"Get them to that shed over there," said Ethan as he pointed. Lennox nodded and shuffled the kids away.

"Go with him now," I said as I pushed Cam and Cass along.

With the weakest of the family out of harm's way, it was time to join the battle. the three of us spun around and shifted.

The moment we did, it seemed like all the fighting stopped as everyone marveled at my father and me.

All the Shadow Walkers immediately shifted their focus to us. When they did that, it gave our warriors the upper hand. Many of them took that opportunity to strike, giving them field advantage. We charged the wolves knowing that this battle was about to be like no other battle in the history of the Moon Valley Pack.

28

Alpha and Luna

As we ran towards the enemy wolves, two of them met Ethan. Three of them met my father. Seven of them met me! *Seriously? I'm the female, here, guys!*

Despite my size, I had no fight training, so I wasn't sure how I was going to handle seven wolves. Right before they got to me, I saw Caroline, Tinsley, and Jessica running towards us. They shifted mid-run, but the wolves reached me before they got to us. I was able to knock one wolf away, but the others attacked. Two of them bit my leg and, to my surprise, it didn't hurt. They didn't even puncture my skin! They were as surprised as I was. They stumbled back, unsure of what to do next.

The others lunged forward. Luckily, I caught one by the neck and bit down hard. His neck snapped in my mouth like a tortilla chip. I threw him to the side. The other three wolves were swiping and biting with all their might at my side. It felt like they were scratching an itch a little too hard. They weren't hurting me very much, but their frenzied fighting made it hard for me to get away from them.

Caroline and her crew finally reached us and the three of them attacked the first wolf I had knocked away. I couldn't believe they'd come to my aid. They weren't great fighters, but with three against one they were giving the Shadow wolf a run for his money.

The two other wolves were running towards me. Ethan caught one by the tail, but the other one plowed right into me, knocking me down. Suddenly I had four wolves on top of me and I had no idea how to get out of it.

One of them bit my ear and that hurt really badly. I yelped and felt a stream of blood running down the side of my face. The sudden pain gave me a surge of strength and I was able to get to my feet, knocking the wolves down. I took that opportunity to pin one down. I bit into his side deeply and ripped it open. He didn't move after that. He just laid there panting and waiting for his slow and painful death.

The other three wolves charged me, but Pax came out of nowhere and knocked them all down. He had two other wolves right on his tail, so he had to turn and fight them, leaving my three. I seized the opportunity and charged one of them. I was aiming for his neck, but he turned his head at the last moment, and I chomped down on his face. I felt my tooth go into his eye. I wanted to puke.

He backed away with half his face hanging off. He turned and tried to run, but his limited vision caused him to run into a pole hard. He went down. Two wolves left to go.

We circled each other and I saw that one was cowering a bit. *Maybe he wants to run but some Shadow Walker creed said for him to fight till the death.* Well, if that was the creed, he was going to die with honor.

It didn't take much. With only two to fight, I was easily able to overcome one and snap his neck. The other wolf latched on to my tail and that hurt as bad as my ear. I snatched my tail from his mouth which caused him to lose his balance and I attacked. With his neck snapped and his body lying motionless on the ground, I ran over to Caroline and her friends and finished taking out the first wolf. They sort of bowed to me and ran off to help others. *I can't believe they came to my aid,* I thought in amazement.

I looked around and one by one, I took out many of the Shadow Walkers, starting with the one Ethan was fighting. With the odds shifting to our side, our Moon Valley warriors decimated the remaining Shadow Walkers. A few of them retreat and ran away. Finally, the battle was over.

There were dead wolves everywhere. We'd lost half of our warriors and a lot of our non-warrior pack members, but we dealt the Shadow

Walkers a massive blow because most of their wolves were lying motionless on the ground. I saw Pax standing a few yards from me. He nodded to me and ran off to help some of our injured warriors. I scanned the grounds for Ethan and didn't see him, but I could feel immense pain coming from him wherever he was. I panicked.

I desperately ran around the grounds looking for him, my panic rising a little more each second that I didn't find him. Finally, I spotted him in the back of the house. He was kneeling on the ground in his human form near a wolf. I ran to him and gasped as I realized who the wolf was.

I shifted to my human form, knelt beside him, and embraced him tightly as tears ran down his face. He hugged me back and we stayed that way for as long as Ethan needed to. I stroked his hair, and I felt him trembling in my arms. I wanted to take his pain away, but I didn't know how.

"I know you're hurting, but everyone's going to be looking for guidance. You're the Alpha now and they need you," I said.

"I can't just leave him here like this," Ethan said through his tears.

"We can have some of the guys come back here—"

"—no, it should be Lennox and me," he said. "This comes first. Find Lennox for me, please." I nodded and went to look for Lennox. During my search, I came across Beta Luke first.

"Umm, hi," I said, not sure how to approach him. "Ummm, you're probably going to have to take over for a while," I said trying to hold back the quiver in my voice. "Alpha Roland...he umm..." I couldn't hold back the tears anymore.

Luke caught on to what I was saying. He buried his face in his hands. "Shit! It was total chaos. I lost track of him. Everything happened too fast." He took in a deep breath. "Ethan is the Alpha now. Where is he? Is he dead also—"

"—he's in no condition to lead right now," I said. "He's the one who found Alpha Roland's body." I sighed. "How are we going to tell Rose?"

"I'll rally the pack right now, but Ethan's going to have to snap out of it and grieve later. He has to take charge. We need a leader now more than ever," said Luke. He walked off to try to begin putting the pack back together and I continued looking for Lennox.

I went to the shed where he took the children. I saw him lying in the grass in front of it and I gasped hard as my breath left me. *No, please don't be dead,* I prayed as I ran over to him. When I reached him, I was relieved to see he was still breathing. It seemed he'd only been knocked out. I shook him and he started coming around.

"Wha—wha—" he started. He sat up slowly, then suddenly his mouth dropped open and he gasped. "The shed! The kids!" He tried to get up, but he grabbed his side, winced in pain, and dropped back to the ground.

"Wait, just sit here and get your head together. I'll check the shed," I said. I ran over to the shed and opened the door. A dozen kids, including Cam and Cass, were huddled together inside. They screamed when I opened the door, but when they saw it was me, Cam and Cass ran to me and hugged me.

"It's okay, guys. You can all come out now," I said. The kids followed me out. Lennox had finally gotten to his feet.

"Why are there kids here?" I asked.

"When we found out the Shadow Walkers were coming, we were trying to get all the kids out of harms way. We were going to hide them in the vault in the house, but we ran out of time. Shit, your ear," said Lennox.

I have to give him the bad news now, I thought.

"What's wrong, Amina," he said. He must have seen the distraught look on my face.

"Lennox, I don't know how to say this—"

"—Ethan! Is it Ethan? Is he okay—"

"—Ethan is fine," I said. "It's not him. He's waiting for you behind the house."

Lennox's brow furrowed, then relaxed as understanding hit him. He shook his head, looked at the house, and took off running as he held his broken ribs.

I told the children to follow me. I headed to the guest house that Ethan and I had called home for so long. Luke was barking orders to some of the warriors. They, along with servants, were dragging bodies off the property and attempting to clean up all the debris from the enormous amount of damage that had occurred.

I got the kids inside, but we weren't the only ones in the house. The house had been turned into a relief station where workers were coming and going for breaks, food, and beverages. I was amazed at how quickly the recovery effort was going. It was very efficient to say we'd just been in a pack war. I got the kids all settled down. Some of them fell asleep almost immediately. Others were hungry and wanted snacks. Cass insisted on following me around. She didn't want to let me out of sight. *I still have to figure out where Star and Skylar are,* I thought.

I spotted Eloise coming out of the bathroom. "Eloise! I'm so happy to see you!" She ran over to me and gave me a big hug.

"Where are the babies? Are they okay?" she asked.

"Luna Rose and Stacey took them to safety. They're fine. I mean, I think they're fine. I'm pretty sure they are." I pointed at the children. "Can you take care of these kids until we figure out where their parents are?"

"Of course, Amina. I got them," she said.

"Can I borrow your phone?"

"Sure," she said. She handed it to me then went over to check on the kids.

When I got a moment to sit down, I called Stacey.

"Hello? Amina! Oh my gosh, we were so worried. Is it over?" she asked.

"Yes, it is. You can come back now. How is Rose doing?" I asked.

"She's stable for now, but she isn't doing so well. She needs a doctor. I tried to take her to the hospital in the next town over, but she wouldn't let me. She insisted we needed to hide," she said.

"That was the right choice," I said, "but now you can bring her home to get help. Are the babies okay?"

"They're sort of crying a lot, but other than that they're fine," she said. I breathed out a sigh of relief. "Thank you, Stacey. Thank you so much."

"No problem," she said. "That's what sisters are for. We'll see you soon." I stared at the phone even after Stacey hung up. *Sisters? She just called me her sister!* I enjoyed that moment for a few seconds, then brought my focus back to the situation at hand. When I did, I could suddenly feel Ethan's despair. I couldn't help but cry. Then it hit me that Cass was right next to me. She was crying also.

"Cass, I need you to stay here," I said as I stood up.

"No, Eliza! Please don't go," she cried.

"I have to handle something, but you're safe now, okay? I promise I'll be back soon. I'm going to find your mom and dad."

I wanted to comfort Cass further, but Ethan needed my comfort more. I ran to the back of the house as quickly as I could. Lennox was pulling a large white sheet over Alpha Roland's body. Ethan was standing over him saying a prayer. I took his hand. He squeezed mine tightly.

I could sense Pax walking towards us. When he realized who was under the sheet, he stopped. Pax kneeled and said a prayer to pay his respects, despite the poor relationship he'd had with Alpha Roland.

Ethan finished his prayer, wiped his eyes, and took a deep breath. *Are you ready to lead this pack?* I projected to him.

It would be a dishonor to my father's memory if I wasn't, he projected back. *I'm ready. Are you ready to be my Luna?*

Yes, I am, I projected back. I couldn't believe that I was saying yes to being the pack's Luna, especially when, technically, Rose was still the Luna. However, something told me she would have no problem turning over her position to me, especially when she found out that Alpha Roland was dead.

Hand in hand, Ethan and I turned and walked towards the front of the house to take control of the pack.

29

Stay

I never knew I could hurt that bad. My perfect life had just been tainted with reality and now I realized that the way I was living was an illusion. Loss has a way of making you grow up in an instant. It opens your eyes to things that people try and fail to get you to see. Seeing my father's mangled body growing cold on the back lawn was the last lesson he gave me, and it was a powerful one. *You can't lose...ever. If you do, you lose everything. Lesson learned, Dad.*

I prepared myself to address the entire pack, or what was left of it for the first time in my life. I could see Lennox, Stacey, the babies, and my mother in the back of the crowd as Lennox gave them the news. Stacey cried out. My mother dropped but Lennox caught her. Two of the male servants went over to help them sit down.

The servants had cleaned up the courtyard as much as they could. They'd even scrubbed the pavement, attempting to get rid of as many bloodstains as possible but so many still lingered. As people filled in to hear our announcements, one of the warriors brought over two large boxes for Amina and me to stand on.

It was time for me to take my place as the Alpha of the pack. I always knew the day would come, but I had imagined it as a happier day when I was older and with both of my parents by my side. Instead, it comes on the heels of my father's death, so instead of feeling like the position was an honor, it felt more like a default position. Still yet, I had to man up.

I took a deep breath and looked at Amina. Even in the middle of all the damage and disruption, she was a sight of pure beauty. I kissed her hand, and she smiled at me. Then I turned to address the crowd. I could see confusion on their faces. They were wondering where my father was.

"Okay, listen up everyone. Our pack has just been through one of the worst moments in our entire history. We were victorious against our brutal adversaries, but our victory was not without many losses." I almost choked up on that part. I cleared my throat. Amina squeezed my hand.

"Unfortunately, my father, Alpha Roland, was killed." There were shouts, gasps, and murmurs from the crowd. Some people started crying. Some started praying. Many were too shocked to react.

"As you know, I had been preparing to take on the position of Alpha when my father retired. As of now…" I had to pause. I almost lost my wits. I took a deep breath. "As of now, I'll be assuming the position of Alpha. If anyone cares to challenge that, now is the time." I looked over the crowd and gave everyone time to challenge me if they so desired, but of course no one would. Not after we'd just been at war.

"If there are no challenges, then I will assume the position starting right now." Normally there would be applause and cheering, but there was only sadness plaguing the crowd.

"This day…should have never happened," I said. "My father was a very wise man, but I can see how some of his choices led to this." Amina shifted next to me. I could tell my comment made her uncomfortable. *Bear with me, baby. I'm not talking about you,* I projected to her.

"As your Alpha, I promise to be more transparent with you. I promise to make better decisions, and I promise to get this pack in a position to defend itself from our enemies. Today will never, ever happen again," I said. "No more secrets. No more lies. We're all hurting right now. We're all broken and bruised. We need to go home, heal our wounds, and come back ready to work."

"How are you going to make sure this never happens again?" yelled someone from the crowd. "We barely won today. What if they send more wolves the next time?"

"You're right, but it's because we weren't prepared. Our warriors weren't prepared for real fighting because..." I looked at Pax, "we've been taking it easy for far too long. The first thing I'm going to do is implement a new training program for our warriors."

"What's left of them," someone else shouted.

"Our pack is plentiful. We can recruit and train more warriors," I said. "In the meantime, I hope my father-in-law would be my new Gamma, especially since the old one is..." I didn't want to finish the statement. The crowd gasped and murmured again as they all looked back and forth between Amina and Pax. I could hear them saying things like, "I thought she was an orphan," and, "I thought she was a rogue."

Pax nodded to me in his usual reticent manner. That was him confirming his acceptance of the position. No cheers or applause needed.

"Who is he?" asked someone else from the crowd.

"I'm glad you asked that," I said with a smile. "The Moon Goddess has blessed us with his presence. He is Alpha Paxton of The Night Guardians."

"The Night Guardians!" someone exclaimed.

"They're a myth," said someone else. The crowd started murmuring.

"Of course he's an Alpha. That's why he's so huge," said another.

"There is so much to tell you," I said to the crowd. "I couldn't possibly tell you everything right here, right now, but trust me when I say that together, Pax and I will get our warriors ready for the next battle. The Shadow Walkers will not prevail under my watch. Now, everyone, please go and rest. Mourn your losses and then let's bounce back and strengthen this pack in honor of our deceased." People in the crowd generally agreed and murmured their approval as they dispersed.

Amina looked at me with pure adoration in her eyes. "I'm glad you approve of my speech," I said.

"You're going to be a great Alpha," she replied as we stepped down from the box and prepared to join our family.

...

I was relieved to see Star and Skye in the crowd. At least I wouldn't have to deliver devastating news to Cam and Cass. Ethan and I already had enough to deal with.

I couldn't have been prouder of my mate as he delivered the speech to the crowd. Maybe it wasn't the most powerful Alpha speech ever, but for someone who was dealing with the sudden violent death of his father and role model, he really came through for the people.

I was also proud of myself. I was no longer the girl I was a little over a year ago. Before, I was broken, alone, scared, and confused. Now I was powerful, loved, and mentally and physically strong enough to protect the very people who had done me wrong my entire life. I had grown so much in a short amount of time. So had they.

I looked out at the crowd of people staring back at us. They were scared and confused, just like I used to be. *We'll lead them back to the happy pack they were,* I thought. *We'll do it together, for my babies' sake.* They deserved a strong family and a strong pack.

Ethan and I stepped off the boxes and joined our family. I looked around at all of them, thinking of how I'd wanted to run away. Ethan convinced me to stay. It didn't escape me that if I had left, Alpha Roland would probably be alive. Perhaps Alpha Roland knew that all along. Maybe that's why he never liked me much. However, if I had left, I'd be the one that was dead. Either way, Ethan would be hurt.

That's how fate and destiny work. The universe can give you all the choices in the world, and you can do your best to choose the best one, but in the end they all lead to the same outcome. I wasn't sure if fate or destiny would be on our side, but what I was sure of is that I no longer wanted to run away. My wish that I'd made at the fountain all those months ago finally came true. I'd found a place I wanted to call home. I finally wanted to stay.

Stay 2:
Rise of the Night Guardians

Coming in 2025!

If you're familiar with the accelerated reader program, you probably remember that kid that aimed to get as many points as possible and always earned the top prizes every quarter. That was D. A. Flowers. She's been an avid reader for as long as she can remember. It's no surprise that writing followed soon after.

She started her writing career as a ghostwriter and freelance writer. Eventually she used her training from the theater program at the University of South Carolina to begin writing plays and scripts. She wrote, produced, and directed her play, Love, Poetry, and Other Missed Connections in 2018 at the Hudson Guild Theater in New York. Now she's evolved to writing romance novels.

@dani.alicia5   @therealdanialicia   @therealdanialicia   @realdanialicia

www.danialicia.com

9 798330 557950